BLOOD and JUSTICE

Rayven T. Hill

Ray of Joy Publishing
Toronto

Books by Rayven T. Hill

Blood and Justice
Cold Justice
Justice for Hire
Captive Justice
Justice Overdue
Justice Returns
Personal Justice
Silent Justice
Web of Justice
Fugitive Justice

Visit rayventhill.com for more information on these and future releases.

This book is a work of fiction. Names, characters, places, businesses, organizations, events and incidents either are the product of the author's imagination or are used fictitiously. Any resemblance to actual persons, living or dead, events or locales is entirely coincidental.

Published by Ray of Joy Publishing
Toronto

Third Edition

ISBN-13: 978-0-9938625-0-2

BLOOD and JUSTICE

PROLOGUE

Eight Years Ago

THE REASON his plan was so good was because it was so simple. He was counting on one fact. Joey was stupid. Not really stupid, like, *stupid* stupid—just dumb.

When Jeremy told Joey he'd found a hidden cache of money and jewels in the woods, probably hidden there by a robber, Joey had been dumb enough to believe him.

Jeremy laughed out loud at the thought.

He looked down, aimed his father's old H&R .22-caliber revolver, and took another shot, this time hitting Joey in the head. The boy on the ground stopped his pathetic whining, crying, and pleading and remained silent and still.

The deed was done; someone had to take care of this. He knew no one would understand. Certainly not his mother, or the police, but Jeremy knew all too well it had been necessary. The bully would torture him no longer.

Shoving the weapon behind his belt, Jeremy Spencer looked around. Except for a couple of birds breaking the stillness, the forest was dim and quiet.

He crouched down and examined the body. The first bullet had entered the victim's stomach. Blood flowed from the wound and darkened the hue of the already red and brown autumn leaves beneath the fresh corpse.

The second bullet had entered just below Joey's left eye. Blood trickled down, followed the path of his cheekbone, down his neck, finally dripping like dew onto the forest floor.

Drip, drip, drip.

He reached out and touched the wound beneath Joey's eye. It felt warm. He looked at the crimson on his finger and gently touched it to his tongue. It tasted sweet and thick. He closed his eyes and tilted his head back, the taste of blood on his tongue somehow making him feel pure, whole, and righteous.

He was filled with a feeling of euphoria, breathing rapidly, his heart racing, excited. He knew at that moment that what he'd done was fully justified.

He remained still for several minutes, pondering the deed, and thought about his father. Father would approve.

Finally, he stood, straightened his back, and took a deep breath. He bent over, grabbed the bloody corpse by the leg, and dragged it to the hole he had previously prepared. A fierce shove with his foot sent the body tumbling over and then down, finally landing with a thud at the bottom of the waiting grave. He picked up the shovel and set about filling in the hole.

Jeremy labored for some time, humming to himself as he worked. Finally, he tossed the last shovelful of dirt, covered the area with twigs, branches, and dead leaves, and stood back.

"That should do it," he said aloud.

He contemplated a moment longer, and then resting the shovel on his shoulder, he turned and hurried for home.

He was expected there by five o'clock, and he didn't want to keep his mother waiting.

CHAPTER 1

Sunday, August 7th, 6:00 p.m.

JAKE DRAGGED another piece of piping-hot apple pie onto his plate and looked across the table. His wife was eyeing him closely, something on her mind, no doubt.

"Next time, honey, I'd appreciate if you'd let me do the talking," she said. "Especially with something so sensitive."

Jake gave her a crooked grin and nodded. "You can handle things like that next time," he said before digging in to the pie.

Annie was right, of course. He'd almost bungled their last task, as simple as it was. They'd been hired to find a man's runaway son. No problem there—a few minutes online and Annie had tracked him down. But going off half-cocked, Jake had made a call to the boy, demanding he return home. He'd almost gotten hung up on, but when the more sympathetic Annie had gotten involved, she'd convinced the boy to contact his father. There was ultimately a satisfactory outcome for all.

"No harm done," she said with a smile that made Jake

wilt. She knew how to tell him off gently.

After he finished eating, Jake helped Annie clean up the table and put the dishes in the sink. He turned to her and sighed. "It's been awhile since we had a real case," he said. "I'm tired of barely making ends meet."

Annie turned to face her husband. She touched his arm and looked up into his eyes. "We're doing okay. Just let me handle the finances."

She was better at that too. She was better at a whole lot of things, and he wondered what he would ever do without her. He took a sideways look at his wife. At just over five feet four inches, she was still about the prettiest thing he'd ever seen. Her midlength golden hair, and the trim figure she'd kept all the years since he'd known her, always made his heart melt. She was his motivating force and he thought the world of her.

The phone jangled on the counter and interrupted Jake's thoughts. He scooped it up. "Lincoln Investigations. This is Jake." It was Annie's best friend from next door. "Hold on, Chrissy. She's right here," he said, holding out the phone. Annie and Chrissy had been friends for a long time, and it seemed to Jake they were always yakking about something.

Annie took the receiver and settled into a chair. "Hi Chrissy. How's everything?"

Jake wandered into the living room, grabbed the remote, and switched on the TV. Just some stupid sitcom. He flicked through the channels but eventually gave up and turned it off again. Tossing the remote back where he'd found it, he stretched out on the couch.

A rocket the size of an eight-year-old boy suddenly landed on his chest. The rocket was named Matty, and he was a bundle of energy, and ready to wrestle his father into submission. The battle soon took to the floor, but before long, Jake surrendered, pinned down and seemingly helpless.

From the other room came a warning. "Don't you guys break anything in there."

~*~

BACK IN THE KITCHEN, Annie finished cleaning up and went to the makeshift office, dropping into her swivel chair behind the desk. The office, formerly an unused bedroom, was sparse. A couple of bookcases lined one wall, filled with read and unread novels, several books on law, and a row of rarely used and obsolete encyclopedias. A few prints hanging on the wall and a well-worn carpet completed the look.

She opened the top drawer of the desk and pulled out the accounting ledger. Jake was right: money was tight. The new camera equipment had set them back, purchased when they had been hired to evaluate the honesty of a department store employee by posing as a customer. The camera had caught the thief red-handed in the act of loading some expensive computer equipment into a waiting van.

Lincoln Investigations was only a few months old, and Annie realized it would take some time to land steady business. The ad in the Richmond Hill Daily Times was pulling in the occasional client, and she was confident in the future of their agency.

Prior to starting their current undertaking, Annie had been doing part-time work as a research assistant for a Fortune 500 firm. The crunch had come when, due to downsizing, Jake had been let go from his job as a construction engineer at one of Canada's largest land developers. But now, things were looking up. Annie had started their new detective agency by taking on freelance research, and they hoped it would eventually allow them both to work full-time.

Most of their clients engaged them to obtain evidence for divorce, child custody, and missing persons cases, or to turn up information about individuals' character or financial status, and Annie's experience had served as a natural progression into their enterprise.

Jake did most of the outside work, chasing leads, or doing stakeouts, but this evening she knew he felt a little restless. There hadn't been much for him to do lately, and he was aching to be useful.

Five Days Ago

JEREMY PUFFED and panted as he maneuvered the bundle from the trunk of his 2005 Hyundai. It dropped to the ground with a dull thump, and he stopped for a much-needed rest.

He'd never grown much. Now at twenty-four years old, he was only five foot three, or maybe four, inches tall, and as thin as a teenager. In fact, he was still often mistaken for one, and he'd had to use his brains rather than his brawn to get anywhere in life.

He took a deep breath and turned his attention back to the task. Dragging almost two hundred pounds of dead weight wasn't easy for someone so small, but he finally managed, with great effort, to heave and roll it to the hole he'd dug earlier. The blanket came loose from its contents, exposing a bloody corpse.

The trees around him snapped and ruffled in the warm afternoon breeze as he stopped again to wipe the sweat from his face with a dirty shirtsleeve. The pungent smell of the nearby swamp permeated the air.

Jeremy preferred to bury the bodies here, in the forest. It was a secluded place, away from prying eyes, making it easier to cover them up and hide them. Here they would never be found.

Good riddance.

He knelt down and stared intently at the body. The blood around the wound looked dry and dark, but as he touched it, it felt slightly moist and still warm. He stood and gazed quietly at the body for a few moments.

Then, bending over, he gave another heave, and the corpse slid to the bottom of the shallow hole. He kicked the bloodstained blanket in after it, filled the grave, then patted the ground flat and covered the area with leaves. The job was done.

But he still had one more thing to do and he was perplexed. The guy had gotten what he deserved, but what about the girl? He couldn't let her go, but hurting her would be wrong, and he had to come up with an idea. But for now, she was safe.

Monday, August 8th, 3:30 p.m.

DETECTIVE HANK CORNING reached across the aging desk and gently touched the woman's hand. "I'm sorry, Mrs. James. We've done all we can do. Your daughter has been missing for almost a week and there's no information to go on. With no evidence of foul play, Captain Diego won't allow us to dedicate any more time and resources."

The woman sitting across the desk from Hank was in her late thirties. She still had signs of true beauty, but right now the grief and anxiety clouding her face were masking her allure.

The woman bowed her head and gave another sob, dabbing at her tears with a soft white handkerchief. "I just know she wouldn't go anywhere without telling me. She's only sixteen, and she's never been away from home for more than a couple of days at a time. And I always knew where she was."

Hank nodded sympathetically and sighed deeply. At forty years old, he'd been doing this job for almost twenty years and had seen more than his share of grief—missing kids, murdered kids, and victims of all kinds. He was tired. Tired of all the pain, and tired of feeling helpless.

He ran his fingers through his short-cropped, slightly graying hair and sat back. "I'm very sorry."

Mrs. James looked intently at the detective, the hope once in her eyes now faded. "Will you keep trying?"

"I'll do what I can, Mrs. James," he promised gently.

The woman clutched her purse, pulling her jacket around her as she stood. "Thank you, Detective," she said, giving him a fragile smile.

Hank's heart broke as he stood and watched her turn and head slowly toward the door. "Mrs. James," he called.

She turned back.

"Perhaps a private detective …"

Monday, August 8th, 9:59 p.m.

SHEETS OF RAIN pounded against the office window. A wind had come up suddenly and threatened to remove the shutters as they rattled and clapped. The big oak in the backyard sighed under the strain.

Jake was in the office, on the phone with a woman who sounded desperate. "We can come to visit you, Mrs. James, or you're welcome to come to our office."

"I prefer you to come here," she said.

Jake arranged an appointment for the next morning and hung up the phone.

Annie poked her head into the room. "Who was that?"

"That was Amelia James. Apparently, Hank recommended she talk to us. Her daughter's missing and the police have nothing more to go on. I told her we would help."

"Another missing kid," Annie said. "Thank God for the Internet. Hopefully, we can track this one down as fast as the last one."

"I'm not so sure this time," Jake said. "The girl's been gone a week. She just disappeared and didn't take any of her things with her. Her mother says it's not like her to do anything like that."

He stood and came from behind the desk toward Annie. She put her arms around his neck and he drew her close, burying his face in her hair. She always smelled good.

"We'll find out more tomorrow morning," he said. "We have an appointment to see her at ten."

Annie looked up at him, nodded, and then said, "By the way, I've invited Mom and Dad over for a barbecue Thursday evening. Is that okay?"

Jake frowned at her and sighed. "You know I don't get along with your mother."

"I know. Just try to be patient."

He pulled away from her, annoyed. "It's hard to be patient when she always gives us instructions on how to raise our own son."

"I don't want the two of you fighting. Besides, she has some good suggestions."

"Like sending Matty to a private school? Who's going to pay for that? I don't know how your father puts up with her either."

Annie shot him a sharp look. "My father's an amazing guy," she said. "He's been through a lot, and he's happy, so leave him out of this."

"I've got nothing against your father. It's your mother. She treats me like a kid and thinks I'm not good enough for you. Maybe I'm not, but it's none of her business."

"I don't want to argue about this," Annie said softly. "It's been a long time since they've been here, and Mom has been hinting at coming over for some time, so I had to invite them." She paused. "And Matty needs to see them once in a while as well. They adore him. Especially Dad. Matty's his only grandson."

Jake plunked into a chair and looked up at her. "All right," he said. "I'll try to keep it under control." He paused. "For your sake."

Annie bent over and kissed him quickly. "Thank you."

Jake stood and drew her close again.

"It looks like we're going to have a busy day tomorrow," she said. "But right now, it's time for bed."

Jake smiled. He was all for that suggestion.

CHAPTER 2

Tuesday, August 9th, 9:58 a.m.

JAKE BROUGHT his 1986 Pontiac Firebird to an abrupt stop under the shade of an ancient maple tree. Annie crawled from the passenger door, stepped onto the sidewalk, and surveyed the house in front of her.

They were in a fairly exclusive part of town in a quiet and safe upper-class family neighborhood. Sitting on about two acres of land, the house was by no means new, but it had been restored to an elegant finish with vintage character.

They made their way up a winding path that led through a well-maintained rock garden and climbed the steps onto a large verandah guarding the front doors.

The solid forged brass doorknocker clanked as Jake knocked three times. In a few moments, there was a rattle of chains and the door swung open. A tall and remarkably beautiful woman appeared in the doorway.

Jake introduced them and handed her a business card. She looked at it briefly and gave a forced smile. "I'm Amelia James. Please, come in."

She ushered them into a fashionable sitting room. Feminine flourishes and modern lines with the absence of a rug created a sparse look and showcased the beautiful, dark hardwood floors. Matching bookcases, with what appeared to be antique books, framed either side of a huge fieldstone fireplace.

"Would you like tea or coffee?" Mrs. James asked.

Jake spoke for both of them. "Coffee, please."

Mrs. James motioned toward a comfortable-looking divan, and Jake and Annie sat. She left the room and returned a moment later, sitting across from them in an overstuffed armchair. She leaned forward and looked intently at them as if sizing them up.

Annie placed a small digital voice recorder on the coffee table in front of her. "Do you mind if I record this interview, Mrs. James?"

"That's fine. And please, call me Amelia."

Jake spoke. "Tell us about your daughter, Amelia."

The woman thought for a few moments. "She's a good daughter. Rarely gets into trouble or anything like that. The occasional party or hanging out with her friends, but nothing worse than we did as kids."

"Does she have a boyfriend?" Annie asked.

"She's very pretty and most of the boys like her, but there's no one steady boy as far as I know. There are a few of them in the group, but there's nobody serious or she would've told me. Jenny and I are close, and we talk about everything."

Annie knew that no matter how close you are to your mother, there are always some things you don't tell her, but she said nothing. "Has Jenny ever gone anywhere without telling you? Even overnight?"

"Never. Like all girls her age, she might occasionally stay

overnight at a friend's house for a day or two, but I always know where she is."

"Is there any one friend in particular?" Annie asked.

"Her best friend is Paige Canter, and they're together a lot. She's sixteen, the same age as Jenny."

"Do you have a copy of the police report, Amelia?" Jake asked. "That may save asking a lot of questions. I'm sure the police have contacted Paige and her other friends?"

"Oh, yes. That was one of the first things they did." She frowned. "And maybe about the only thing." She paused. "However, Detective Corning has been kind, but there's a limit to what he can do."

Amelia got up and opened a small drawer beside the bookcase. She pulled out two or three sheets of paper stapled together. "Here's the police report. It has all the names and addresses of her friends."

Jake reached for the papers. "Thank you. That should help."

Annie glanced over and scanned the pages as Jake leafed through them. She looked back at Mrs. James. "Would you have a picture of Jenny we could borrow?"

Amelia sat back down, reached toward a nearby end table, and picked up a photo. "Here's a recent picture of her," she said, handing it to Annie.

Annie looked at the picture. Jenny's mother certainly was not biased. The girl in the picture had long blond hair like her mother, a great figure, and a beautiful smile. She was a very pretty girl, indeed.

The entrance of a tiny Filipino woman, who appeared to be the maid, briefly interrupted them. She carried a tray that held three cups of steaming coffee, with cream and sugar, and set it on the table in front of them. Jake helped himself, and the others followed.

"Do you have another picture? Perhaps a close-up of her face?" Annie asked.

Amelia looked around the room, her eyes stopping at the fireplace. She stood and retrieved a framed picture from the mantel. "You may borrow this." She removed the photo from its frame and handed it to Annie. She smiled. "I'd like it back, though."

Jake asked, "When was the last time you saw Jenny?"

"It was last Tuesday morning, August second. She left for school as usual. Richmond Hill Public School. And that was the last I saw or heard from her." Amelia bowed her head. When she looked up, a tear or two was on her cheek. "Oh, please, I hope you can find her. I'm so afraid she may be in some danger."

"We'll do what we can, Amelia," Annie said gently. "I can't promise we'll find her, but we won't give up."

Annie sipped her coffee and glanced at the police report again. All of the vital information seemed to be there. Full name, date of birth, nicknames, height, weight, hair color, etcetera. The report contained a lot of other questions regarding the missing girl's habits and personality, but Annie wanted a little more information. "Does Jenny have a cell phone?"

"Yes, she had it with her as far as I know, but the police were unable to track it. She must have turned it off, or maybe it was lost."

"And what about social media? Facebook and so on?"

"Like just about everyone she knows, she has a Facebook page. She doesn't spend a lot of time on the computer, it's mainly for homework, but I know she chats with friends on occasion."

"We can't rule out online predators," Annie said.

Amelia looked fearful. "She's careful about things like that."

"I'm sure she is," Annie said. "We just don't want to miss any possibilities."

"And your husband?" Jake asked. "Jenny's father? Is he …"

Amelia forced a smile. "My husband, Mr. James, is … was … Jenny's father. He passed away a little over three years ago."

"Sorry to hear that," Jake said.

"He was a good man. A good father." Amelia looked around the room. "He provided for us very well." She sighed. "He just worked too hard I think. Winston had a weak heart and it couldn't take the stress of his job."

"What was his work?" Annie asked.

"He worked for a private investment firm. Private banking, asset management, hedge funds, things like that. He had some very wealthy clients and had to work long hours to keep up. But he always had time for us."

"And Jenny … how did she cope with his death?"

"She loved her father very much. She was his pride and joy. She took it very hard, but we've worked through it together. At first, I was unable to provide emotional support for both of us, so we saw a counselor, but we're okay now. We made it through the rough part together. She's a very strong girl and very sensible. I know she didn't just leave. She's out there somewhere."

Jake nodded. "Don't worry. We'll find her."

After a moment of silence, Annie spoke. "I believe that's all for now, Amelia. We'll keep you updated as we proceed. If there's anything else we need to know, we'll contact you."

Jake gulped the last of his coffee and stood. Amelia followed them to the door, handing them a piece of paper. "Here's my cell phone number where you can reach me if I'm not at home."

Jake stuffed it into his shirt pocket as they left.

CHAPTER 3

Tuesday, August 2nd, Eight Days Ago

JEREMY SPENCER didn't know what to do with the girl. He couldn't go on keeping her locked up, feeding her, and attending to her needs. He had things to do. But he couldn't let her go, either. She could identify him in a second.

He hadn't counted on her being there. She wasn't supposed to be around when he got the guy, but she had been, and now he was stuck with her.

Her boyfriend had been easy to catch. Like before, Jeremy had planned everything quite skillfully. A simple plan for sure, but sometimes the simplest plans were the best.

He knew the guy would drive out of town and then along County Road 12, a seldom-used road, on his way to King City. It was there Jeremy had put his plan into effect.

He had seen the car coming about a quarter mile away, around a curve. He climbed from his vehicle, parked on the shoulder, and lay down in the center of the road, his leg curled underneath him. He looked twisted and broken, like perhaps he'd been hit by a truck.

Jeremy heard the car screech to a stop just a few feet from him. He heard the door slamming, then footsteps coming toward him. A figure bent over, and then he heard an explosion as the bullet left his gun and shattered the skull of the scumbag.

He heard a scream and he jumped to his feet. The scream came from the guy's vehicle. There was a girl in the car, but she wasn't supposed to be there. What had happened to his oh-so-wonderful plan?

He ran to the car and pointed his gun at the girl. "Stop your noise," he said. "Get out of the car."

The girl did as she was told. She opened the door and stepped out slowly, keeping a distance between herself and him. She looked terrified. "What … what do you want?" she managed to ask.

"I already got what I want," he said, frowning. "And more than I want." He pointed toward the rear of the guy's car. "Get over there."

She obeyed, her body trembling. He kept an eye on her as he moved toward his car and popped open the trunk. Digging in a cardboard box, he found a plastic cable tie, then came back and fastened her wrists securely together in front of her.

He stuffed his hand into her side pocket and brought out a cell phone, which he switched off and shoved into his own pocket.

"Get in the trunk."

Jenny climbed clumsily inside and he slammed the lid. His first priority was to get the guy's car off of the road, leave her inside, and hide the vehicle somewhere. She would be okay in the trunk for a few minutes while he returned to move his own car. Then he would take her someplace safe until he figured out what to do with her.

Tuesday, August 9th, 4:06 p.m.

ANNIE HAD ARRANGED a meeting to interview Jenny's best friend, Paige Canter. Jake was at home, in the garage with Matty, fixing the leg of an end table that had come loose during one of their wrestling bouts.

She arrived at the Canter house just after four o'clock. She parked her Ford Escort on the narrow street in front of the modest house and walked up a short pathway bordered by flower beds stuffed with carnations, lilies, and bright red geraniums. She rang the doorbell. Mrs. Canter answered the door and, after introductions, led her to the kitchen.

The smell of something newly baked hung in the air. A vase of freshly cut flowers sat in the middle of the kitchen table, giving off a subtle fragrance.

A young girl sat at the far side of the table. She stood and introduced herself as Paige. She was an attractive girl. Maybe not as pretty as Jenny, but certainly appealing enough to turn the heads of most boys. She was dressed modestly in a colorful printed t-shirt and faded jeans.

Mrs. Canter took a seat at the end of the table, while Annie and Paige sat across from each other.

Annie dug a notepad and pen from her small valise and placed them on the table in front of her.

"We're worried about Jenny," Mrs. Canter said. "She's such a nice girl. Whatever we can do to help, we certainly will."

Annie smiled. "Thank you, Mrs. Canter." She turned to Paige. "When did you see Jenny last?"

"She came to school as usual last Tuesday," Paige said. "It was just an ordinary day. She has been seeing this guy. I wouldn't call him a boyfriend. Nothing romantic or anything like that, but they had started hanging out. She left with him right after school that day. She wanted me to come too, but I had lots of homework to do, and I told her I needed to get right home."

"What can you tell me about him? What's his name?" Annie asked.

Paige stopped to think. "His name is Chad Brownson ...

or Bronson … something like that." She leaned forward. "I think he's from King City."

"Have you seen him since last Tuesday?"

"No, he didn't come around as far as I know. They didn't see each other every day, just two or three days a week, but I haven't seen him since last week." Paige paused. "You don't think he had anything to do with her disappearance, do you? He seemed like a nice guy. Very polite and all that."

"It's too soon to say anything, but we have to check him out. He may have been the last person to see her." Annie paused. "Do you know what kind of car he drives?"

"I'm not too good with cars, but I know it's a Toyota. White." Paige frowned. "I don't know what year, though. But not that old."

Annie scribbled something in her notepad and then looked up. "Would anyone else know Chad? Someone you hang out with, perhaps?"

"I don't think so. He seems to be kind of a loner. He always came by himself."

"Where did Chad and Jenny meet?" Annie asked. "Do you know?"

Paige thought a moment and then replied slowly, "I really don't know. I'm surprised she didn't tell me more about him, but I think it may've been at a party somewhere. I told all this to the police," she added. "But nothing seemed to come of it."

"The police are limited, Paige. They did what they could, but they're so busy they can't do much beyond a few interviews and phone calls," Annie explained. "But right now, we're dedicated to finding Jenny and nothing else."

Paige leaned forward. "Please find her," she pleaded, looking worried.

"We will. By the way, do you know if she had her cell

phone with her? If she did, it seems to be turned off."

"I'm sure she did. She always carries it," Paige replied.

Annie skimmed quickly through her notes before looking up. "That seems to be all for now," she said. She dug a card from her valise and handed it to Paige. "If you think of anything else, give me a call. Anything at all."

"I will," Paige promised.

Annie turned to Mrs. Canter. "Thank you, Mrs. Canter. This has been a big help." She packed up her notepad and pen. "I'll be in touch," she said as she stood.

CHAPTER 4

Tuesday, August 9th, 4:46 p.m.

ANNIE SAT AT THE desk in the small office of Lincoln Investigations. She stared intently at the computer screen, a frown on her face.

"There are only a couple of Brownsons and several Bronsons in King City," she said. "We'll have to try them all."

"I think this guy is the key to it all," Jake replied. He was slouched back, his bulk burying a small leather chair, one foot resting on the desk. "If we find him … we'll find her."

"Mrs. James seemed certain Jenny would never go anywhere without telling her." Annie looked at Jake and sat back. "But it seems certain that wherever she is, she was with Chad."

"And it doesn't seem to be a kidnapping," Jake added. "At least, not for ransom. The kidnapper would've contacted someone by now if it was."

"So … if she wouldn't leave without telling anyone, and she wasn't kidnapped for ransom, then …" Annie hated to say it. "She's either dead or in grave danger."

Jake leaned forward and grabbed the phone. He hit a speed dial button and covered the mouthpiece with his hand.

"Let me see what Hank can do."

After several rings, the voice mail on Detective Hank Corning's cell phone greeted Jake. "This is Hank. Leave a message."

Jake and Hank had been friends since high school. They'd played together on the school football team, where they'd met and hit it off right away. After that, Jake had gone on to university while Hank wanted to be a cop. Hank had wanted Jake to go to Police Academy with him, but Jake knew all too well the social life of a cop wasn't much. Besides, Jake and Annie were already a couple, and she would be attending the University of Toronto as well. That had done it for Jake. He chose Annie over Hank. "No hard feelings, Hank," he had said. "But she's better looking than you."

Jake had great faith in Annie's expertise online. He knew when it came to research, if Annie couldn't do it, nobody could … except maybe Hank. But only because the cop had access to more resources than Annie.

Jake spoke into the phone. "Hank, it's Jake. I need some info. What can you find out for me about a guy from King City? Chad Brownson, or maybe Bronson. Probably the last one to see Jenny. Get back to me ASAP."

He slowly hung up the phone. "In the meantime," he said. "There's not much we can do."

Annie was staring at the computer again. "There's nothing on Chad Brownson or Bronson on Facebook. At least not from around here. The names do pop up in a few other places elsewhere online, but mostly hundreds of miles away. Certainly not our guy."

Tuesday, August 9th, 4:52 p.m.

BENNY FLANDERS had been a bum and a petty thief for most of his long life. He could never seem to settle down.

Didn't want to. He liked the freedom of doing his own thing, stealing what he needed, bumming for cash, and doing the occasional break and enter. Most houses were easy to get into. There was always an unsecured window or some other means to help him find his way into an unguarded residence.

He'd been in and out of jail a few times. Nothing serious. He didn't care. Actually, jail was a pretty good place to spend a night or two. The cells were warm and there was enough to eat. They never seemed to be able to pin much of anything on him and life was pretty good.

And right now, he was as free as the air. There was nobody to tell him what to do, and that's what it was all about.

A half-full bottle of cheap wine obtained from this morning's begging jutted from the right pocket of his filthy overcoat. An unlit stub of a cigar was stuck in his face.

And today was a day just like any other.

Benny was patrolling the parking lot of the huge Walmart store centrally located in Midtown Plaza. He peeked in car windows, looking for unlocked doors, searching for anything to claim as his own. Maybe he could find something to sell, or wear, or eat, or whatever the occasion provided.

He wasn't having much luck so far.

Benny leaned down and scanned the front seat of a white 2000 Toyota Tercel.

"I can't believe it," he said, his mouth hanging open, the cigar stuck to his lip. "They left the keys in it."

Benny hadn't driven for many years and he didn't know whether he should even attempt it. But the keys dangling there in front of his astonished eyes, and a chance to break up the boredom of the day, were just too much for him.

He took a quick look around. Nobody was in sight. He grinned as he lifted the door handle, opened the door, and slipped into the driver seat.

He sat there for a minute with a stupid smile on his face, then turned the key and the motor purred to life.

He backed carefully from the narrow parking spot his newfound toy was occupying. He cut the wheel slightly too sharp and dinged the front fender of a sleek black Mercedes beside him.

"Oh, nuts," he said to himself. "Be more careful, boy."

There were no more mishaps, and in a couple of minutes Benny steered the Tercel from the lot and headed toward a side street away from Walmart. He bounced up and down in the seat with glee, chuckling to himself as he sped down the street. Not too fast. There might be cops around.

He spun through a stop sign, not noticing it until it was too late. A quick look in his mirrors assured him he was still safe. Nobody else was in sight.

He didn't want to keep the car. Of course not; it was stolen. And he couldn't sell it. He wouldn't know where to sell a car. It probably wasn't worth much anyway. He just wanted to go for a little ride. Or a long ride. Whatever. He wasn't thinking that far ahead. He didn't care and didn't want to care.

The officer in the cruiser who tossed his donut into the box beside him, pulled from the side street, and hit his siren didn't care either. All he knew was he'd seen a car run a stop sign and that was against the law.

Officer Spiegle was new on the job. He felt important. He wasn't too bright and had only gotten the job because his daddy was a cop. The other cops called him Yappy. He didn't know why. He didn't talk much, but it was a name, and he didn't care, so it stuck.

But he was a cop, a symbol of authority, and he was going to get this guy.

When Benny heard the siren, he glanced in the rearview

mirror and swore. He cursed the cop and then swore again, pushing the gas pedal to the floor. He didn't care about stop signs now.

He should never have taken the car. But he had, and now he had to get away from the cop.

The vehicle weaved back and forth across the narrow street as Benny did his best to control it. His best wasn't good enough. The engine whined. The car seemed to skid out from under him, spun around, and planted itself into a row of well-manicured hedges.

Benny rolled from the car and sprang to his feet. He wasn't a big guy, or brawny by any means, but he spent most of the day on his feet, so he had strong legs. Those legs helped him jump over the hedge and carried him past the house, then through the backyard and away. He was gone.

Officer Spiegle couldn't do much of anything. By the time he was able to remove himself from the cruiser, Benny was out of sight.

He swore, jumped back into the car, and called dispatch.

He would let them handle it.

CHAPTER 5

Tuesday, August 9th, 5:25 p.m.

DETECTIVE HANK CORNING slouched at his tired desk in the precinct, surrounded by a steady buzz of activity. Footsteps clattered on the well-worn hardwood floor as officers moved to and fro. A photocopier quietly whined. Complaints were being handled, phones were ringing, and constant chatter of all kinds filled the room.

He hit the message button on his cell phone.

"Two new messages," the machine informed him.

Hank listened to the first message. It was from Amelia James. He smiled at the soft, pleasant voice. He couldn't help but picture her face. Her long blond hair framing her beautiful features, her gentle manner, and her graceful walk. Then he felt guilty for thinking about her that way when she was going through so much pain.

She had called to keep in touch. "I know you're not actively pursuing this anymore," she had said. "But I'm anxious to see if anything turned up."

Hank returned her call. When she answered, he

apologized, explaining there was nothing new.

"I've contacted Lincoln Investigations as you suggested," she said hopefully. "They sound confident they can help."

"I've known Jake and Annie for many years," he assured her. "They're good at what they do."

"Thank you, Detective. They promised to let me know if anything develops. I just feel so helpless and wish there were something I could do."

"Mrs. James," Hank said suddenly. "I want to help you and I'm going to contact Jake Lincoln and offer to assist them in any way I can. Officially, I can't do anything unless there's a solid lead, but unofficially … well, that's a different matter. And please, Mrs. James, call me Hank," he added.

"Thank you again, Hank. You may call me Amelia." She sighed deeply and Hank felt her sadness.

After hanging up, Hank's chair groaned and squeaked as he leaned back. At a little more than five years away from retirement, he was ready for it. He would do a little fishing, maybe some hunting, and just generally take it easy for a while. Then he could do something less stressful, like working as a security guard, or consulting of some kind.

But right now, something had drawn him to this case. Maybe it was because Amelia felt so helpless. Maybe it was the thought of a missing girl, or maybe it was because his own daughter would've been about the same age as Jenny.

He knew the captain would cut him some slack on this. It wasn't just a spur of the moment decision. He'd been thinking about this for some time. Maybe he would take some time off—he needed it anyway—and see what he could come up with.

He hit the "Next Message" icon on his cell and listened intently to Jake's message.

Leaning forward quickly, he tossed his phone on the desk

and thumped a few keys on his computer terminal. The name Chad Bronson appeared on his screen. From King City. Eighteen years old and no record to speak of. Just a pair of speeding tickets. Hank tapped a couple more keys and a picture appeared. He touched the print button, and in a moment, a page came whirring from the printer.

Hank stared at the screen. A further search showed a car registered to Bronson had just been involved in an accident. The driver had fled the scene and the car was now on its way to the pound.

He snapped up his cell again and hit the "Return Call" button. After a couple of rings, Jake answered.

"Jake, it's Hank," he said, dispensing with small talk. "I may have something here. A car registered to a Chad Bronson has just been in an accident. No sign of the driver." Hank scanned the online police report. "The attending officer described the fleeing driver as a white male. Approximately fifty to sixty years old. That doesn't sound like Bronson. The vehicle is on its way to the pound right now. I can meet you there if you come right away."

"On my way," Jake replied. "I'll just let Annie know, then I'll see you soon."

Hank printed a couple more pages, scooped them from the printer, and hurried from the building.

Tuesday, August 9th, 5:55 p.m.

THE SUN GLEAMED sharply off the hood of the bright red Firebird as Jake brought it to a quick stop beside where Hank stood waiting for him.

"Park that thing and let's go," Hank said.

Gravel flew as Jake spun into a nearby parking space and joined the cop.

The auto pound on Cherry Street was the only one in Vaughan, used to store vehicles that had been used in the commission of a crime and required additional investigation or were on hold for evidentiary purposes. It also held unclaimed vehicles that had been towed away for one reason or another. The enclosure was surrounded by a huge chain link fence and guarded by a massive gate.

Hank flashed his badge to the attendant and was given the location of the white Tercel. A tow truck crawled past them, exiting the lot, as Jake and Hank slipped through the gate and made their way toward the back of the area.

The auto had been deposited head first against the rear fence, the keys still in the ignition. Hank slipped on a pair of surgical gloves and retrieved the keys, handing them to Jake along with another pair of gloves. Jake forced on the one-size-fits-all gloves, ripping the back of one hand, and thought about faulty advertising.

"Be careful what you touch," Hank said. "If Bronson was the last one to see Jenny, then this vehicle is evidence."

A quick search of the backseat revealed a faux leather case stuffed with CDs. A McDonald's bag was on the floor, a couple of coffee cups jammed under the seat.

"Hank, look at this," Jake called. He stood at the rear of the car, the trunk wide open, pointing inside. He had lifted the mat to reveal a small gold pendant necklace. Hank picked it up carefully.

"I bet that's Jenny's," Jake said. "And look … it wasn't broken or ripped off. The clasp is undone." He looked at Hank. "She left it there on purpose. She was in this trunk." He dug his cell phone from his jacket pocket and snapped a picture of the pendant and a couple more of the outside of the vehicle.

Hank dropped the necklace into an evidence bag, peeled

off the silver strip, and sealed it. "I'll get the forensic guys down here," he said. "They need to go over this car completely, especially the trunk. This is not just an abandoned vehicle anymore. It's a crime scene."

Hank called dispatch and gave the information. He put the bag containing the necklace back in the trunk and shut the lid. "Let's go pick this Bronson character up," he said.

CHAPTER 6

Fourteen Years Ago

THIRTY-TWO-YEAR-OLD Quinton Spencer sat in the visitors' center of Kingston Penitentiary. He watched the door where families came and went, eagerly awaiting the arrival of his wife and young boy. It had been five years since he'd seen his son. The boy was now ten years old, and he ached to hold him in his arms again.

And when he finally got out of this life-robbing place, he would hold them both and never let go.

As he waited, he thought back to that night six years earlier. Back to the events that had brought him here, back before this all started.

He'd done a good job of keeping the farm up. He'd been successful, and the mortgage on their property was paid off. He had a beautiful wife and a little boy, and life was pretty good.

Then one night their life was shattered.

Annette Spencer was awakened suddenly, sure she'd heard something. She reached over and gently awakened her husband.

"I think there's somebody in the house," she whispered.

Quinton was immediately alert. He didn't hear anything, but he dropped carefully out of bed, went to the closet, and retrieved his Remington Model 7 hunting rifle. He crept across the dim bedroom and gently opened the door to the hallway. As he felt his way silently toward the stairs, he peeked inside Jeremy's room. His son was fast asleep. When he reached the top of the steps, he heard rustling from downstairs.

The house was old, and the steps creaked a little as he gradually made his way down and toward the kitchen. The half-moon was bright enough to allow him to safely avoid chairs, tables, and other furniture.

The rustling noise was coming from the living room. The sound of drawers opening and closing. Hugging the wall, he inched steadily toward the sound of the intruder. He held his rifle in a firing position, bolt back, safety off, ready to fire.

A careful glance around the corner showed a shadowy figure dressed in black, holding a flashlight, snooping in drawers, violating his home.

Quinton raised his rifle and carefully aimed. "What are you doing in my house?" he demanded.

He got off one shot as the invader ducked. Then, crawling, stumbling, and diving toward the open window, the thief plunged outside head first, landing with a thud six feet down.

Quinton raced to the window. A second shot winged the villain in the shoulder as he tried to rise. A third shot and he was down, flat on his face, a bullet through his head. Dead.

It is said those with the most money get the most justice, and that appeared to be true in Quinton's case. In fact, his lawyer wasn't up to much, and the end result was a hanging judge handing down a sentence of ten years. Tried and convicted of manslaughter. Sent to Kingston Penitentiary. Locked away.

~*~

JEREMY SPENCER could hardly contain his excitement, pleased to finally be seeing his father again after so many years. He and his mother arrived a half hour early to the prison's visitors' center, a small building situated outside the prison grounds. His mother showed her identification, which was scrutinized by a squinty-eyed attendant, and then they were allowed into the waiting room. There they had to put everything they were carrying into a locker.

In a few minutes, a corrections officer escorted them to the main prison, where they were searched.

Jeremy didn't like being searched. He didn't like the man doing the search. He was rough, and he didn't like it when the man touched him in a place where he knew nobody should touch him. It made him afraid and all cold inside.

After the search, they were taken to the visits hall. The room was filled with rows of tables, seated inmates, and visitors. There was a guard in each corner of the room. Jeremy saw his father already seated and waiting for them.

Jeremy had been a lot younger when his daddy was taken away, but he still remembered his father's face. After five years in Kingston Penitentiary, his father appeared much older and had a rougher exterior. His short-cropped hair showed some silver at the temples. He looked worn out.

A guard eyed them closely as his father stood, kissed his mother, and gave Jeremy a quick hug. That's all that was allowed.

Seated at the table in the visits hall of the correctional institution, Jeremy couldn't hold back his tears. Seeing his father in this place made him sad. And his mother didn't deserve this either.

"Hi, Jeremy," his father said gently and smiled. "You've grown a lot."

"When are you coming home, Daddy?"

"It'll be awhile yet, son."

Jeremy looked around him at the families, the loners, and some old guy fidgeting with his hands, sitting straight as a rail on a seat at the far wall. People of all kinds. Jeremy had never seen so many scary characters. Some looked like they could bite the heads off nails. The glare from a bearded and heavily tattooed man caused Jeremy to cower in fear and cling to his mother. Tattoo gave Jeremy a menacing grin. The boy looked away quickly. It was a terrible place, and he wondered why his daddy was there.

Before long, their time was up and they had to leave. Leaving Jeremy's father behind.

On the long drive home, his mother explained how this had all happened. She explained about the intruder, how he'd entered through the window, and how his father had shot him while he was trying to escape. She explained that his father didn't deserve to be in prison; he was only protecting his home and his family.

Jeremy wasn't stupid. He knew what that meant. He realized the burglar who had invaded their home deserved to die. His father always did the right thing, and he had killed someone who deserved it. He was glad the boy was dead. He wished he could've been the one who did it. It made him angry.

"Mommy, Daddy did the right thing, right?"

"Yes, honey, he did."

Jeremy looked out the side window as they sped down the highway toward home. He was deep in thought.

Tuesday, August 9th, 6:22 p.m.

JAKE ACCOMPANIED Hank to King City. The building on Canderline Street that the printout showed as Bronson's residence was an ancient apartment complex. They took the elevator to the third floor, and Jake followed behind the cop as he approached 3B.

The door was opened to Hank's knock by an elderly woman wearing a faded housecoat. That, and the rest of her attire, appeared to have been scrounged from Goodwill. She looked at them blankly. As she spoke, the ash fell from a cigarette dangling from her mouth, landing on the filthy carpet. "What is it?" she demanded.

Hank showed the grizzled old woman his badge. "We would like to talk to Chad Bronson," he said.

"He ain't here."

"Can you tell me where he is?" Hank asked.

"Ain't seen him 'round for a week or more," she said. "What's he done this time?"

Hank avoided the question. "This is important," he said. "Can you tell me where he might be?"

"Don't know."

"Are you his mother?"

"The only one he has." She blinked a toothless grin.

Hank eventually convinced her to tell him where her son worked. After a little more coaxing, they were allowed in, and she led them to Bronson's bedroom. She let them open a few drawers, check the closet, and perform a basic search. There wasn't much to go through—just a few clothes in a narrow closet, a dresser with more clothes, and a few knickknacks, along with a picture of Chad posing with his car. Nothing appeared to be out of the ordinary.

"If you see him, tell him to get his butt home," the old

woman said as they were leaving. "Ain't been outta this place for a week, an' I need my meds."

Hank assured her they would.

The factory where Bronson worked was only a couple of blocks away, and they arrived at King City Foods in a few minutes.

Hank flashed his badge to the evening supervisor and they were led into a small office at the front of the building.

The supervisor consulted an obsolete computer perched at the back of his desk. He squinted at the tiny monitor. "Bronson works the graveyard shift. Midnight till eight a.m.

He hasn't shown up for work in several days, though," he said. "That appears to be unusual for him. No matter what else he is, he seems to be a steady worker. Always on time. Never takes a day off."

"When was the last time he was here?" Hank asked.

The supervisor squinted again. "He showed up August first. Clocked out the next morning. Hasn't been here since."

Hank was taking notes. "Do you have any contact phone numbers for him, besides his home phone?"

"Nope. Just his home number."

"Residence at 266 Canderline Street, 3B?"

"Yup."

Hank stared at his notes. "That's all for now. Thank you."

They were at a dead end. No one had seen Bronson.

Chad Bronson and Jenny were both missing.

On the way home, Hank said, "I hate to say it, but it appears they may've run off somewhere together."

"Maybe," Jake said. "But where could they go without a car?"

Tuesday, August 9th, 6:22 p.m.

JENNY WASN'T uncomfortable. She wasn't cold, or hungry, or in need of anything. But she was afraid. Afraid because she'd seen Chad brutally murdered. She was afraid because when her assailant had let her out of the trunk and led her here, she'd seen his face. She could identify him. And she was afraid he would likely have to kill her to protect himself. To keep her from turning him in. But then, why hadn't he killed her yet? Why had he kept her here all this time, caring for her, bringing her food, and talking with her? He seemed to be going out of his way to make sure she was comfortable.

The room where she was held was nice enough. Sure, everything was old, antique, maybe, but it was functional. The closet was even filled with clothes. And the drawers as well. It seemed obvious to Jenny that the room had once been the bedroom of a woman. Or maybe a husband and wife, because the room contained a double bed; however, there were no signs of a man's presence.

The walls were covered with wallpaper, creamy and pink roses, rather faded, but still pretty. The dark hardwood floor needed a fresh coat of varnish. A large curtained window was on one side of the room, covered with bars on the outside of the glass, fastened in tight. They wouldn't come loose. Jenny had tried. The only other means of exit was the bedroom door, but it was securely bolted from the outside.

She loved to read, and the room was well supplied with books. A massive, overstuffed bookcase took up half of one wall of the large room. She had perused a few books, but couldn't settle her mind long enough to actually finish one.

Jenny had tried screaming for help earlier, but a look out the window told her it was no use. On the other side of a massive unkempt lawn, there was a decaying and weather-beaten barn, surrounded by fields of emptiness, and then what appeared to be an endless forest. She knew she was in a secluded spot. It did no good to call for help—no good at all.

She sat on the edge of the bed and cried. She thought about her mother. Surely her mother wondered where she was. And the police—were the police looking for her? She thought fondly of Chad. Why had he been murdered? And who was this little man who had killed him and was terrorizing her? He had said his name was Jeremy and he wasn't going to hurt her.

With a sob of despair, she threw herself onto the bed, her gasps filling the room. She prayed. Prayed God would get her out of this place and away from this terrible man.

Her prayers were interrupted by the sound of an approaching vehicle. Gravel crunched under its tires as it drove in and squeaked to a stop near the house. She didn't need to look out the window; she knew it was him. It was late afternoon, maybe early evening, just about the time he always arrived. She turned on her side and soaked her pillow with tears.

CHAPTER 7

Wednesday, August 10th, 8:20 a.m.

CRANSTON'S DEPARTMENT Store was a valued new client, and they had already turned some work toward Lincoln Investigations. When the head of security at Cranston's called Annie, she was obliged to drop all she was doing and head there immediately to consult with them.

Cranston's was the anchor store of the busiest mall in the area. The security office was located on the main floor of the massive store. Annie tapped on the door and a burly man opened it immediately. An enormous grin threatened to split his face when he saw her.

"Annie," he almost shouted. "Come in. Come in."

Annie smiled back at him. His exuberance was almost overwhelming. He pointed to the only visitor's chair in the small room. "Have a seat," he said as he slouched down in a swivel chair behind the desk. "So how's the most beautiful girl in Canada?" The grin still hadn't left his face.

Annie chuckled. "Jake and I are doing well."

"Jake? Are you still with that guy? If you ever need a real man, I'm your guy."

Annie laughed. She and Jake had known Chris for some time, and had assisted him in his job as head of store security on several occasions. He was a harmless flirt. She knew he had a wife he loved dearly, and a young boy who was his pride and joy. "I'll let you know," she said.

"Good enough," he said, and turning more serious, he continued, "But in the meantime, we've got a small problem on our hands. It's in the jewelry department. Seems like we've had some stuff go missing lately. A couple rings, a necklace or two. Security cameras haven't caught anything." He frowned.

Annie leaned forward. "We ran all of your jewelry people through a security check. They came back clean."

"We have two shifts during the day, then a couple of different girls work evenings and weekends. But we're not necessarily suspecting it's one of our girls. It could just as likely be a customer."

Annie knew exactly what to do. A few strategically placed mini-cameras, with close-ups on the cases, should do the trick. "We'll set up some camera surveillance," she said. "If we can get in here this evening after you close, it shouldn't take too long. We've got the equipment."

"Excellent," he said. "I knew I could count on you." The grin was back.

Before she left, they arranged to meet again just after nine o'clock that evening.

On her way home, she thought about Jenny. Jake had filled her in on their unsuccessful attempt the day before to locate Chad. She felt she should update Mrs. James on their progress, or lack thereof. In the case of a missing child, for a mother, any news was better than no news at all.

When she arrived back at the office, she called Mrs. James immediately, arranging for a meeting just after noon.

Jake was still at home, and she informed him of the task

for Cranston's. They needed a few more mini-cameras in order to do the job right, so Annie sent him down to Techmart, a store that dealt in everything electronic, including a wide range of security and surveillance equipment.

She knew Jake wouldn't mind that mission. It made him feel like a kid in a candy store.

Wednesday, August 10th, 11:05 a.m.

"HANK WANTS TO meet us at Amelia's," Jake informed Annie. Jake had returned from Techmart and had dumped his purchases out on the kitchen table.

"That's fine," she said. "Amelia will see he's still taking this seriously." Annie eyed the pile of electronic equipment. "This looks good," she said. "But did you really need this pen camera? You're not quite James Bond, you know."

"I thought it would come in handy," Jake replied sheepishly. "Plus, it was on sale."

Annie glanced at the clock on the wall; they still had a while before their appointment. Jake helped her prepare a quick brunch before heading to Amelia's.

When they arrived at their destination, Hank was waiting for them, parked across the street, still sitting in his dark brown Chevy. He swung from the vehicle when they pulled up, greeting Annie with a warm smile and a smothering bear hug.

They made their way to the front door of the house, and when Annie knocked on the door, Amelia opened it almost immediately and led them into the lavish sitting room. There was a box of tissues on the stand beside where Amelia sat. A look at her face showed she appeared to have been crying. The lack of sleep was evident on her face as well. Photo albums were spread out on the coffee table. The room was quiet and still.

They sat down and Hank fumbled with a package he was carrying. He withdrew the picture of Chad and handed it to Mrs. James. "Amelia," he said. "Do you recognize this man?"

She took the photo and studied it carefully. "No," she said. "I don't believe I've seen him before." She looked up at Hank, a question on her face.

"This appears to be one of Jenny's friends," Hank informed her. He withdrew the necklace from the bag, looking at Jake and then back at Amelia, and reluctantly added, "This was found in his car. Do you recognize it?" Annie noted Hank didn't mention the necklace had been found in the trunk.

Amelia gasped and took the necklace, fondling it gently. "It's Jenny's. I'd recognize it anywhere. Her father gave that to her on her thirteenth birthday." She looked at Hank again, puzzled, waiting for an explanation.

Hank continued in a soothing voice, "Amelia, we have absolutely no evidence any harm has come to Jenny." He pointed to the photo. "Apparently, she was seen with this man, Chad Bronson, several times in the past. He seems to be missing too, although we were able to locate his vehicle. It appears they may've been together the day she went missing." He quickly added, "There could be a perfectly logical explanation."

Annie interrupted, pointing to the necklace. "As you can see, it's undamaged. It wasn't forced or broken off. The clasp was undone, and we believe it was removed by Jenny herself."

Hank spoke. "And we have an APB, an all-points bulletin, out on Bronson. If he's around anywhere, we'll pick him up."

A mixture of hope and despair was in Amelia's voice as she spoke. "Jenny's out there somewhere. Please find her."

Hank leaned forward and gently placed his hand on

Amelia's. "Don't give up hope," he said. "Just don't give up hope."

Amelia smiled weakly and thanked them.

After they left, Hank followed them to their vehicle. "I didn't want to mention this to Amelia," he said. "But I got the forensic report back on the vehicle this morning. They found some hair in the trunk as well. It matches Jenny's. I think we can definitely conclude she was in that trunk."

Wednesday, August 10th, 1:25 p.m.

EARLIER THAT afternoon, Hank had faxed over a copy of the Police Forensic Report. Annie grabbed it from the machine and studied it for some time. There were several pages, and she went over it thoroughly.

Picking up the phone, she dialed MacGlen Forensic Services. MacGlen was a private forensic firm located in the downtown area. As a licensed forensic service, MacGlen could gain access to Bronson's vehicle. It was not that she didn't trust the police forensic report, but she had a question the report didn't cover. Specifically, she wanted a botany test of the tires and underside of the car.

She spoke with Sammy MacGlen. Sammy was an expert she'd dealt with in the past, and he took her call immediately. "Annie, what can I do for you today?"

She explained the situation to him and outlined her needs. He agreed they could get at it right away and try to get back to her in a day or two. As a private, for-profit firm, they were unhampered by red tape and backlogs. With a team expert in every forensic field, she was confident she would get accurate results, and fast.

CHAPTER 8

Wednesday, August 10th, 1:55 p.m.

AMELIA PICKED up the phone. "Hello," she said.

"Hi, Amelia. It's Hank Corning. I have something I'd like to talk to you about. Is this evening fine for you? Say about seven o'clock?"

"Seven would be fine," she answered.

"Actually, if you'd like to get away from the house for a while, there's a quiet little deli I know. You can have a break, and we can have some dinner and talk."

Amelia hesitated. Jenny could call at any minute, and she wanted to be home if she did. She hadn't wandered far from home these last few days. All she did was worry, pace the floor, and cry. And wait for the phone to ring with some good news. It never did. Would it be all right to go out for an hour or so?

Amelia thought a moment. "That sounds fine," she said. "I'm sure I could use some time out." Suddenly she felt guilty and considered changing her mind.

Hank interrupted her thoughts. "See you at seven," he said.

She hung up the phone and dug in the kitchen junk drawer for a manual. She consulted it and, with a few clicks, enabled call forwarding to her cell phone. She tested it. It worked fine. If her daughter called, she wouldn't miss the call.

~*~

BEFORE DRIVING TO Amelia's house that evening, Hank visited the local car wash around the corner from his apartment. After the wash, he spent a few dollars on the two-dollar vacuum machine and gave the inside of his car a well-needed cleaning. Then he dashed home and changed into a pair of slacks and a matching sport jacket. No tie.

He knew about the death of Amelia's husband from his first interview with her a week or so ago, but he wasn't sure what his intentions were, just that he was attracted to her very much. She could use someone to talk to right now, and he could always use a little feminine company. He wasn't much of a ladies' man. Just didn't seem to have met anyone, and never went out of his way to. Besides, his job kept him busy most of the time. It was easy enough to work overtime to keep his mind occupied.

But today was different. He definitely needed a break. He hoped he wasn't being too forward at this difficult time, when Amelia's mind was consumed with thoughts and worries of her daughter.

He steered his Chevy into her double-width driveway at a couple of minutes before seven. A last look at himself in the mirror, a quick brush of his hand through his hair, and he stepped out and made his way to her front door.

Amelia answered his knock wearing an attractive, but not too elegant, black skirt, matching high-heeled shoes, and a simple white blouse. She carried a small handbag, just big enough to hold a few necessities. A small gold chain and pendant hung at her throat, her long hair in a ponytail. Hank refrained from telling her how beautiful she looked.

Instead, he just said, "Hi."

She offered him a weak but wonderful smile as he held out his hand to help her down the stairs. He followed her to the car and opened the door for her. He felt self-conscious about picking her up in his wreck when she probably had a Mercedes, or maybe a Porsche, parked in her garage.

"Buckle up," he said. "I'm a cop." And then he thought how lame that must sound.

But she laughed—a real laugh, and it made him feel better.

They didn't have time to more than exchange a few pleasantries, talk about the weather, and traffic, before Hank pulled up in front of the deli a couple of blocks away.

Center Street Delicatessen was a popular Jewish deli, tucked over in the corner of a small strip plaza. It was small, but served great food, and though it was busy, they were able to find a quiet booth near the back.

After placing their order, Hank said, "Amelia, I don't have much progress to report, but the good news is, now that Bronson's car has been found, with some evidence Jenny had been in the vehicle, the Captain has taken more interest. Though there's no official police investigation, he has given me a handful of men to work with and I'm going to push them to their utmost."

"But what about if she's … I mean, do you think she's all right?" Amelia asked.

"We have no reason to think otherwise," Hank said softly. "There's no evidence any harm has come to her."

Hank filled her in on Bronson's car and how it had been found. "Jake and Annie got information on Chad from Jenny's friend, Paige," he informed her. "Annie also said

Jenny and Chad had been seeing each other off and on, but nothing serious."

They were interrupted briefly as a bubbly young waitress brought their meal. She slid it onto the table in front of them. "Enjoy," she said with a smile.

"Jenny never told me about that boy," Amelia said, frowning.

"According to Paige, there was nothing romantic between them. Perhaps Jenny didn't feel it was important enough to mention. Just another casual friend."

Amelia looked thoughtful. "Yes, I'm sure you're right."

"Don't worry, Amelia. We'll find Jenny."

Amelia was silent for a while, eating in silence. Finally, she spoke again. "I don't mean to pry, but have you ever been married?"

Hank put his sandwich down. He leaned back in his seat, took a deep breath, and studied Amelia a moment, gathering his thoughts. Finally, he said, "A long, long time ago."

Amelia waited for him to continue.

"We were young, but very much in love, or so we thought. Perhaps we were. I know we certainly enjoyed being together as much as possible. So we got married and things were great. I'd just graduated from the academy. She'd just graduated from the University of Toronto, and our future looked wonderful, without a care in the world."

Amelia picked at her food and waited patiently. "Go on." She encouraged him with a smile.

"Before too long, we found out we were going to have a baby. Our nice life was even nicer. We were over the moon. We soon found out it was going to be a girl, and we spent so much time running around, getting stuff for the nursery, all those things expectant parents do."

Amelia leaned forward. "I remember doing that too," she

spoke wistfully, a faint smile. "I loved every minute of being pregnant." She interrupted her own thoughts, "Go on."

"Before we knew it, the baby was born. We named her after my wife, Elizabeth. Beth, we called her." Hank's eyes were unfocused, a faraway look with a twinkle of moisture. "She was the most beautiful creature I'd ever seen." He moved his head slowly back and forth a few times, amazed at the thought. "As a new father, looking at this little baby, this person I'd helped create, it was an indescribable feeling."

He looked away, watching a couple walk by, his eyes unseeing.

She touched his hand. He looked intently at her and lost a tear. He rubbed it away, cleared his throat, and took the last bite of his sandwich.

Amelia pushed back her plate. She sat back, dabbed at her lips with the cloth napkin, and smiled weakly at Hank. "That was delicious. Thank you."

"You're welcome," he said. "It's been a pleasure."

CHAPTER 9

Wednesday, August 10th, 8:45 p.m.

ANNIE'S FRIEND, CHRISSY, had dropped over from next door to watch Matty for a while. Annie called Jake in from the other room where he was helping Matty put the finishing touches on a Lego mansion. The boy came trailing along behind in his pajamas as Jake answered the summons.

Jake grabbed a duffel bag from the kitchen table. "All ready," he said.

"We should be back in a couple of hours," Annie said to Chrissy, and then turned to Matty. "Don't forget to brush your teeth."

"I will, Mom. You know I always do."

Right on time, Jake and Annie arrived at Cranston's Department Store. Jake tapped lightly on the door of the security office and eased it open. Chris rose from his chair and slapped Jake on the back. "Good to see you, buddy." He offered his hand and a grin.

Jake shook the hand and returned the grin. He dropped the duffel bag full of tools and equipment on the desk.

"We're all set here any time you are," he said.

"Got all your spy stuff in there, do you?" Chris asked, pointing to the bag.

"Enough and more."

"We'll give it a few minutes to let the cashiers check out, and then we can get this thing done."

Before long the huge store was empty, save for a few security guards patrolling the aisles, making sure all the customers were gone. Jake and Annie followed Chris to the jewelry department.

Three of the showcases contained the most valuable items. Necklaces, rings and bracelets made from gold and containing diamonds and other precious jewels. These were the cases that had endured the losses.

The cameras were tiny and could be put almost anywhere without being obvious. They would wirelessly send what they saw back to a special bank of digital recorders already set up in the security office. The recordings were timestamped and could be viewed live on monitors or played back at a later time.

They fitted two cameras inside each showcase, one at either end. Another went on top of the case, fastened to the cash register. A couple more went behind the counter to cover a larger area, and they were done.

Chris glanced over the inventory control sheet. "Nothing missing today," he said. "Yesterday we had a diamond ring disappear. It's usually about every couple of days."

"We're done here," Annie said, zipping up the bag. "Now it's just a matter of waiting."

Chris let them out the front door of the megastore, locking it behind them.

They got in the Firebird and Annie turned to Jake. "I'm

glad that's out of the way for now. I'm anxious to do whatever we can to find Jenny as soon as possible."

Jake agreed.

Wednesday, August 10th, 9:00 p.m.

HANK SPUN THE wheel and the car veered to the right. He swung into Amelia's driveway, squealing to a stop in front of the double garage.

Amelia looked at her watch. "Would you like to come in for a coffee?" she asked.

"Sure," Hank said.

He climbed from the car, moved around to the other side of the vehicle, and opened Amelia's door. He offered his hand as she stepped gracefully out. Approaching the house, she fumbled briefly in her purse, and in a moment the front door swung open and they stepped inside the foyer.

Lilia, the live-in maid, greeted them at the door. She'd been with them for many years and was a cherished helper, treated like one of the family. Amelia asked her to make a pot of coffee, and Lilia nodded slightly, smiled, and headed for the kitchen.

Amelia excused herself a moment and followed Lilia. She checked the phone. No one had called. There were no messages and no missed calls. She didn't know whether to be relieved or not. She checked the phone to be sure it was still working and the call forwarding was still in place. It was.

Coming back to the foyer, Amelia motioned toward the sitting room. Hank followed her and they took a seat on the divan. He propped up one knee on the couch, turned sideways, and faced her, his arm over the back cushion. She sat at the other end and crossed her legs.

Seeing the photo albums still on the coffee table, she

breathed a sigh and looked at Hank. "Jenny loves this room," she said. "She used to come in here to read or do her homework. She loved … loves … to have the fireplace going and just sit here and talk."

Hank agreed. "It's a beautiful room," he said. "And comfortable. I can see why she likes it so much."

Just then, Lilia eased into the room, her feet in soft ballet slippers, barely making a whisper. She slid a silver tray gently onto the coffee table, carefully moving one of the albums aside to make room. As well as coffee, cream and sugar, the tray contained a plate of fruit-stuffed scones. Just big enough for a bite or two. Lilia poured two cups and smiled sweetly at them, slipping again from the room.

Hank fixed up his coffee with cream and lots of sugar before sitting back, cup in hand. He looked at Amelia.

Amelia turned to face him. "Hank, tell me about your daughter, about Beth," she asked cautiously.

She caught a faraway look in his deep brown eyes as he sipped his coffee thoughtfully before speaking.

"Our daughter, our beautiful daughter Beth, was diagnosed with brain cancer at six months. She had started to refuse food and wasn't thriving very well. She had an MRI scan which showed she had a brain tumor. Chemotherapy to reduce the size of the tumor didn't help much. She grew constantly weaker. The specialist recommended surgery, but it wasn't effective due to her weakened condition, and she died less than a week later."

Amelia was silent and encouraged him with a compassionate look.

He looked down, brushing some invisible dust from his pant leg, and then looked up and continued. "Naturally, it was a hard time. For both of us. We were devastated. And now the happy future we had envisioned was just dark. I know time heals all wounds, and it pretty much does. At least the pain gets less, but at the time, we sure didn't think so. I guess everybody grieves in their own way. I buried myself in my work, but Elizabeth just wanted to cling to me. She wanted to always be talking about it. I just wanted to be busy. Neither one of us understood the other. We grew apart. Just like that."

Hank cleared his throat again and took another gulp of coffee, then poked a scone into his mouth. He chewed slowly, assessing his thoughts. She watched him.

He continued, "Though of course I was still in a lot of pain, I could come to accept it after a while. But Elizabeth never could. I didn't expect her to just forget it. Of course not, but she couldn't deal with it. The amount of help and encouragement I tried to give her, and the support from her family, just wasn't enough."

He shrugged his shoulders and spread his hands, palms up, as if resigned to the past he couldn't control. "And so we separated. She went back to live with her parents. I thought it was only temporary, but it didn't work out like I thought, so I just went my own way. Back to work, and tried to move on with my life. And here I am." He smiled. "I'm okay now."

Amelia studied him momentarily. He seemed like such a caring man in the little time she'd known him. Compassionate, and always sympathetic toward others. Now she understood why. Those who experience pain can best understand the pain of others. She touched his hand, smiled, and nodded slowly. "Yes, you're okay now," she agreed.

Hank popped another scone and downed the rest of his coffee. He stood and said, "I'd better go."

As she rose, he thanked her and moved toward the door.

"Hank," she said, as his hand was on the doorknob.

He turned. "Yes?"

"Find Jenny for me."

"We will," he promised. "Finding your daughter is my top priority. Every available officer I could scrounge is canvassing the city round the clock. If even the remotest lead is found, I'll be all over it. I'm going to give the Lincolns my full support as well, and they've assured me they'll spend as much time as possible looking for Jenny."

CHAPTER 10

Thursday, August 11th, 10:20 a.m.

JAKE WAS FIDDLING with his car in the garage. Annie knew it had something to do with the mufflers, but she wasn't sure what the problem was. He always had some emergency adjustment to do, something that couldn't wait to be fixed. His car always seemed to run smoothly to her.

She backed her Ford Escort from the driveway, heading for Mortino's. The large grocery store had the best selection of meats, and a good load of red meat was necessary to fulfill Jake's cravings. Especially during barbecue season.

She picked out four nice big steaks for the barbecue that night. Then she put two back and selected a couple of smaller ones. Lettuce and tomatoes for a salad. Some chubby potatoes for baking. She consulted her shopping list, moving aisle to aisle, gathering what they needed, and only what they needed. Mostly.

"Hello, Mrs. Lincoln."

Annie turned around. "Hi, Jeremy."

She looked at the little man grinning up at her. Slightly

shorter than her, he was an odd specimen, but always polite and helpful. He knew where everything was in the store, always bustling around restocking, and was quick to point out special sales. Today he thought the tomatoes were especially nice.

"Local grown," he said. "Early ripening tomatoes. Nice and juicy."

Annie pointed to her cart. "Yes, I have some."

"You should see my tomatoes," he said. "I planted a whole crop of them this spring. They're just getting ripe now. Big ones. I have great soil. I can grow anything. I have lettuce and carrots growing too. Not ready yet, of course."

Annie smiled. He was too helpful sometimes, rambling a lot, but she couldn't help feeling sorry for him. Normally she wouldn't have paid much attention to him, let alone known anything about his personal life.

When Jeremy's father had been sent to prison when he was young, she hadn't been aware of it. When he was found dead in his cell, a shiv fashioned from a sharpened toothbrush protruding from his heart, no one heard about it. At least she hadn't.

But when his mother had been found in the barn, hanging from the rafters, with a length of strong rope noosed about her neck, one shoe lying quietly on the straw below her lifeless body, Annie had heard about it. That didn't happen every day. And so, Annie felt some compassion for the young man, odd though he was.

"I'm sure your garden is nice," she said. "It's great you can still put the land to some use."

"Yeah, can't let it go to waste. Mother always had a nice garden. We took care of it together. We had to, you know, with Father not able to be there. She's buried out near the garden with Father. And my grandparents too, you know."

He added thoughtfully, "Guess I'll be buried there someday too."

"I expect that won't be for a long time, Jeremy."

"Yeah, I guess not. Well, I'd better get back to work. Goodbye, Mrs. Lincoln."

"Goodbye, Jeremy." She watched him bustle over to the next aisle and disappear behind a stack of baked beans.

Thursday, August 11th, 11:00 a.m.

JAKE WAS IN THE basement doing his daily workout routine. Annie found a message propped up on the office desk from Sammy MacGlen from MacGlen Forensic Services. The message said he'd found something interesting and could she please call him back.

She took a seat, tapped in the phone number written on the note, and after two rings she heard, "MacGlen Forensic Services. Sammy speaking."

"Hi, Sammy. It's Annie Lincoln."

"Hi, Annie. Glad you got back to me right away. As I told Jake, I found something."

"Yes?"

"We did a sampling for any botanical material found on the tires and underneath the vehicle, as you asked."

"Yes?"

"Not surprisingly, the tires didn't show anything unusual at first, but the underbody did. We found evidence of partially decomposed plant materials, like water lilies, fern, and cypress, resulting in a buildup of peat and rich soil. There are fragments of plant tissue, excluding live roots, which have retained recognizable cellular structure of the original plant."

Annie chuckled. "So what does that really mean?"

"The materials examined came from an area that had

probably been a swamp at one time. The breakdown suggests many years ago, possibly hundreds. And so, we examined the tires again and found small traces of the same soil in the treads. Not enough to be remarkable on its own, but there nonetheless."

"Excellent work, Sammy. Will you fax me a copy of that report?"

"I'll send it over right away," Sammy said. "I'll fax a copy to the police as well."

"Hang on to the samples for now," Annie asked.

"Sure will. I'll put them in storage."

After hanging up the phone, Annie pulled in her chair and powered on the computer. She needed to find an area, probably locally, that had once been a swamp. It appeared Bronson's car had been driven in a spot with that description. It wasn't much to go on, but it seemed to be all they had.

She searched through topographic maps online. No luck there. A geological map looked more promising. After a few minutes research, she found an area west of Richmond Hill, toward King City, which fitted the description. A lot of it was now government-protected land because of the wildlife that flourished in the area, and much still contained swamp, but in many places the swamp had receded and the land was thriving and heavily forested.

Annie printed out the maps and sat back, staring at the monitor. She had to go on an expedition.

Thursday, August 11th, 12:00 p.m., Noon

JAKE STEPPED FROM the shower and dried himself off on the way to the bedroom. After getting dressed, he wandered down to the kitchen where Annie was putting together a light lunch.

"Did you call Sammy?" he asked.

"Yes, I did, and he found out something interesting. The vehicle had recently been driven through an area that was previously a swamp. There were bits on the underside of the car body. I did some checking, and it looks like there are three possible areas."

Jake whistled. "Nice call."

"According to the maps, two of the three areas are near roads, but one is much further away from any traffic areas and probably not reachable by vehicle. I doubt if it would be the spot. If you're game, I think we should take a look at one of the two possibilities and see if we can find anything."

"I'm ready," Jake said.

"We'll take my car," Annie said. "I know how picky you are about yours. We'll bring a shovel just in case. I might want to take some soil samples."

After lunch, Jake and Annie changed into some hiking gear. Jake threw a shovel, a length of rope, and some kitchen garbage bags into the trunk of Annie's Escort. "All set," he said, getting in the vehicle.

Annie climbed in the passenger seat and studied the map. They had to start a couple of miles west of Richmond Hill, where the city met the country. Four main roads, making a rectangle enclosing about eight square miles, surrounded the area. It was in this rectangle that the swamp was located.

The two possible options were along the north road or the south road, where the swamp, as well as the reclaimed areas, came closer to the back roads. She was sure the place where Bronson's vehicle had been was along one of those two roads. There were some farms in the area, but none especially close to the swamp, and she ruled them out.

"We'll take the north road first," she said. "That may be all we have time for today." She looked at her watch. Matty would be trudging home from school by three thirty, and they needed to be back by then.

There was little traffic on the roads, and they only met a few vehicles after they left the city and made their way toward Service Road.

"Go slow," Annie said. She was looking for any possible route off the road.

Going slow wasn't something Jake was good at, but he tapped the brake and the car crept along.

Annie motioned toward the side of the road. "Stop here."

Jake brought the vehicle to a standstill on the shoulder and Annie stepped out. She had noticed a spot where the fence was broken down and there seemed to be a narrow access path into the tree-covered fields. She stood at the side of the road and studied it. It was too narrow for a vehicle, and there were no wheel ruts, tire marks, or other indications it had ever been used for anything other than a footpath or a deer crossing.

She climbed back in the car. "Keep going," she said.

Jake threw the car into first gear and pulled back onto the road, peering at her over his sunglasses. "Well?"

"Nothing there," she said. "Get your eyes on the road."

A couple minutes later, Annie spied another possibility. "Maybe there," she said. "But keep going. We're almost at the end. We can come back later."

After a couple more minutes, they reached an intersection where a north-south road marked the border of the block of land they were interested in.

"That's all there is," Jake said. "I'll turn around." He made a three-point turn and headed back the way they came. He pulled over when they reached a path that led from the main road, stretching through the bramble of vegetation, into the trees beyond. Wide enough for a car, but just barely. A carpet of wildflowers ran along the fence beside the path.

Jake got out and stood by the side of the road, examining the pathway. "This may be it." He knelt down and studied the ground, testing it with his fingers. "The ground is hard, but something has been through here. It may've been a car, or perhaps a tractor."

"Can we drive in there?" Annie asked.

"Sure can," Jake said, climbing back into the car.

Annie's Ford did just fine on the highway, but it wasn't designed for off-road driving. They bumped and jarred their way through the overgrown foliage. In places, the vegetation threatened to hide the road, but Jake held the vehicle on the trail, moving slowly toward the timberline.

When they reached the treed area, the greenery thinned out, and the course progressed into an expansive forest of maples. Fallen trees, branches, twigs, dying leaves, and a still quietness surrounded them. The thickness of the leafy trees above darkened the afternoon sun.

"Let's look around," Annie said as they stepped from the vehicle.

Jake pointed. "Over there."

Just barely visible, maybe fifty yards away, past an elevated area, a chimney could be seen. As quietly as possible, they moved forward toward the top of the rise. Looking down, they saw a small cabin. There was no sign of anyone around.

Jake whispered, "I'll go take a look."

"I'm coming too."

Jake frowned at her. Then, avoiding twigs and branches, they made their way down the rise, working around to the side of the cabin to a small window. Jake and Annie crouched below the window and listened. A pair of squirrels chased each other a few yards away. A bird twittered, looking for a mate somewhere in the near distance.

Rising up slightly, Jake peeked in the window. The cabin was dim and quiet. A pile of empty metal pails sat along the far wall. In the center of the room stood a large cast-iron stove. Chopped wood was piled along one wall.

"It's a sugar shack," Jake whispered. He moved quietly around to the front of the building, testing the door. It was unlocked.

"Stay here," he said. He turned the rusty knob carefully and eased the door open. A mouse skittered across the dirt floor and found safety under the pile of wood.

He entered and glanced around. "Nobody here," he said.

Annie stepped inside the shack and they poked around. A shelf contained glass jars. Wooden boxes on the floor were stuffed with taps. Two or three large boiling kettles were piled in a corner. It looked like no one had been here since maple syrup season had ended three or four months earlier.

"Let's look around outside," Annie suggested.

The track ended just behind the building, the ground flat and untrodden beyond that. They spent a half hour combing the ground around the cabin, thirty yards in each direction.

"Looks like a dead end," Jake said.

Annie knelt down and brushed away some of the dead leaves and twigs, retrieving a clot of soil. She placed it in a plastic bag she dug from her side pocket.

She stood and looked at her watch. They still had time to get home before Matty arrived.

CHAPTER 11

Thursday, August 11th, 3:00 p.m.

JENNY LAY ON her back, reliving the events that had brought her into this dreadful situation.

She remembered the trunk of Chad's car finally swinging open, and she was half-blinded from the sudden intrusion of the lowering evening sun. She struggled to sit up and look around. She was in a forest somewhere. Digging in the trunk, her tormenter found an oily rag and blindfolded her. Her protests and pleading went unheeded.

Her wrists were still tied, but her feet were free. She thought of trying to jump from the trunk and run, but quickly realized it would be futile. Even if she got to her feet and was able to run, she could blindly hit a tree, and then where would she be?

He forced her back down with a hand on her head, and she heard the trunk bang shut again. A car door slammed, the engine roared, and the vehicle bumped its way across rough ground for several minutes. It came to a stop, started again, and she heard the unmistakable whine of tires on blacktop.

Then it slowed, swerved around a curve, traveled along more rough ground, then stopped again.

She was helped from the trunk. He checked her blindfold, and she stumbled and faltered as he led her across the stony ground, then up three stairs. She was taken into a building and across a wooden floor.

"Watch your step," he said.

She nearly lost her balance a couple of times as she was pushed and prodded up a flight of stairs and down a hallway. A door slammed behind her. She felt a tugging at the back of her head and the rag slipped free. She was in a bedroom, and she spun to face her captor. Now more than afraid, she was angry, sure his intent was to rape her.

She lashed out at him with her voice and her bound hands. "Why are you doing this?" she screamed. "Who are you? Why did you kill Chad?" She beat at him with her arms, flailing uselessly.

He grabbed her by the wrist. "Calm down," he demanded. "Just calm down. I'm not going to hurt you."

"Then what do you want?" She sobbed in desperation.

Instead of answering, he retrieved a hunting knife sheathed to his leg, cut the tie holding her wrists, then turned and left the room. The door slammed behind him and she heard the sound of metal on metal—probably a dead bolt lock. His footsteps grew fainter, and then silent. She banged at the heavy wooden door and screamed until her hands were numb, her voice tired. Then she collapsed on the floor and cried.

And now a week later, as she lay on the bed, she still tried to make sense of everything, struggling to understand why she was being held. Over the past days, though not resigned to the situation, she'd accepted it somewhat, and her bouts of panic and anger had subsided. Less panic, less crying, now lots of boredom, but she was still filled with a pervading sense of helplessness and exasperation.

As she lay on her back counting the ceiling boards for the millionth time, she had a thought. Perhaps there's a way out through the ceiling. Above her was an air vent, or maybe it was a heat vent. She sat up and peered at it. Even if she could get the vent cover off, the hole was too small. The rest of the ceiling was covered wall to wall in hardwood, stained and yellowed with age, but solid, with no way through.

She slipped open the closet door and looked up. The ceiling was covered in hardwood as well, and the walls of the closet were solid.

In frustration, she threw herself back on the bed. The antique headboard squeaked and wobbled, whacking against the wall. She heard the sound of crumbling plaster trickling to the floor and caught the smell of its dust in the air.

Flipping on her back, she stared again at the ceiling, this time unseeing. Thinking. Then suddenly, "That's it," she shouted. "The walls."

It was so obvious, why hadn't she thought of it before? Jenny's father had put an addition on the house a few years ago, and she had enjoyed running through the unfinished walls, between the studs, just generally getting in the way, but having a wonderful time.

Jumping from the bed, she half stumbled to a spot near the door that led to the hallway beyond.

The ceiling was solid, and the floor, and the door as well, but the walls were just plaster and empty space. The easiest way out of there was right through the stupid wall.

She pounded madly at the wall with her fists and then kicked with first one foot, then the other, until her toes were sore. She barely made a dent in the hard plaster.

She calmed herself down and looked around the room.

The old wooden chair might work, or maybe some of the heavy books. No, there had to be a better idea.

She dashed to the bed. With a lot of effort, she managed to lift one edge of the mattress and sent it swinging and spinning, landing with a whoosh near the dresser. She inspected the bed frame. The rails were held to the corner posts of the headboard and footboard by a notched area near its center, slid in, and fastened by downward force—no screws and no bolts.

She twisted, turned, and tugged, and finally managed to free one end of the rail. The other end received the same treatment, and a side rail was free. She tested the weight of the iron in her hands. Not too heavy. Just about right. Pulling off a pretty pink pillowcase, she wrapped it around the middle of the rail. Holding it with both hands on the padding, she tested her grip.

She looked quickly at the clock. It was just after four o'clock. She could make it.

She knew there were studs in the wall. She didn't know how far apart they were but assumed twelve or eighteen inches. She chose a spot waist-high from the floor, tightened her grip on the iron rod, and brought the end crashing into the wall. The brittle wallpaper cracked. It was barely a ding, but it was something. With one more try the rip became a dent. Once more and dust trickled from the bruised wall.

Frantic and euphoric at the same time, she continued to hammer away at the small hole, the weapon swinging rhythmically back and forth. Then it was through. It caught, and she twisted it to wrench it free. The small hole became larger, and then pieces came away in chunks. Inspecting the hole, she saw it was close to a stud on the left side. If she worked to the right, the hole would soon be large enough for her to squeeze through.

In a couple more minutes, she was satisfied with the size of the space, but now the wall on the other side of the studs had to be done. After more hammering, swinging, dust, and falling chunks, she finally tossed the makeshift tool aside.

She peered through the hole, the dust causing her to choke. She coughed it out and looked through again, seeing only a hallway beyond. But it was freedom. She struggled through the tight space, catching her shirt on a nail head. She carefully worked it free, and then, after more squirming and pulling, she was through. She landed in a heap on the other side and inspected herself. She had a badly bruised elbow, and a cut along one arm where she'd scraped it on a piece of sharp plaster, but otherwise, she felt fine.

She smiled grimly. "I'm free," she whispered, as if not believing it. She jumped to her feet and threw her hands in the air, her voice rising in triumph. "Free!"

She knew the wicked little man who had held her captive wouldn't be home for a while, but she was cautious as she made her way along the hallway toward the stairs descending to the main floor. Listening a moment, she heard nothing. Holding the bannister with one hand, she took each step carefully. They squeaked in protest as she rested her weight on each tread. She stopped often to listen and then continued, one slow step at a time, until she reached the landing.

The house was still and quiet. She could see the kitchen off to one side, the living room at the other. She waited a minute, contemplating her quickest means of escape. The back door off the kitchen would be her best choice.

She crept along the wall, moving slowly toward the kitchen. She saw a telephone over by the fridge and knew she should call for help instead of dashing madly out. She didn't know where she was, but she pulled the phone from the wall clip and quickly dialed her mother's phone number.

The phone rang. Once. Twice. Three rings. "Hello?" It was her mother's voice.

"Mom, it's Jenny. I'm okay. I don't know where I am but—" Her voice froze in shock and terror.

She had heard a noise behind her and she turned at the sound. She hadn't heard the back door being unlocked, and she hadn't seen when Jeremy swung the door open and stepped inside.

He had a pair of earphones on, his back to her as he plunked a couple of grocery bags on the kitchen table. She dropped the phone, let it hang, and slunk back to a spot at the end of the cupboards where he couldn't see her.

She tried to control her breathing as she shivered in fright. She heard him removing things from the bags and dropping them on the table. Her mind ran at full speed, deciding what to do. Any moment now, he could come to the fridge and see her. She had to take a chance now.

Half rolling, half crawling, she scrambled across the floor toward the entrance to the living room. She ducked around the corner and sat there a moment panting. She glanced around the room and made a swift decision. The couch. Behind the couch.

She heard a gasp from the kitchen, and then swearing. The phone jangled as he slammed it back onto its spot. Then she heard him dash furiously upstairs. In a moment, he was down again.

"Jenny," he called. "Where are you?" His voice was half-angry, half-mocking.

She crouched behind the couch, trying to think, then rose up slightly and peeked at the front door. It was a double door, securely closed and chained. She would never have time to get it open before he found her.

"Oh, Jenny," he sang.

He was in the living room now.

"I know you're here. The kitchen door was locked and the front door still is, so I know you're here. Come out, come out, wherever you are."

Her mind frantically searched for a plan, anything that would give her a chance. She wished she had a weapon. She should've grabbed a knife from the kitchen, but she hadn't, and all she had was a hiding place—an unsafe one.

Her breathing was rasping, ragged, and uneven, her heart like thunder in her chest. Her leg was going numb from crouching in an awkward and cramped position. She dared to take another breath, letting the air out slowly. It sounded like rushing wind.

She heard him now, in the small room, maybe an office or spare bedroom off the living room. He still called her name, taunting her. A closet door slammed.

It was now, or maybe never.

She slid off her shoes and pushed them carefully underneath the couch, then eased from her hiding place and tiptoed towards the front door. Carefully sliding back the chain, she turned the knob and, thank God, the door didn't squeak. The outside door was a little trickier. It had a slide lock on it she had to ease back.

The lock opened with a bang and she stood motionless.

"Jenny, Jenny, Jenny." He was still mocking her, but now frustrated. He didn't seem to have heard the noise.

She pushed gently at the door.

A voice behind her. "There you are."

She caught a glimpse of him across the room as the door exploded open. With a mad dash, she stumbled down the steps. If she could get to the trees, she would be safe; she could hide there. She dashed across the back lawn and through the garden. A look over her shoulder showed he was close behind. She doubled her effort and headed for the forest. The hard ground bit into her stockinged feet as she ran, and with each step it seemed further and further away.

Seeing a rock the size of her fist on the ground, she dove for it. He was only a few feet away now. Swinging her arm as hard as she could, she threw the rock at him. It caught him hard on the right shoulder and momentarily drove him back.

"You little witch," he screamed. "You're going to be sorry now."

His anger may have given him more energy, more determination, because before she could run more than a short distance, she felt a hand on her arm, grabbing her. She twisted away and changed direction. He lost a little ground, and then made it up and was right behind her again. She felt a tugging on her hair, and she was brought to an abrupt stop, yanked backward, landing with a painful thud on the hard-packed ground.

He was on her. Sitting on her chest. She tried desperately to protect herself as he beat madly at her face and head. "You little witch," he screamed again and again. His fists pummeled her, and she tasted blood in her mouth. She struggled in vain as he continued his crazed barrage, inflicting more pain.

As suddenly as the beating started, it stopped. She couldn't move as he held her hands against the ground and breathed heavily. She looked into his depraved face through her one unswollen eye. The uncontrollable fire she had seen in his eyes a moment ago seemed to be dying down, as if extinguished by a dose of her tears.

"Now look what you've done," he said.

Jenny managed to draw some saliva, mixed with blood, together in her mouth. She spit at him with all the strength she had. He sat back and raised his head, laughed, and wiped the mixture away. His face was speckled with blood. Some dripped from his chin.

Reaching out, he touched her mouth where the blood trickled out. He looked at the dark smear of red on his finger, then closed his eyes, moved his hand toward his mouth and shuddered. Then his eyes snapped open, and he wiped his finger on her shirt, sighed, and then smiled.

"I'm sorry I had to hurt you," he said, his voice almost gentle now. "You shouldn't have run. Why'd you run? You shouldn't have run."

She was exhausted and weak, not able to offer any resistance as he helped her to her feet. He held her firmly, leading her back through the garden, then down a gravel path toward the barn. He swung open the decaying barn door and pushed her inside.

"Over there," he ordered, pointing to a spot near the far wall. "Move over there."

She stumbled obediently across the rough wooden floor, the dusty straw kicking up clouds as he prodded her along.

He pointed to a huge beam, far above, running the length of the barn. Tatters of rope still clung to the grizzled wood. "See that beam up there?" he asked. "That's where Mother died. They said she hanged herself. Maybe she did. That was a while ago. She's buried now." He looked menacingly at her. "You wouldn't want to die there, would you?"

She glanced up and shivered, then looked at him, realizing who he was. She had heard about the woman who hanged herself in a barn. This barn. This was the place mentioned in the papers, and on the lips of everyone in town for several weeks.

She hugged herself and took a step backwards, stopping with her back against the wall of the barn. What was he going to do? She quivered in fear, expecting at any minute he would throw a noose around her neck and hang her from the very spot his mother had hung.

He laughed. "I'm not going to hang you. Just do as you're told."

Jeremy crouched down and picked up a length of chain fastened securely to an upright post against the barn wall. The loose end had a wide leather collar, and he tested the chain in his hands.

"We had a dog once," he said. "She went crazy. Father wanted to shoot her, but I didn't want him to, so he chained her up here so she wouldn't hurt anybody. But then the stupid dog bit me. Not hard, but still it hurt. I knew Father had been right when he said we should shoot it, so I killed it. But I used a board to whack it, then my knife. There was a lot of blood. It's buried now, you know. It can't hurt anybody now."

He snapped open the collar and removed a padlock hanging through a hoop in the leather band, the key still in it. "Hold still," he said.

She meekly obeyed.

He wrapped the collar around her neck and fastened the lock through a metal loop, clicked it shut, and removed the key. He stood back and surveyed her, cocking his head to one side, stuffing the key in his pocket.

"That should do it," he said.

"Are … are you going to leave me here?" she managed to ask, looking at the floor, avoiding his eyes.

With a hand under her chin, he raised her head, forcing her to look at his face. "I don't know what I'm going to do. You have to stay here for now. Maybe not long. Maybe a long time. I don't know. It's your fault, you know."

He grabbed a horse blanket tossed across a stall door and

threw it her way. "This will keep you warm. You need to keep warm. And you'll need to sleep."

In a moment, he was gone, his short legs carrying him swiftly across the barn floor, closing the door behind him as he left.

CHAPTER 12

Thursday, August 11th, 6:00 p.m.

JAKE PLOPPED THE packet of steaks down on the end of the barbecue and admired them—red, juicy, and thick, just as he liked them.

The Master Chef barbecue was already hot, flames licking at the grate, the smell of charcoal filling the air. A container of tangy barbecue sauce was ready when needed. A pot of coffee percolated noisily on the side burner.

A few feet away, a solid homemade picnic table was covered with a plastic cloth, the table piled high with paper plates, utensils, salads, and other summertime treats.

A pair of large speakers on the deck was softly pumping out the mellow voice of Johnny Cash singing about a ring of fire. Somewhere far away the rumble of a lawnmower could be faintly heard.

Matty was running around the backyard chasing a soccer ball. Annie and her mother stepped out the back door carrying more plates of food, arranging them on the already overloaded table.

"There's enough food there for an army," Jake said, eyeing the table.

Andy Roderick glanced at Jake and grinned. "I, for one, am going to eat more than my share."

Annie's father was tall, unlike Annie and her mother, Alma. And unlike his wife, he spoke softly most of the time. His looks were deceiving. He could be mistaken for the CEO of a major firm, a banker, or a highflyer on Wall Street. He was none of those, but content to manage his small trucking company, doing mainly local deliveries.

Matty came running up. "Grandpa, come and play soccer with me."

Andy looked down at Matty and grinned. "Sure, mate," he said, taking the offered ball and kicking it toward the back fence. They chased after the ball.

Annie approached Jake as he dropped the last steak onto the sizzling grill. "As soon as those are ready," she said. "We can eat."

Jake looked over his shoulder. Annie's mother was fiddling with something at the table. He grinned at Annie. "So far, it's been a wonderful night."

Annie slugged him on the shoulder. "Just be good."

"I'll try," he said with a wink.

In a few minutes, the steaks were done to juicy perfection. They took a seat at the table. Jake thanked the Good Lord for the food and they all dove in.

Matty was chattering away about having too much homework. Annie and Alma were talking about some boring stuff the guys had no interest in, while Jake and Andy discussed football, and Thrush's new, bright red "mad hot" performance mufflers.

Jake's cell phone buzzed in his pocket. He stood and moved away from the chatter. "Hello?"

"Jake, it's Amelia James." She spoke fast, excited. "I tried your regular number but got voice mail, so I called your cell. It's Jenny. She called. She's okay, but I don't know where she is."

"Try to calm down, Mrs. James," he said. "Do you remember exactly what she said?"

"She said, 'It's Jenny, I'm okay, but don't know where I am.' And then it went quiet. She was gone, but it sounded like the line was still open. And then I heard a voice. A man's voice. He swore, and then I was disconnected. I dialed star 69, but it was a private number and I couldn't return the call."

"That's good news, Amelia. It's been almost two weeks and it proves she's still safe somewhere. We've been following a few leads. Nothing firm yet, but we're still confident we'll find her."

"What can I do? Can I do anything?" The excitement in her voice was still there, mixed with anxiety. "I've already called Hank and filled him in."

Jake looked at Annie who was watching him. He covered the phone and said in a loud whisper, "Jenny called. She's okay."

Annie stood and came over to Jake. She was smiling, her eyes lit.

"We'll let you know. We'll keep in touch, Amelia," Jake said into the phone. "Let me talk to Annie about this and decide where to go from here." He said goodbye and clicked off the phone, shoving it into his pocket.

Annie looked at him and waited.

"Jenny called her mother," he said. "Jenny said she was okay but didn't know where she was. Then she was cut off."

"At least that's some good news. Actually … that's great news."

Jake glanced at the table. Annie's mother was looking at

them and scowling. When they returned to the table, Alma gave Jake a frown, then raised her chin and looked down at Annie. "I thought tonight we were supposed to relax. Is it necessary to mix business with pleasure all the time?"

Annie looked sharply at her mother. "Mom, a girl is missing and we're trying to find her."

"Well, I'm sure it can wait until tomorrow."

With some difficulty, Jake held back his comments. He opened his mouth a couple of times to speak, and then clamped it shut. He looked at Andy, who seemed uncomfortable enough to hide under the table.

Andy frowned and shook his head briefly at Jake as if to show his disagreement with his wife. Jake nodded at him and reached for another baked potato, stabbing it savagely in two. He bit his lip and doused the potato with butter and sour cream.

"There's nothing we can do right now. Yes, it'll have to wait until tomorrow," Annie said. "And hopefully, tomorrow isn't too late. This poor girl has been missing for more than a week, and her mother is frantic with worry. Have a heart, Mother."

Alma sniffed and looked away. "It can wait another day." She looked at Matty. "Sit up straight. You're slopping ketchup all over."

Jake felt like telling her to mind her own business, but instead he took another bite of salad and held back his comments.

He was relieved when the evening was over. The company was gone, all was cleaned up, and Matty was safely tucked in bed.

Annie and Jake were in the kitchen. She threw her arms around his neck. "I know you were bursting at the seams, but thank you for keeping your mouth shut." She kissed him gently on the lips for a long time.

Jake was glad then, that he had.

Friday, August 12th, 8:33 a.m.

"ANOTHER RING went missing yesterday," Chris said.

"I'll get down there this morning and take a look at the recordings. We'll see what shows up."

Jake clicked off his cell phone.

The phone had been on speaker and Annie heard the conversation. She pushed her chair back from the kitchen table and stood. "Do you need me there?" she asked.

"I think I can handle this one. Do you have some plans?"

"I need to do some client billing and sort out a few other things."

Jake leaned back and looked up at Annie. "I spoke to Hank," he said. "A judge wouldn't issue a court order for the release of the phone records of Jenny's call to her mother because there's no evidence she's in danger, and there's no official police investigation. Hank also said, since Jenny appears to be all right, the police still aren't making it a priority to find her."

"I want to make it a priority." Annie looked at the ceiling a moment and then continued, "I think I'll check out the road on the other side of the swamp this morning. That's about all we have to go on."

Jake looked worried. "I don't like you to go out there alone," he said. "Can't you wait until we can go together?"

Annie smiled at him. "I appreciate your concern, but I'll be quite all right."

"Just be careful."

"Jake, there's nothing to worry about. Just because

Bronson's car may've been in that area at one time doesn't mean there's anything dangerous there now."

"You know what's strange?" Jake was thinking as he spoke. "Jenny appears to be all right, but Bronson is missing. If he abducted her, what's his reason? Why do we have his car? Did he abandon it? If so, why?"

"It's possible he has her held somewhere and his car was stolen. We know the driver of the vehicle wasn't him."

"If we could find that driver and find out where he got the car from, that could lead us to Bronson, then possibly to Jenny."

"That appears to be a dead end," Annie said. "The description of the driver is too vague."

Matty wandered into the room. "Ready for school, Mom."

Annie leaned down and straightened the collar of his shirt. She kissed him on the forehead. "Got your homework?"

"Of course, Mom."

Jake gave him a bear hug. "See you later, kiddo. Be careful crossing the street."

Matty rolled his eyes. "I'm not a little kid, Dad."

Jake laughed out loud as Matty swung his backpack over his shoulder. "Bye, Mom. Bye, Dad."

Annie watched him leave. The front door banged. "That kid is about as smart-mouthed as his father," she said.

Friday, August 12th, 9:05 a.m.

JAKE PARKED the Firebird in the last spot of a row of parking spaces, as far away from other vehicles as possible. He didn't want another driver to open their door and ding his machine.

Chris was leaning against the wall outside the security office door, his arms folded. A grin split his face as Jake approached. He beckoned for Jake to enter the office, following behind.

Jake offered his massive hand and they shook. "Good morning, buddy," Chris said.

Jake grinned. "Good morning. Now let's get to the bottom of this."

He looked across the room to where a small table was set up, holding a bank of equipment and a couple of monitors. A control board contained a row of electronic switches, allowing the view on the monitors, during playback, to switch from one camera's recording to another.

Jake sat and hit a couple of buttons. The monitor showed the top view of all the showcases. "Which case is the one with the missing item?" he asked.

Chris pointed at the monitor. "That one."

That left four recordings that would be of interest. The two inside the showcase, the one fastened to the register showing the top of the case, and the overhead camera. Jake stabbed at the controls a couple more times, isolating the recordings he wanted to view.

Starting with the overhead camera, he watched from the beginning, the recording running at fast speed. Each time a customer finished viewing items at that case, Jake stopped the recording and examined the interior cameras, showing a clear view of the inventory at the same timestamp.

On the third check, something was gone. A ring had been removed. Switching back to the overhead recording, he could see a customer had purchased the item.

"False alarm. Next."

He continued the ritual, switching back and forth between recordings, clicking buttons, leaning in, pausing, viewing, staring. He sat back and yawned.

By now, Chris had returned with a couple cups of coffee.

Jake worked off the lid and took a few sips before continuing.

Click, pause, view.

"Got him."

Jake back-stepped the recording a few minutes. "Watch closely."

Chris leaned in as Jake switched one monitor to the overhead view, the other to the register view, then set it to play in slow motion.

The overhead view showed a man in his midthirties. He was tall, with dark hair and a goatee. He stood at the case holding a large envelope. The salesgirl removed a tray of rings from the case and set them on the counter. The register camera showed a clear view of the tray.

Jake and Chris watched, looking back and forth between monitors. The thief held the envelope in his left hand. He moved it horizontally above the tray as he distracted the girl's attention by looking at her and speaking. When her attention was diverted, his right hand moved under the envelope, hidden from view. The register camera clearly showed him slip a ring from the tray, then draw his hand back. The move was invisible to the girl as well as the overhead camera.

Jake zoomed in on the man's face and hit a button. In a moment, a photo of the thief zipped from the printer.

"I'll slip down to the police station and make a report," Jake said. "Maybe this guy's been around awhile, so I'll run through some mug shots as well. I have a friend there and I'll get him to check for shoplifters in the database and see if he pops up." He pointed to the monitor, which showed a live view of the jewelry area. "In the meantime, get somebody to keep an eye on that and see if he shows again."

Chris sat back and grinned. "Will do."

"We'll get this guy," Jake said.

CHAPTER 13

Friday, August 12th, 9:45 a.m.

ANNIE WORKED HER way across town, heading east. There wasn't much traffic to contend with at this time of day—everybody who was going to work was already there. She zipped her Escort deftly through the steaming city streets and made it to the outskirts in a few minutes. She headed for County Road 12, the south road bordering the swamp. It was a few miles and a few minutes before she reached the remote stretch of country blacktop.

This time, she planned to take a slow ride along the two-mile section, make some mental notes, then work her way back, checking out any possible places she had noted.

Driving with one eye on the unkept road, the other one studying the landscape to her left, after a couple of miles, she reached the north-south intersection. That was as far as she wanted to go. She had noticed two spots of interest, and she spun into a lane to turn around. She recognized the property as the old Spencer farm. She could make out the barn and shuddered at the thought of Mrs. Spencer, who'd been found there, dangling by a rope from the overhead beam.

Then she thought of Jeremy, probably at work at Mortino's right now, and how hard it must be for him to keep the place up by himself, especially with the low wage he earned as a stock boy.

Suspending her thoughts, she backed out and returned the way she'd come. She hadn't seen any traffic yet, but she kept to the right and crept along the narrow shoulder. After about a mile, she pulled over and stopped, the right side of the car tilted, almost in the ditch running along the edge of the road.

She climbed from the vehicle and studied a pathway leading into a field. It had looked like a possible place of interest, but there was no way a car could pass through there. Perhaps a 4x4 could make it, but certainly not the low-slung Tercel Bronson drove.

She had one more spot to try. She drove a few hundred more feet and pulled over. A small rutted track leading from the road, through a weeded field, and into the leafy forest of maples, looked more promising. If her memory was correct, it was just about parallel to the sugar shack they'd seen yesterday, a mile or so through the forest, and probably on the other side of the swamp which filled the interior.

Jumping from her car, she examined the narrow track. It didn't appear to be an often-used lane. The ground was firm. A few weeds struggled through the baked soil, and potholes marred the wheel tracks.

She walked slowly down the pathway. To her left and right were rocks and weeds. Wild berry bushes and juniper shrubs dotted the field, sparsely at first, then growing thicker as she reached the tree line. A breeze whispered through a patch of grass, causing the tops to dance in the sun.

Then, as if carved with precision by a master sculptor, there was a sudden retreat into shadows at the edge of the dense forest. The cloudless morning sky disappeared under an impenetrable sheet of leaves above.

Peering ahead, Annie could see the pathway continued on, winding among the trees. She couldn't see how far, but she kept on. A flock of blackbirds peeled themselves away from the treetops, squawking and screeching as they went, probably looking for another private perch away from unwanted intruders.

She calculated she was in about a quarter of a mile when the path petered out into a small clearing. Around her were untold acres of leaves, branches, and rotting tree stumps.

She was confident she was on the right track. The soil samples from the underside of Bronson's vehicle had to have come from this area. There was nowhere else for miles around fitting the botanical forensic report. She was confident in Sammy's expertise and determined to keep looking.

Friday, August 12th, 10:12 a.m.

JAKE'S PHONE buzzed in his pocket. He dug it out.

"This is Jake."

An excited voice came over the phone. "Jake, it's Chris. He's here now. The security cameras just caught him coming in the front doors."

"Are you in your office?"

"Yup."

"Keep an eye on the live monitor and see if he hits the jewelry counter. In the meantime, I'm about finished here, so

I'll head on over. I'm on my way as I speak. See you in ten."

A uniformed cop, just leaving the station, whipped his head around and frowned as the Firebird backed out and squealed away. Jake never worried about speeding tickets. He always managed to avoid them. Almost always. And right now, he made double time as he shot the few blocks to Cranston's and screeched into the taxi waiting area in front of the store.

He knew Chris could probably handle the situation, but he wanted to earn his pay. Besides, it could be fun.

Chris saw him coming and beckoned frantically. "He's there now. It's a different girl at the counter today. He probably wanted to avoid seeing the same one."

They watched the monitors.

Jake grinned. "Look at the envelope he's carrying. He's gonna try again."

"And it'll be the last time."

They saw the girl reach into the showcase and remove a tray of rings. They saw the large envelope put into play. They saw the distraction, and the grab, and finally they read his lips: "Not today. Thank you very much." with a nod and a smile as he moved away.

"Let's go," Chris said. "I'll take the front door, you take the side."

"Remember, wait until he leaves the store," Jake warned.

"No problem. I've done this before."

Chris walked quickly toward the front of the store while Jake hurried to the side, zipping past the line at the cash registers. He took a quick look back. The thief wasn't coming yet, so he stepped outside and moved around the corner out of sight.

He called Chris's cell. "I'm out here now. Any sign of him there?"

"Not yet."

"Hey, don't you guys have any walkie-talkies for this?"

Chris laughed. "Cell phones work better."

They waited a few minutes. Jake could hear Chris humming some '80s tune. Or was it from the '70s? He wasn't sure.

The doors whirred open and closed a few times. Mothers with babies. Some old guy. A couple of girls, probably skipping school.

"Okay, I see him," Jake whispered. "He's coming out."

Jake moved in behind the suspect and tapped him on the shoulder. "Excuse me," he said.

The man spun around. "Yes?"

"I need you to come with me."

The man frowned and cocked his head. "What's this all about?"

"Just come with me, please." Jake grabbed him firmly by the arm. "Back inside," he ordered.

The thief tried to pull free but Jake's grip allowed the man no possibility of escape.

As Jake escorted the man inside, Chris came their way and grabbed the other arm. "Care for this dance?" he asked.

The man scowled but offered no resistance as he was marched across the store into the security office. Chris shut the door quietly behind them.

"Empty your pockets," Chris said to the suspect.

"You have no right to hold me," the man said arrogantly.

"Actually, we do. You're on private property and we have proof you stole a ring from the jewelry department." Chris pointed to the monitors. "Right there, scumbag."

There was a tap on the office door, and a security guard pushed it open and poked his head in. Jake and Chris turned at the sound.

The thief must have been waiting for any opportunity. He dove headfirst to the floor and, scrambling and rolling, he slipped past the legs of the guard, spinning to his feet. He stumbled a moment, caught his balance, and ran.

Jake reacted, Chris right behind him. They chased the man down a long aisle before he came to a quick stop and vaulted over a counter leading to the hardware department. He stumbled as he landed, but quickly gained his feet, pushing aside a couple of kids as he ran, knocking one crying to the floor. Jake vaulted the counter behind him, but the man had taken another turn and headed for the stockroom.

Chris was still behind, calling on his cell for the other guards to watch the doors. "Don't let anybody out," he yelled.

The large metal doors leading to the stockroom burst open as the thief hit them, barely slowing down. The impact caused him to stumble and fall, but he landed like a cat and was up again.

Jake dove for him and caught him by the pant leg. His grip slipped and he was left holding a shoe. The man was up and running, but Jake reached back into his football years at high school and the shoe flew from his hand, smashing the runner squarely in the back of his head.

He went down face first.

Jake had him. He twisted the man's right arm securely behind his back and forced him to his feet.

Chris walked over. He was steaming. Whacking the thief in the chest with his open hand, he rammed him back against the concrete wall. The blow caused the thief's head to bounce a couple of times. His eyes rolled.

Chris's face was two inches away. "You run again, you scumbag, and next time you'll go right through the wall."

The scumbag just glared back, held securely.

Another guard came running.

"Call the police," Chris said. "Let's get this guy out of here."

Friday, August 12th, 11:15 a.m.

ANNIE HAD SPENT the last few minutes walking back and forth, up and down, combing the area where she was sure Bronson's vehicle had been. She was looking for tire tracks, footprints, anything unusual at all.

The rich, earthy smell of the nearby swamp filled her nostrils. She watched a squirrel scamper up a tree and disappear in the foliage above. A sparrow chirped. A woodpecker tapped.

What had Bronson been doing here? There had to be something she was missing.

She examined the forest floor several yards ahead. Near the edge of the clearing, she noticed a slight dipping of the earth as if the ground had sunk. Walking over, she bent down and brushed away some of the dead leaves and twigs. She felt the soil below with her fingers. It was rich and soft.

She brushed away more of the decaying undergrowth.

A footprint.

It was a child's footprint. Barely detectable, but unmistakable. She stared at it a moment, and then carefully swept more.

There were a lot of footprints.

She pulled out her cell and snapped a few pictures of the

whole area, and then a close-up of the clearest footprint. Tucking away her phone, she scooped up a handful of soil and frowned. Why were there undecayed twigs and leaves under the soil? It was as if the ground had been disturbed recently.

She stood and stepped back, wishing she had brought the shovel. It was still in the trunk of her car, so she'd have to go back and get it. She looked at her watch. She had plenty of time.

Annie hurried back to her car and popped the trunk. A vehicle zipped by on the road, heading for the horizon. She removed the shovel, slammed the trunk, and made her way back to the trees, the tool slung over her shoulder.

Using the shovel, she scraped back the ground, layer by layer, working meticulously for several minutes. It was cool under the canopy of leaves and branches, but she stopped to wipe her forehead on the sleeve of her shirt. She swatted at a mosquito buzzing around her head.

Then dug some more.

Even down a couple of feet, there was still a trace of undecayed leaves mixed in with the soil. She was on the right track.

Her shovel hit something solid. She tossed it aside and dug at the area with her hand. Digging and scraping and brushing.

It was a shoe.

Pointing upward.

She jumped back in horror, stumbling over a branch, and fell on her buttocks. She sat there a moment, mouth and eyes wide, breathing fast, staring at the shoe in disbelief.

She was afraid what she might find attached to that shoe.

She wanted to get out of there, but gritting her teeth, she summoned her bravery, edged over to the hole, and gently brushed away the soil around the shoe, bit by bit.

Then she realized she had found what she hadn't wanted to. What she'd thought might be hidden in this forest but had hoped wasn't here at all.

She wasn't wrong.

There was a leg attached to that shoe.

She called 9-1-1.

CHAPTER 14

Friday, August 12th, 11:55 a.m.

OLD EDNA BELLOWS was rather a kindly soul. Always optimistic and cheerful, but lonely. Everyone she had known was dead now. She'd had so many funerals to attend she couldn't get to them all. Her savings had long run dry, and now, at eighty-nine years old, she had to settle for living in a small apartment in a wretched old building that should've been condemned long ago. The government check she received each month barely covered her rent, with little left for food to keep her energy up.

Nonetheless, life goes on. She sighed to herself as she counted out the few remaining coins rattling around in her cookie jar. Just enough for a bit of bread, maybe a pack of chicken wieners, the no-name brand, and perhaps a jar of marmalade.

"Sounds like a feast to me," she said aloud.

She tied a scarf over her thin, gray hair, fastening it firmly under her chin. She was too proud to use one of those silly walkers the old folks were using these days. She grasped the handle of a well-worn cane as she removed it from the doorknob, then grabbing her handbag, she made her way out to the hallway, locking the door carefully behind her.

She was glad to be on the second floor. That meant she only had two flights to climb. With the elevator not working, as usual, it took her some time to make it to the street. Then, hugging her cane with one hand and clutching her handbag in the other, she moved haltingly down the sidewalk toward her destination.

She hummed a happy tune as she went. She smiled a sweet hello to everyone passing her on the sidewalk, but most of them didn't have time for a useless old woman. She didn't care. It was a lovely day and she felt refreshed.

The door at Mortino's opened automatically as she approached it. She was still amazed at how that could possibly work, but it always seemed to, so she slipped confidently through the door.

Picking out her purchases didn't take much time because her list was so short. Passing by the meat department, she thought, *Oh my, that looks good.* Her eye had been on a nice, juicy pork chop, nestled securely in its styrofoam coffin, covered with a blanket of thin plastic wrap. It seemed to be calling her name. She dug in her purse again and counted her coins. She didn't have enough money. She moved along the counter. She looked back. Her mouth watered.

A devil appeared on her shoulder, probing her with its wicked thoughts. Tempting her. Goading her.

Poor Mrs. Bellows had never stolen anything in her life, and she certainly hadn't intended to start now. But the vision of that lovely chop sizzling on her grill, the smell of hot juices filling her nose, her fork and knife ready, were more than her feeble will could take.

With a quick look in either direction, she deftly slid the

awaiting feast to the front of the case and into her handbag. She immediately felt a touch of guilt, but it was insufficient to cause a change of mind. She walked her slow walk toward the checkouts at the front of the store, now empowered by the devil on her shoulder.

Friday, August 12th, 12:35 p.m.

JEREMY HAD BEEN busy. The boss was working him hard today. One thing after another. Right now, he was busy piling up cartons of macaroni and cheese as high as he could reach, maybe higher. He had to get a stepladder to help him.

He stood on the top rung, hoping the ladder wouldn't wobble and send him crashing down. From his vantage point, he could almost see the whole store—crowds at the registers, people picking at vegetables, and some old hag looking at the meat.

Then he frowned and stared hard. He couldn't believe it. The old hag had stuffed a package of meat in her purse and was now making off with it.

He sighed and climbed off his perch, taking one careful step after another, and followed the woman toward the front of the store. As he walked past her, he peeped slyly into her handbag. The stolen meat was still there.

"I've got a delivery to make. Be back soon," he said to the manager as he neared the front of the store.

The manager grunted and went on reading from his clipboard.

Jeremy slipped past the registers and out the front door. He stood outside around the corner, against the wall, where he couldn't be seen from the front.

In a few minutes, the old hag, working her cane, hobbled through the exit. He knew stealing wasn't stealing until they left the store, so just to make sure, he walked past her again and checked her bag. It was still there. He ducked into an alley and let her get ahead of him, and then strolled out and followed her.

Because she moved so slowly, it took some time, but finally they reached the run-down dwelling where he supposed she lived. Jeremy slipped inside behind her as she sweetly held the door open for him.

"Thanks," he mumbled.

She went to the right, so he went left. As she opened the stairwell door, he turned around and headed back in her direction. Keeping out of sight, he made the slow uphill climb, one plodding step after another.

Two floors later, he watched her go through the stairwell exit into the hallway and stop in front of the second door. She fiddled with her handbag and pulled out a single key on a rabbit's foot chain. She worked it into the lock, pushed open the door, and entered her humble living space.

Jeremy hurried up the hallway, held out his foot to stop her door from closing, and then pushed it open a couple of feet. She faced him, holding her cane out as if about to hang it on the doorknob.

Her eyes, and then her mouth, popped open. She asked, "What is it, young man? Are you the new neighbor? I always like meeting the new neighbors. People come and go in this place, but I like to meet them all."

Jeremy let the door close behind him. "No, I'm not your neighbor," he said. "I'm from Mortino's and I know what you did." He looked menacingly at her.

She quivered in fear.

"I saw you take the meat. You shouldn't take the meat. That's stealing. You're not supposed to steal."

Poor Mrs. Bellows seemed to be in too much shock to see

Jeremy reach down, lift his pant leg, and pull his top-quality Bowie knife from its sheath. She only grunted as the knife entered her body. Her eyes were still wide as she slumped to the floor.

Jeremy bent down. He wiped the knife clean on her dress and put it back into its sheath.

The blood from the wound in her chest soaked her dress, the warm, thick liquid pooling on the worn-out carpet.

He reached out and touched the wound. The tip of his finger was crimson. As he put it to his tongue, he closed his eyes and immediately felt a swelling of exultation and ecstasy.

He remained silent. The excitement caused his breathing to become rapid, and his heart raced as he relished the euphoric feeling overtaking him.

The blood on his tongue soon mixed with his saliva and was gone.

He opened his eyes slowly, then stood and watched her.

Her eyes flickered and remained still, unseeing, soon to join her long-gone friends.

CHAPTER 15

Friday, August 12th, 12:55 p.m.

JAKE GOT THERE before the cops did. Annie had called him after reporting her discovery to the police. She was waiting in front of her car when he roared up. He pulled a U-turn and stopped behind her vehicle.

As he stepped out, she ran to him and held on. He felt her shaking, and he tried to soothe her, to calm her down.

"It's all right now. Relax, honey," he said, his strong, safe arms around her.

"I didn't get a look at the face," she said. "I only saw one foot. It looked like a man's shoe."

"At least we know it's not Jenny."

In the distance, Jake saw some approaching vehicles, and soon three police cars pulled up. He waved the first one over. A uniform was driving, Hank in the passenger seat.

Jake pointed to the lane by the road. "In there," he said.

"Jump in," Hank said. "Annie, get in."

They climbed in the backseat of the cruiser and Annie pointed. "Drive up this lane and into the forest, then it's just past there."

The uniform drove, and the other cars followed.

They stopped in the clearing and climbed from the cruiser. Hank warned Jake and Annie to stand back from the immediate area, and in a few minutes, the clearing was buzzing. One cop stretched yellow crime scene tape while others milled around, one taking pictures, one on the phone.

Hank bent over the partially uncovered corpse. Richmond Hill didn't have a large robbery/homicide division. When Hank joined the force, there hadn't been a murder for years, and there'd been few since. His training and experience took over now.

Officer Spiegle was there, bending curiously over the grave.

"Don't touch anything," Hank warned. "Get back over there." He looked up at the cop. "Spiegle, make yourself useful. The ME is on her way. Go out to the road and make sure she finds us all right."

Spiegle wandered away.

Hank watched him and shook his head.

Jake and Annie were sitting with their backs against a tree. Annie followed Jake as he got up and approached Spiegle, holding out his hand. "Hi, Yappy," he said.

Jake knew Officer Spiegle. He didn't think much of him, but he liked to keep a cordial relationship with everybody. Especially cops.

Yappy gave Jake's hand a limp shake. "Hey, Jake."

"I want to ask you a little bit about the car you chased the other day. The one that drove into the bushes."

"Yeah?"

"The guy who was driving it. I know you reported he was fifty or sixty."

"Yeah."

"Can you tell me anything else about him?"

Spiegle looked up at the treetops, and then back. "Maybe he was drunk," he said.

"Drunk? How do you know?"

"Don't know really, I just think he was. He looked like a bum, too. Had on this old overcoat. He ran fast, though. I wasn't that close and he was gone before I had a chance to catch him."

Jake squinted at Yappy and asked thoughtfully, "Do you think he was just out for a joyride?"

"Yeah, probably. Anyway, it wasn't his car." Yappy looked over toward Hank. "I gotta go," he said.

"Thanks, Yappy. You've been a big help."

Spiegle waved it off. "Don't mention it." He walked toward the road.

Jake looked at Annie. "I lied," he said.

Annie cocked her head.

"He was no help at all."

Friday, August 12th, 1:33 p.m.

THE SUNLIGHT SEEPED through cracks between the boards, casting long strips of white diagonally across the heavy plank floor of the vast storage area. The air inside the barn was warm but not uncomfortable. The tin-covered roof high above the hayloft deflected most of the heat. An old tractor, unused for years, sat decaying beside the large double doors. Other forgotten farm implements were scattered about.

Jenny had worked at the thick leather collar until her neck

was sore and raw. The chain holding her allowed a few feet of freedom, and she had searched as far as she could reach for something sharp, anything at all that might cut into the leather band. She found nothing.

She picked away at the peanut butter sandwich Jeremy had left her that morning. A half-eaten apple lay on the plate. She didn't feel much like eating.

She slept little the night before, and any attempts to sleep now were useless, though she tried.

She used the pail he'd left her for a toilet. There was no tissue; she had to use straw, and she felt dirty.

He'd left her with a good supply of drinking water. There were several bottles of spring water in a small cardboard box. Removing her shirt and bra, she dumped one over her head in an attempt to wash, then dried herself on the tattered horse blanket and dressed again.

He'd been to see her that morning and said he couldn't stay long—he had to get to work. She didn't care. She didn't want him to stay. Or did she? Maybe a bit; she was lonely.

She touched her right eye. The swelling around it seemed to have gone, and the pain from the beating she'd received the day before had subsided.

Her hair felt like the straw surrounding her. She needed a comb and a toothbrush, and she wanted to see her mother again.

Thoughts of her mother made her wonder. Surely they were looking for her. She was thankful at least she'd been able to contact her. She wondered whether the call could be traced. Probably not. It was too short.

In a fit of desperation, she tugged violently at the chain holding her to the post. The sudden frenzy caused her face to contort, and she gritted her teeth. Emitting a low throaty scream, she thrashed the chain back and forth, up and down.

It rattled and sang as if mocking her. Then she collapsed on the straw, the dust settling around her.

Chained up like a mad dog, she had no tears left.

Friday, August 12th, 2:11 p.m.

THERE WAS MORE traffic on County Road 12 than it had seen in a month. Channel 7 Action News had arrived at the scene, no doubt picking up the report on their police scanner. It was the biggest news in a decade, and they wanted some of it. Other news stations and local newspapers were represented as well. Reporters and camera operators milled around outside the taped-off area, cameras humming, trying to shove microphones in faces.

Hank made a brief statement and informed them there would be a press conference later. The cameras kept humming. The reporters kept milling.

The ME was there as well. The soil was painstakingly swept from around the body, which was then hoisted from the hole and onto a gurney. A bloody blanket was found and carefully removed from the grave.

Hank peered at the corpse. The face was a mess. What appeared to be a bullet hole was visible just below the nose. He found a wallet in the victim's back pocket. Flipping it open, he dug through the papers inside.

"Chad Bronson," he read. From the picture of Bronson he'd seen, even by what was left of his face, he could clearly tell this was indeed Bronson.

He flipped the wallet closed, and then bagged and tagged it, slipping it into his pocket. With the big mouths around here, he knew enough to keep the information private until the ME could make a positive identification and Bronson's mother could be told. He didn't want her to have to hear about this on the news.

Bronson's body was covered with a snow-white sheet and placed into the waiting ambulance. The vehicle drove away, red lights flashing.

Hank walked over to where Jake and Annie were watching. A camera followed him. He turned and glared, and the camera operator went to bother someone else.

He turned back to Jake and Annie. "It's Bronson," he said quietly. "Shot through the head."

Hank turned again, annoyed as a brave reporter shoved a microphone at him. "No comment right now." He frowned and turned back. "I'm done here. Forensics can finish up. Meanwhile, let's go somewhere where we can talk without being bothered by reporters."

He beckoned to a uniformed officer. "Charlie, let's go."

They walked out to the road.

"I'll be there in a minute," he said to the uniform.

The cop leaned against his vehicle and lit up a smoke, while Jake, Annie, and Hank went and stood behind Jake's car.

Annie spoke. "Now there're more than just Jenny and Bronson involved here. Someone killed Bronson, so we have a murderer out there somewhere, and Jenny is still missing."

"It seems doubtful Bronson had anything to do with Jenny's disappearance," Hank said.

Jake added, "Unless Bronson stashed her somewhere first, and then somebody killed him."

"Maybe, but I can't see that happening," Annie said. "It seems more like somebody killed Bronson and then grabbed Jenny."

"I think you're probably right, Annie," Hank said.

"Or … what about a kidnapping?" Jake suggested. "Perhaps Bronson had a partner and they kidnapped Jenny for ransom. Then something went wrong. There was an argument, and Bronson's partner killed him and held on to

Jenny. Perhaps Bronson was the brains behind it, and now he's dead, and the partner doesn't know what to do with Jenny."

Annie frowned. "If Bronson had a partner who was cold-blooded enough to kill him, then why wouldn't he just kill Jenny instead of holding on to her?"

"I'm no expert," Hank said. "But it looks like Bronson has been dead about a week. So Annie, I think you're right. If it was a kidnapping for ransom gone wrong, that means the partner has been holding Jenny for a week. That seems doubtful."

Annie said, "Maybe the original intent was for the killer to grab Jenny, but Bronson was in the way and got himself killed."

Jake looked thoughtful, and then spoke slowly, "So that brings us back to where we started. What's the kidnapper's motive?"

"A sex slave?" Hank suggested.

"Let's hope not," Annie said.

Friday, August 12th, 2:48 p.m.

JEREMY WAS TAKING a break. He'd been hard at work, stacking stuff up, restocking, and running around doing all the crap his boss had demanded, and now it was break time.

He sat back and propped his stubby legs up on the table. He munched slowly on his peanut-butter-and-tomato sandwich and looked at the tiny television mounted on the wall in front of him.

He thought about how much he hated his job.

He thought about that old woman he'd had to punish that morning.

He thought about how boring TV was during the day.

A reporter came on the television and Jeremy sat up

straight. He recognized the spot where the reporter was standing. He opened his mouth and stared, his sandwich slipping to the table.

"A body has just been discovered buried in a wooded area off County Road 12.

"The victim hasn't been identified yet, but it appears to be the body of a man, possibly in his early twenties.

"I spoke to the detective in charge briefly, but he declined to comment.

"We will bring you breaking news as it happens. In an exclusive report, I'm Lisa Krunk, live for Channel 7 Action News."

Jeremy's mind buzzed at a thousand miles an hour, his mouth still hanging open. Abruptly, he leaned back again and relaxed. He put his feet back up on the table and nibbled at his sandwich. He realized they couldn't possibly know who was responsible.

He looked at his watch, then packed up the rest of his snack in a brown paper bag and put the bag in a small locker by the wall. Yawning, he trotted back out to his boring job.

On the way from the break room, his boss, Mr. MacKay, stopped him. "Jeremy, you have blood on your shirt." He pointed and frowned.

Jeremy looked down at his shirt. There was a patch of blood on one side. Oops. He should've been more cautious. Now what could he do?

The boss continued, "I told you to be more careful around the meat. You know the packages sometimes leak. Now go and change your shirt."

Jeremy looked meek. "Sorry, Mr. MacKay," he said, then turned and smiled.

He went and changed his shirt.

CHAPTER 16

Friday, August 12th, 3:00 p.m.

ANNIE KNEW SHE would have to fill out a police report detailing how she'd found the body and the events leading up to it.

She looked at her watch. Matty would be coming home soon. She didn't have time to get to the precinct, fill out the report, and get home before Matty arrived.

She had instructed him in the past that, if nobody was there when he got home, he should go next door to the Pascuals' house. Chrissy was almost always there this time of day, but she wanted to be sure.

She dialed Chrissy's number and explained that she would be late. Would Chrissy please cover for her?

"No problem," her friend said cheerfully. "I'll watch for him."

Annie thanked her and hung up.

She looked toward the woods. They were still busy there. It might be a while longer.

She climbed into her car and steered carefully around a

cruiser protruding greedily into the roadway. She drove towards town, heading for the precinct.

Friday, August 12th, 3:10 p.m.

JAKE PARKED the Firebird in a vacant slot adjoining the apartment complex on Canderline Street.

Hank looked at Jake from the passenger seat. "This is the worst part of the job," he said. "Informing the victim's family their loved one is dead."

Jake nodded. "I don't envy you."

Hank climbed wearily from the vehicle. "Let's get it over with."

They took the elevator to the third floor and stopped in front of 3B. The door opened a crack at Hank's knock. Mrs. Bronson peeked around the chain. The door closed, the chain rattled, and then the door swung open. She wore the same faded housecoat, and she pulled the belt tighter and ogled them.

"Yeah?"

"Mrs. Bronson, I'm Detective—"

"Yeah, I remember you."

"May we come in a moment, ma'am?"

She sniffed. "I'm not a ma'am." She said the last word with a note of distaste. "But come in. Watch the floor. Don't trip over the rug."

Hank avoided the bulging rug as he stepped inside. Jake followed.

"Well, what is it this time? I told you, I don't know where Chad is at."

"May we sit down, Mrs. Bronson?"

She frowned, then turned and walked into the small kitchen beside the hallway and sat at the table. Jake saw a plate with an unfinished meal on it. It appeared to be eggs or something. A cigarette butt protruded from a piece of toast, with ashes decorating the rest of the plate. She pushed it aside and propped her elbows on the table, staring at them.

Jake pulled a chair back and sat carefully. The air smelled of something stale. Maybe rotting food as well. He tried to avoid the odor as he watched Hank sit and pull his chair in to the table.

She lit a cigarette and blew smoke at them. "Did you find Chad?"

Hank looked at her. "Mrs. Bronson," he began, and hesitated, covering her hand with his before continuing. "I'm sorry I have to inform you, your son has been killed."

She looked at him in disbelief. "Are you sure?" she asked.

"Yes, Mrs. Bronson. We're sure."

She continued to stare at him. Finally, the reality hit her. Her eyes moistened, a tear rolled free, and she jammed the unfinished cigarette into the toast.

"How?"

"I'm sorry, Mrs. Bronson, but it appears to be homicide."

She cocked her head at him. "What's that?" she asked.

"He was murdered, Mrs. Bronson."

Again she was silent and only stared, unseeing and vacant. Jake watched as the second revelation finally hit her.

Hank spoke again. "I'm sorry, Mrs. Bronson." His voice was low, soft, and sympathetic.

"Who done it?" she whispered hoarsely.

"We don't know yet, but we're doing everything we can to find out."

She was crying freely now. "Can I see him? He's my only boy." She sobbed and pulled a well-worn tissue from the pocket of her housecoat.

"Yes, you can. We need you to identify the … him, just for the record."

"All right," she managed to say.

Hank leaned back and looked at Jake. Jake looked at the floor, and then the walls, and then around the room. His eyes were moist and unfocused.

Hank made arrangements for an officer to pick her up later that day and take her to the morgue to identify her son's body.

As they were about to leave, Hank said, "We'll let you know as soon as we find out anything, Mrs. Bronson."

She thanked them and let them out.

As Jake pulled the car onto the street, Hank looked over. "Are you getting a cold?" he asked. "I thought I heard you sniffling in there."

Jake laughed. "Must be contagious. I think I heard you sniffling too."

Friday, August 12th, 3:25 p.m.

BASIL WRIGHTSON trudged up the two flights of stairs to his apartment. A small brown terrier scampered around his feet, up one step, and then back, as if trying to hurry his master up. The dog's nose was on the floor, constantly sniffing, and he yipped a small dog yip, tugging and testing the length of his chain.

Basil had been for a long walk that morning. It was a beautiful day, so afterwards, he'd sat in the park for quite some time, munching on a small lunch he'd brought with him. He'd watched the kids try to injure themselves on those infernal things they climbed around on. Oh, to be a kid again. He fed some pigeons from his lunch, scooped up dog poo, and had a wonderful time.

But he was tired. He needed a cup of tea and a quick afternoon nap. Then he would feel better. But first he had to get up the dern stairs. They needed to fix the dern elevator someday.

He finally reached the top of the steps and opened the door to the hallway. The dog dashed through, yanking on the chain, still yipping away.

He passed doors with dumb homemade signs on them, like "Home Sweet Home" and "Welcome to My Humble Abode." Mostly made from wood or leftover stuff lying around. One said, "Please Use Other Door," and pointed to the neighbor. Basil enjoyed knocking on that door sometimes as he passed, just because it was such a stupid sign.

But today he kept on walking.

The terrier tugged at his chain, two steps behind him.

Basil pulled. "Come on, Pup."

Pup just kept tugging, his nose to the floor, sniffing near the bottom of a door.

Basil pulled a little harder.

Pup pulled back.

Basil stopped tugging. "Whatyu diggin' at there?" He leaned over and screwed up his eyes. "What the heck is that?"

He saw some thick red stuff oozing out from under the door. He stared at it a moment, scratching his head.

"Looks like blood."

He stood, looked at the door, and read, "Don't Worry, Be Happy." He looked underneath the sign and said aloud, "Number 204. That's Mrs. Bellows."

He cocked his head, pulled at his earlobe, and tested the door. It was unlocked.

He gently pushed at it, but it only opened halfway; it seemed to be hitting something. He poked his head around the door and looked inside.

"Oh dern," he said.

Thirteen Years Ago

JEREMY SWUNG OPEN the school door and stepped

outside. He huddled his shoulders, trying to force the already upturned collar of his coat a little higher. The cold air snapped at his ears as he tucked his hands into his pockets, sniffled, and hurried down the steps.

"Jeremy, you little faggot."

He didn't look. He knew who it was. He paid no attention to the voice as he jumped the last step onto the sidewalk, hurrying for the parking lot where the busses waited.

"Faggot. Faggot. Faggot."

He glanced over quickly this time, long enough to see three boys heading toward him. He walked faster.

His tormentors were closer. He started to run. Too late. One had his arm wrapped around Jeremy's neck, choking him.

"Leave me alone, Joey," he pleaded, trying to breathe. "I didn't do nothing to you. Just leave me alone."

Joey laughed and mocked him. "Leave me alone, Joey. Leave me alone, Joey."

One of the other boys grabbed his feet. They lifted him up, swung him back and forth, finally tossing him into a snow bank running along the edge of the pathway.

Joey jumped on him, holding him down. "Wash this faggot's dirty face for him, Cole."

Cole scooped up a handful of snow and rubbed it vigorously in Jeremy's face. The snow was hard-packed, and Jeremy tried to wiggle free at the discomfort. The cold bit into his face.

"Let me up," he gasped.

Joey looked at him and sneered. "Your father's a murderer, isn't he?"

"No, he's not. He's not."

"And your mother's a whore."

Jeremy struggled again, the words hurting more than the cold.

"My mother is not a whore. Yours is," he screamed.

Joey smacked him across the face. The hit dazed him, made his face more numb, and he winced in pain.

"Your father killed somebody. That's why he's in jail. I hope somebody kills him," Joey said.

Joey rubbed another handful of snow into Jeremy's face and stood. "See you around, Jeremy," he said, then laughed and walked away.

Jeremy got up, rubbed his sleeve across his face, sniffled, and cursed to himself as he hurried to catch the bus.

CHAPTER 17

Friday, August 12th, 3:50 p.m.

TO AVOID DRAWING onlookers and the media, who would undoubtedly be monitoring the dispatch frequency, the radio message Hank received was brief, not revealing the full nature of the incident.

When he arrived at Mrs. Bellows' apartment complex, the entire building was taped off. Sentries had been put in place at all entrances, and admittance to the building was tightly controlled.

A uniformed officer was leaning against the door frame at the main entrance. Hank showed his badge and was directed to the scene of the homicide.

He climbed the stairs two at a time and stepped into the hallway. He sniffed, testing the air. It smelled stale, musty, not unlike the odor from a wet dog—or dirty socks—Hank wasn't sure which.

He made his way down the passageway, covered in faded carpeting, and eased open the door of 204. The medical examiner was already there. The crime scene investigators were evaluating and collecting physical evidence.

Hank made a visual survey of the apartment. It was a basic one-bedroom unit with a small living room adjoining an open kitchen. It was clean and neat and felt quite comfortable despite its aging appearance.

Mrs. Bellows' body was slumped down a couple of feet inside the doorway. She was half on her back, one leg bent and folded under the other. Her handbag had fallen to the floor and lay near her left hand, a wooden cane by her right. A large puddle of blood had formed, trickled across the uneven floor, and oozed under the door.

Looking around, Hank couldn't see any visible signs of a struggle or footprints in the blood.

He bent down and addressed the ME as she hunched over the body. The victim's dress had been cut back, revealing the wound.

"Cause of death?" he asked.

"Appears to be a single stab wound penetrating the heart," she answered, pointing.

Hank examined the injury.

The ME continued, "A severe wound, and almost always fatal."

"So the killer seemed to know exactly where to cause the most damage?"

"It appears so."

"Weapon?"

"I won't know exactly until we do the autopsy, but it looks like a fairly broad instrument, probably a knife." She pointed. "See these ragged edges around the wound? The killer seems to have used a serrated knife, causing severe damage to the surrounding tissue."

"Killer was right-handed?" Hank asked.

"Almost certainly. And by the angle of penetration, taking into account the height of the victim, the killer was probably about the same height. Hard to tell exactly, but certainly not a tall person."

"And the time of death?"

"I can't be sure yet, but it appears to be within the last two or three hours. I'll know more later."

Sliding a pen from his inner pocket, Hank used the tip to lift up the top edge of the handbag. He peered in. A neatly packaged pork chop lay inside on top of a plastic grocery bag. He squinted his eyes at the label on the chop.

"Mortino's," he read aloud.

He eased open the plastic bag and was able to work the receipt free. He studied it a moment. Wieners, marmalade, a loaf of bread, but there was no pork chop on the receipt. He frowned thoughtfully, took a shot of it with his cell camera, and tucked it back into the bag.

"Who called this in?" he asked.

"Apparently, a guy down the hall. In 212. A Mr. Basil Wrightson."

Hank stood and looked around the apartment. "Anybody talk to Wrightson yet?"

Nobody had.

Hank squeezed past the exit door and stepped into the hallway. Yellow crime scene tape draped across the area leading further down the hall toward other apartments. An officer leaned against the peeling wall, chatting with a few old-timers who stood on the other side of the barrier, trying to get a glimpse of what was going on.

Hank addressed them. "Mr. Wrightson?"

An old woman pointed. "Down there. 212."

Hank ducked under the tape. He walked past a couple of doors, reading the numbers, and stopped in front of 212. He knocked. A dog's yelp came from inside.

In a few seconds, an elderly man appeared, a small dog

squatting behind him. The man squinted at the badge.

"Mr. Wrightson?" Hank asked.

"Yep."

"I'm Detective Corning. May I talk to you for a moment?"

Wrightson swung the door back. "Come in," he said.

Hank followed him into a tiny living area, almost a carbon copy of Mrs. Bellows' apartment, but not as clean and tidy. He noticed the air was fresher than in the hallway. A window was open on the outside wall, and the afternoon breeze fluttered the plain blue curtains.

He sat on a hard chair as Mr. Wrightson took a seat in a comfortable lounge chair facing the television. Wrightson silenced the TV with a remote on the stand beside him.

The dog laid his head on his front paws beside Wrightson's chair and studied Hank.

"You called in the report about Mrs. Bellows, is that right?" Hank asked.

Wrightson sighed and nodded. "Yeah, I called it in from here. Then I went back and hung around the hall until the police came. Couldn't take it anymore. Had to leave."

"Did you know Mrs. Bellows?"

"Sure. People come and go, but a lot of us are lifers."

"Lifers?"

"We're here for life. Till we're dead."

"How long have you lived here?"

"Well, put it this way. I remember when this building was in great shape. And the elevator worked. So, probably about twenty years, maybe more."

"You're not a suspect, Mr. Wrightson, but for the record, I have to ask. Where were you before you found the body?"

"I was gone for a long walk, most of the day. I was at the park there, just down the street, enjoying the day. Took my lunch with me."

Hank dug a well-worn faux leather notepad from his pocket. He flipped it open and scribbled something in it.

"Did anyone see you there?"

"Sure did. Lots of people."

"And when you returned," Hank asked, "did you see anyone else outside or inside the building?"

"Nary a soul."

Hank scribbled in his pad.

"When you opened the door to Mrs. Bellows' apartment, did you move the body in any way?"

"Nope. I opened the door slow, because I wasn't sure what was up, and when the door hit her, I just poked my head in."

"And that's when you saw her?"

"Yup."

"And what made you suspect something was wrong? In other words, why did you open the door?"

Wrightson looked at his dog, then back at Hank. "My little dog, Pup, was sniffing at her door, and when I looked, I saw some blood coming out underneath. So I opened the door."

Hank made another note.

"You said you knew Mrs. Bellows. Did you ever have occasion to talk to her?"

"Sure. Lots of times. She was always such a nice, happy person, much like me, I think, and so we had a cup of tea together sometimes. We just chatted about the old days. Stuff like that. I'll miss her, that's for sure. I don't really have a lot of close friends left anymore and she was the closest I had."

"Would you say you knew her rather well?"

"Pretty well, I think." Wrightson laughed. "Weren't nothing sexual or anything. I don't think either of us could even remember how to do that."

Hank's lips formed a half smile and he continued, "Do

you have any idea who might have wanted to kill her? Anyone who didn't like her?"

Wrightson looked at the ceiling a moment and shook his head. "Can't think of anybody. Weren't nobody around here didn't like her, least I can say that much."

Hank consulted his notebook and scribbled something again.

"Thank you, Mr. Wrightson. That's it for now. You've been a big help. I'll let you know if I need anything else."

"Any time. Glad to help. I sure hope you find the guy who did this." Wrightson shook his head sadly. "Mrs. Bellows had such a good soul. She didn't deserve this."

Hank stood and let himself out. Pup followed him to the door, his tail wagging.

CHAPTER 18

Friday, August 12th, 4:22 p.m.

JAKE PEERED THROUGH the windshield. Red and blue lights blinked some distance ahead and traffic had come to a standstill.

His cell phone buzzed in his pocket. He reached over and turned down the smooth voice of Kenny Chesney.

"This is Jake."

"Jake, it's Hank."

"What's up?"

"You're not gonna believe this."

"Try me." Jake eased his car ahead a few more feet.

"There's been another murder," Hank said. "I just came from the crime scene now. An old woman. Stabbed to death in her apartment." He filled Jake in on some of the details.

"Any witnesses?" Jake asked.

"Nobody saw anything. They're still working the scene, but there are no suspects at this point. Strangest thing, though."

"What's that?"

"It appears she had just come from the grocery store. She bought three items, but also had a pork chop in her handbag, not listed on the receipt."

Jake chuckled. "So, the victim is a thief."

"Can't see it, though. She's eighty-nine years old and we don't see a lot of eighty-nine-year-old shoplifters."

"Maybe she bought it somewhere else," Jake suggested, as he touched the gas pedal and steered into the adjoining lane.

"Nope. The receipt, as well as the label on the chop, both said they came from Mortino's."

"But you don't think that had anything to do with her murder, do you?"

"Sounds unlikely," Hank said. "But it's rather strange, nonetheless."

Both lanes were just as slow. Now the other one was speeding up. Jake steered back into the first lane and moved ahead a few spots.

"And here's another odd fact," Hank continued.

"Yeah?"

"As you're probably aware, there hasn't been a murder in this city in a long, long time. And now there are two within a week of each other."

"I know cops don't believe in coincidence, but this has gotta be one." Jake slapped on his blinker and weaved through the oncoming traffic, making a quick left turn. He knew a shortcut.

"Maybe," Hank replied. "Maybe not. Sure doesn't seem related, though. Different MO. Different everything."

"There's one good thing about this," Jake said.

"What's that?"

"At least you'll earn your paycheck now."

Friday, August 12th, 5:05 p.m.

ANNIE WAS AT HER desk in the office when she heard the rumble of Jake's Firebird as the vehicle pulled into the driveway. In a few moments, she heard Matty squealing, running to meet his father at the door. Then she heard grunts, roars, and other guy noises coming closer.

Jake ducked as he came through the office doorway. Matty was on his shoulders, holding on with his hands weaved together, wrapped around Jake's forehead. Jake took a seat in the guest chair in front of the desk, Matty still clinging.

Annie dropped her pen, sat back, and smiled at her two boys, one big and one small.

Jake reached up with two hands, grabbed Matty by the waist, and lifted him up. He whirled him over and deposited him feet first onto the floor.

"Why don't you go ahead and lift a few weights, Matty," Jake said. "I'll be down in a minute. I just need to talk to your mom."

"Sure, Dad," Matty said, heading for the basement.

"Don't hurt yourself," Annie called.

"Oh, Mom," he called back. "Don't worry so much."

Jake laughed and Annie frowned.

Jake leaned forward and put his elbows on the desk. "Hank called me a few minutes ago," he said. "An interesting development."

"Oh?"

"You know those old apartment buildings down there on Carville Street? An old woman was murdered there. Hank said she just got home from Mortino's and somebody did her in right there. Just inside her apartment."

"Somebody followed her," Annie said.

"Probably. Her purse was right beside her, with her shopping inside of it, and the door was unlocked."

"When did this happen?"

"Just a couple of hours or so ago." Jake scratched his head and looked up a moment. "Actually, I think Hank said the timestamp on the receipt was twelve forty-two."

Annie thought, then said, "Those buildings are maybe a five or ten minute walk from Mortino's. So she probably got home around one. Maybe slightly before."

"Sounds right to me," Jake said. "Unless she stopped somewhere else on the way home."

"Like where?"

"Dunno. I'm just saying. Maybe."

"Well, anyway, that's a shame," Annie said.

"Sure is," Jake said. "Hank is wondering if it's related to Bronson's murder somehow, but he doesn't see the connection. Different MO and everything."

Annie leaned forward, silent a moment, looking at Jake. Finally she said, "I'll have to put some thought into that idea, but in the meantime, we need to concentrate on finding Jenny. That's our top priority."

CHAPTER 19

Tuesday, August 2nd, Ten Days Ago, 12:00 Noon

IT WAS SUCH a beautiful day outside and Jeremy was sick and tired of stocking shelves, packing, unpacking, doing this, doing that, doing everything around there, it seemed.

It was lunchtime. He hurried to the back room, opened his locker, and grabbed a small paper bag. He was going to leave this dump and eat lunch in the park.

There was a nice little spot just a couple of blocks away from Mortino's, right across from the high school. He hurried out the back door and down the street to his destination.

It was nice there. Just like at home. Lots of trees around, birds singing, and pretty quiet. For a city.

He sat down, leaned up against a tree, and closed his eyes. He was kind of tired. A nap would be nice, but he only had forty minutes. Best not dawdle too much.

He pulled a napkin from his bag and spread it neatly on the ground beside him. He dug out an apple and a tomato and laid them carefully on the napkin. Lastly, he brought out a sandwich, wrapped up nicely in plastic wrap. He looked at it. Peanut butter and jam. Delicious. He unwrapped the sandwich, took a big bite and, tilting his head back against the tree, he closed his eyes and chewed.

He frowned and opened his eyes again, peeking around the tree. A couple of noisy kids had sat at a bench a few feet away. Their backs were to him, but he could hear them chattering away. He shook his head. So much for peace and quiet.

A girl was talking. He wasn't the least bit interested, but he could hear her plainly as she spoke. "It's so nice here," she said.

Then a guy spoke. "It sure is."

Jeremy thought, *Yeah, it was until now.*

She spoke again. "It's really nice to see you again."

Jeremy peeked around at her. She was pretty.

Then the guy said, "It's nice to be with you."

Jeremy rolled his eyes.

"You were telling me before," she said. "About the problem you had?"

"It didn't amount to much. It was a couple of years ago, and I'm ashamed of it now."

Jeremy thought the guy looked like a jerk.

"Yes?" She urged him on.

"I don't want you to think bad of me, but I did something stupid."

Jeremy could see her looking at him, waiting for him to continue.

He did. "A friend and I, we broke into some guy's house."

She caught her breath.

"It was real dumb. I admit it," he said. "I wouldn't do anything like that again. We had a couple of beers and weren't thinking straight."

She was frowning at him now. "So what happened?"

Jeremy was frowning now too.

The jerk continued, "We took some stereo equipment. And his TV."

Jeremy's frown deepened.

The jerk put his hand on her shoulder.

Then she spoke. "Chad, how could you do that?"

"I know, Jenny. You should be upset. It really was dumb."

Silence a moment and Jeremy waited for somebody to speak.

"So then what happened?" Jenny asked.

"We got caught. Somebody saw us coming from the place and called the cops."

Jeremy hoped the judge nailed him good.

"But because we were only sixteen at the time," Chad continued, "they couldn't release our name to the public and we basically got off with a warning."

Her eyes were wide. "Wow."

"Yeah, we got lucky."

Jeremy was so busy eavesdropping he'd forgotten to eat his lunch. He took a big bite of his sandwich, leaned back against the tree, and chewed thoughtfully.

He took another peek as she said, "I really like you, Chad, but what you did scares me." She looked worried.

"I know," he said. "You have every right to feel that way. But it's over. Done with. It won't happen again."

"Promise?" she asked.

"Promise." He stroked her hair. "I promise."

Jeremy rolled his eyes again.

Jenny looked at her watch. "I need to get back now."

"I'll drop by at three o'clock and give you a lift home before I head back to King City. I need to catch a little sleep before work."

"I'm counting on it." She smiled, and they stood and headed back toward the school.

Jeremy slowly packed up the rest of his lunch as they left. He was deep in thought as he walked back to his boring job.

Tuesday, August 2nd, Ten Days Ago, 2:50 p.m.

JEREMY HAD BEEN keeping an eye on his watch ever since he'd gotten back from lunch. He took another look at it now. It was ten minutes before three.

He walked to the front of the store. His boss was busy with a customer. Jeremy hung back out of sight until the boss was free, and then he approached him.

Jeremy looked anxious. "Mr. MacKay," he said. "My aunt is real sick. She needs me badly. Is it all right if I leave a little early today? Please, sir. She's sick. She's real sick."

Jeremy didn't have an aunt. At least, not one he knew of. Didn't matter. MacKay didn't know.

MacKay frowned.

"I'll make it up later," Jeremy said.

"All right, then," MacKay said reluctantly. "Run along."

"Thanks. I appreciate it. Thank you, sir."

Jeremy hustled to the back of the store. He got his half-eaten lunch from his locker, stuffed it into his backpack, and headed out the back door to the employee parking lot.

He climbed into his Hyundai, adjusted the fat cushion under him, backed from the space, and drove onto the side street. He took a left, and another left, and in a minute, he approached the school.

He pulled over into a space by the side of the street, some ways back, but close enough so he could see what he wanted to see.

He waited.

There were a couple of cars parked where the sidewalk leading from the school doors touched the street. He kept an eye on the cars.

In five or ten minutes, he saw her smiling as she came down the walk. She looked pretty.

One of the cars he'd been watching was a white Toyota Tercel. He wasn't sure what year it was, maybe a few years old.

He saw the jerk get out of the driver seat, go around the vehicle, and open the passenger-side door. Then Jenny got in the car and the jerk went around and got in his side.

Jeremy kept watching. They were talking about something. Then the Toyota pulled away from the curb. Jeremy followed, keeping back.

He wasn't nervous. He was too busy putting his simple-but-genius plan into place.

He knew from the conversation he'd overheard that the jerk was going to drive her home and then go home to King City himself. There was only one direct route to King City. That's the one he would take, for sure.

He had a few minutes to get ready.

At the next street, the jerk turned left and Jeremy turned right. He drove carefully across town, heading for County Road 12.

Jeremy lived on County Road 12, so he knew exactly where he was going. At one spot, there was a hill, and then a curve before the road straightened out again. Any cars had to slow down at that spot, just enough to make his plan perfect.

He drove over the hill, rounded the curve, drove about a quarter mile, then pulled over and stopped.

He shut off the car and waited patiently.

Tuesday, August 2nd, Ten Days Ago, 3:20 p.m.

JENNY'S CELL PHONE rattled out a hip-hop beat tone. It was her mother.

"Hi, Mom."

"Jenny, I'm just at the hairdresser's. It may be about another hour or so before I get home."

"Sure, Mom."

Chad took his eyes off the road and looked at her.

"Mom's at the hairdresser's. She's going to be awhile," she said.

"Do you want to go straight home?" he asked.

Jenny thought a minute. "There's no hurry," she said.

Silence a moment.

"Do you want to go for a spin?" he asked.

"Sure."

"How about King City? It's only about ten minutes. There's this great little coffee shop I want you to try."

Jenny smiled. "That sounds nice."

Chad swung the car to the curb, glanced in his mirror, and then spun around and headed back the way they came.

"I'll have you back by four," he said.

CHAPTER 20

Friday, August 12th, 5:17 p.m.

HANK LEAFED THROUGH the autopsy report. There was a lot of technical stuff he skimmed over, as well as details of a complete external examination of the body of Chad Bronson. The toxicology report revealed nothing unusual, and the cause of death was as he suspected.

> *Gunshot wound to the head, perforating the left temple four inches from the top of the head.*
>
> *Wound path, right to left, upward, and slightly backward.*
>
> *In my opinion, Chad Allen Bronson died of a gunshot wound to the head. Manner of death is homicide.*

It was signed by Nancy Pietek, Deputy Medical Examiner.

There was no exit wound. The bullet, ascertained to be of .22 caliber by the ballistics report, had been retrieved from inside the skull. The low-velocity, penetrating bullet had ricocheted inside the skull, continuing to cause damage until it stopped moving.

The approximate time of death was listed as being ten to twelve days prior. That fitted in with the witness statements that Bronson had last been seen on the afternoon of August 2nd.

Hank leaned back in his chair and stared at the report. There weren't too many surprises.

The forensic report was completed as well. Hank was interested in the blanket found along with the body, but it didn't appear to have anything unusual about it.

There were fibers on Bronson's clothes and on the blanket, determined to be from floor mats used in car trunks. The make of car could not be determined as most manufacturers use the same supplier.

The most interesting fact to Hank was that, according to the crime scene investigation, the homicide had happened elsewhere, the body carried to the grave and buried.

That Bronson had been dead at the time of burial was also noted.

Hank snapped open his briefcase and slipped the papers inside.

Friday, August 12th, 5:40 p.m.

JAKE FLIPPED onto his back. He lay on the exercise mat, pulled up his knees, and reached for his cell phone.

"Jake here."

"You sound like you're out of breath." It was Chris.

"Just doing a few push-ups."

"Yeah, maybe a few hundred."

Jake chuckled. "What's up, Chris?"

"A couple of things. First off, I'm faxing you over two names I need a background check on. Prospective employees."

"No problem. That's Annie's department. She's a whiz at that. What's the other thing?"

"I wanted to update you on the jewelry thief," Chris said. "It seems he accumulated quite a stash of goodies."

"I'm not surprised. He was pretty brazen."

Chris howled with laughter. "Yeah, he was that. After the cops got through with him he wasn't so brazen anymore. With the video proof, they easily got a warrant and searched his apartment."

"And?"

"They found thousands of dollars' worth of stuff. Maybe tens of thousands. It appears he'd been hitting stores all over."

Jake whistled. "Was he holding everything?"

"It goes deeper than that. Apparently, the stuff they found was just recent acquisitions. They think he has a connection somewhere in Toronto where he gets rid of a lot of stuff."

"A fence."

"Yeah, a fence. But they couldn't get a name from him. He clammed up and asked to see his lawyer."

"That's great news. I'm glad we could help."

"The bosses here are pretty pleased with you guys, too," Chris said and then laughed. "And they're pleased with me, too."

Jake chuckled. "As if you had anything to do with it."

"I was smart enough to hire the right people, wasn't I?"

Friday, August 12th, 5:55 p.m.

THE POLICE ARE never wrong. They always identify the body correctly, but under normal circumstances someone who knows the deceased makes a personal identification.

At least, that's how it was in Richmond Hill City Morgue.

Mrs. Bronson shivered as she stepped in front of the glass window. It was cold inside the morgue, but out here on the other side of the glass where she stood, it was comfort-controlled. The shiver was not due to cold. It was the atmosphere.

She lifted her head and peered through the glass. The large white autopsy room was full of peculiar equipment. Tables for autopsies and dissecting. Racks of instruments, saws, and a large bank of refrigerator units.

She shivered again.

Someone in a white gown pushed a bulging cart her way. As it drew closer, she could see a toe tag attached with string to a big toe of a foot, protruding out from under the white sheet covering the body.

The body of her son.

She covered her face with both hands, peering with dread through her slightly spread fingers.

The cart drew closer. She felt a tiny thud as it came to a stop against the wall.

She dropped her hands, straightened her composure, and looked at the officer beside her.

"Are you ready, Mrs. Bronson?" he asked gently. His hand was around her shoulder, as if to protect her.

She nodded slightly and turned back to face the glass.

The officer nodded to the morgue attendant.

The sheet was lifted, exposing the face.

She looked down slowly, praying she wouldn't see what she knew was there.

The face she forced herself to look at was white and wrinkled, not like her son should look. But it was him.

She turned away and bowed her head, sobbing quietly at first, and then hysterically. The officer kept her from collapsing. With one arm still around her shoulder, the other holding her arm, he turned her away from the window and led her to a chair. She dropped into it, bowed her head, and wept.

The cop held her hand patiently, and in a few minutes she calmed herself. She cleared her throat and looked at the officer.

"It's him," she said weakly.

CHAPTER 21

Friday, August 12th, 6:20 p.m.

JEREMY DIDN'T know what to do about Jenny anymore. She'd seemed like such a sweet person at first. He thought maybe he was falling in love with her, but now he wasn't so sure. The way she'd thrown that rock at him, and cursed him, and spit at him, made him confused. Maybe he would kill her after all. That would solve all his problems.

He dumped the remains of his macaroni and cheese dinner into a small container and popped the top on. He washed up the dishes, packing them neatly where they belonged, and looked around the room.

The kitchen was exactly like Mother had left it almost seven years ago. It was spotlessly clean, and neat as the day she left. The day she was forced to leave—the day she died.

He thought back to the funeral. Nobody had come. It was just him, his mother, one friend of hers, and some preacher from a church in town that agreed to say a few words at the small service.

Then he buried her beside Father. He never cried—he

couldn't. Then he went on with his life.

He brushed his teeth carefully, slipped his runners on, grabbed the container of leftover supper, and stepped out the back door.

His vegetable garden was coming along nicely. The tomatoes were turning red and growing, and he looked forward to enjoying them.

He strolled contentedly toward the barn, enjoying the cool of the early evening, then swung open the small entry door beside the huge double doors of the barn and stepped inside. Jenny was lying down, curled up on the blanket, over by the far wall.

She looked at him without moving as he came nearer.

Picking up a folding chair, he set it a few feet away from her. He sat and put the container of food on the floor beside him, then leaned over with his chin in his hands, watching her.

She sure was pretty. Even though she probably needed a wash, and maybe some clean clothes, she still looked awful pretty.

He glared at her and didn't speak.

Neither did she.

Finally, he sat up straight and said, "I brought you something to eat."

He picked up the container, stood, and moved over to her. He set the meal beside her and returned to his chair without speaking.

She ignored the food.

"It's good," he said. "Macaroni and cheese. I made it myself. You should try it. It's very good."

She ignored his suggestion and closed her eyes, remaining silent.

"You should talk to me," he said.

She opened her eyes. "Why?"

"Because I need your help."

"What kind of help?"

"I don't know what to do with you." He sighed.

She said nothing.

Then she spoke. It was a statement, but almost like a question. "You can let me go."

He was quiet for a minute, then said softly, gently, "I can't."

"Why not?"

"Because you would tell the police what I did to Chad. They wouldn't understand. Nobody seems to understand what I did was for the best. Only Mother and Father would, but they're dead."

Silence a moment.

"I understand why you had to do it," Jenny said.

He thought a moment, then frowned at her and asked, "And why'd I do it?"

Finally, she said uncertainly, "Because he deserved it."

Jeremy stood and glared at her. "Deserved it? Why? Why'd he deserve it?"

Jenny was silent.

He sat again and folded his arms. "You're lying to me."

Nobody spoke.

"You're pretending to understand, just so I'll let you go," he shouted.

"Sorry," she said calmly. "I didn't mean to lie to you. I don't know why, but I realize you must have a good reason or you wouldn't have done it."

Jeremy looked at her skeptically out of one eye. Should he believe her? No, probably not. *She's a liar.*

"I'll tell you the reason," he said, calmer now.

She waited. He hesitated.

"He's a criminal. He broke the law. He's a thief."

Jenny widened her eyes. Then she blinked and asked in disbelief, "That's why you killed him?"

"Yes."

"But you don't even know him."

"Doesn't matter. I know what he did."

"How … how did you know?"

"I have my ways. I see things. I hear things. I know things."

Silence.

"Have there been others?" Jenny asked.

"Just two others, so far."

"Who were the others?"

"It doesn't concern you."

"Were they the same? You know, criminals too?" she asked.

"Yes, they were."

"I'm not a criminal," she said.

"Yes, I know. And that's why I have such a problem. I don't know what to do with you."

CHAPTER 22

Friday, August 12th, 6:40 p.m.

AMELIA WAS IN her massive kitchen when the knocker clanked. She had just cut some fresh flowers from the flower beds behind the house and was arranging them. She dropped the flowers into a tall vase on the table and went to the foyer.

Lilia had already answered the door. Hank was standing inside, and he grinned when he saw her.

She smiled back and motioned for him to go into the sitting room. "Come in."

She asked Lilia to bring some coffee, then followed him, and they took a seat on the divan, facing each other.

Hank glanced at the photo albums, still on the coffee table, now closed.

"How've you been?" he asked.

She sighed. "Fairly well, considering the circumstances."

Hank nodded slowly and asked, "Have you seen the news?"

She cocked her head. "No."

"The body of Chad Bronson has been recovered."

She caught her breath.

"The medical examiner reports he was likely killed about the same day he was last seen. Ten days ago."

She waited for him to continue.

"He was murdered," he said. "Shot in the head."

Amelia was horrified. "And Jenny?"

"Still no word on Jenny, but absolutely no reason to think she has come to any harm."

She looked hopeful. "If Bronson died ten days ago, but Jenny was still fine as of yesterday, then—"

"Then she's still fine today," Hank assured her.

Amelia feared the worst. "But why was Jenny kidnapped? She said she's all right."

"That's what we don't know."

"Where was Bronson found?"

"Annie found his body. She was doing some investigating and found him buried in the woods along County Road 12."

Amelia's brow rose. She opened her mouth and stared at Hank.

"I'll tell you something, Amelia. Annie and Jake really know what they're doing. If anyone can find Jenny, they can."

Lilia eased into the room, set a tray with a pot of coffee, two mugs, and a plate of sugar cookies on the coffee table, then silently left.

Hank poured two cups of coffee and fixed his up with cream and sugar. He selected a cookie and sat back, holding his cup, sipping at his coffee.

Amelia sat back, holding her cup with both hands wrapped around it, staring blankly inside.

Hank looked thoughtfully at her. Something seemed to be on his mind. He put his arm on the back of the couch and cleared his throat as if making a decision.

"As you know, Amelia, we live in a pretty safe city. There

hasn't been a murder here as long as I can recall, but—"

She looked up.

He moistened his lips and continued, "An old woman was killed today as well. There doesn't seem to be any connection, but we're still looking for one."

Horror gripped her face.

Hank pulled out his notepad. Flipping it open, he withdrew a photo of Mrs. Bellows, held it up, and showed it to her.

"Can you recall, have you ever seen this woman, or heard the name Edna Bellows?" he asked.

Amelia looked thoughtfully at the picture a moment and shook her head.

"The face doesn't look familiar," she said. "And neither does the name. Is that the woman who was killed?"

Hank nodded.

"I don't think Jenny knows her either, but I can't be sure," she said.

Hank finished his coffee, set the cup back on the tray, and stood.

Amelia stood as well.

Hank placed his hand gently on her arm and looked intently at her.

"We're all making Jenny's disappearance a top priority," he said. "But I have to go. I promise you, I won't rest until Jenny is home."

Friday, August 12th, 7:00 p.m.

ANNIE WAS AT her desk in the office of Lincoln Investigations when the doorbell rang.

Matty called from the other room, "I'll get it."

She dropped her pen, slipped the desk drawer shut, and

then stood and walked through the doorway of the office just as Matty came running back.

"Mom, there's a woman here to see you."

Annie went to the front door and swung it open. She frowned when she recognized the caller. A cameraman stood beside her, his camera pointed her way.

"Mrs. Lincoln," the woman said. "I'm Lisa Krunk from Channel 7 Action News. May I ask you a few questions?"

Annie was still frowning when a microphone was shoved in her face. She hesitated, and then said, "Yes?"

"I understand you're the one who found the body of Chad Bronson this morning?"

"Yes."

"And you and your husband are private investigators, is that correct?"

Annie nodded. "Yes, we are."

"Can you tell us a little more about that? What led you to Bronson's body?"

Other newspapers and TV stations hadn't been so demanding, but Lisa Krunk was known for being pushy. Annie was annoyed and didn't know how much she should say about the case. The murder of Bronson was still an ongoing police investigation, and they hadn't released all the details to the public. She had to be careful.

"Bronson's car was found abandoned a few days ago," Annie said. "And forensics showed it had recently been in an area we determined was along County Road 12."

"And so you went there alone?"

"Yes."

"Weren't you concerned?"

"There was no reason to believe I was in any danger. Besides," Annie added indignantly, "I am capable of taking care of myself."

"Yes, it appears you are," Lisa said, and waited for Annie to continue.

Annie remained silent.

Lisa said, "Sources tell us Bronson's death is related to the disappearance of sixteen-year-old Jenny James. Is that correct?"

Annie thought a moment. "That's yet to be determined," she said.

"Have you made any progress on finding Miss James?"

"Yes, we're making progress and we expect to find her soon."

"Given the fact she was known to be with Bronson, who is now dead, you still believe Miss James has not been killed as well?"

"Definitely not," Annie said sharply. She decided not to mention Jenny's phone call, but added, "We have reason to believe she's in no danger."

"Is there anything else you'd like to add, Mrs. Lincoln?"

"No, that's all for now."

"Thank you for your time."

The cameraman swung the camera over to Lisa.

"We will bring you breaking news as it happens. In an exclusive report, I'm Lisa Krunk for Channel 7 Action News."

The cameraman shut the camera off and lowered it. Lisa Krunk waved a "thank you" as Annie shut the door.

CHAPTER 23

Friday, August 12th, 8:02 p.m.

THE MEDICAL examiner's report Hank received didn't seem to shed any light on the murder of Edna Bellows.

He frowned as he leafed through the pages of the report. The observations Nancy Pietek had made at the crime scene proved to be correct.

The cause of death was stated to be a fatal wound penetrating the left atrium. The weapon used was a broad serrated knife, possibly a hunting knife or similar.

The time of death was determined to be approximately 1:00 p.m. on August 12th.

Hank had requested to view the evidence collected from the crime scene. He pulled the box toward him. Lying on top was a handbag. He removed it from the evidence box and tipped out its contents onto his desk.

There wasn't much there.

Along with the groceries in the bag, he took another look at the package of meat, now turning a brownish, sickly hue. *Better get this into cold storage*, he thought grimly.

He snapped open her change purse. There were a few coins inside, along with ten dollars in bills. The only other thing in the handbag was a single key; it was undoubtedly for her apartment.

Other than from Mrs. Bellows, no fingerprints had been found inside the apartment or on the door and doorframe.

The building had no security cameras, so that was a dead end too. Everyone in the building had been questioned and no one had seen anything, or anyone, unusual.

Hank sat back and scratched his head, staring intently at the box of evidence in front of him, trying to determine his next course of action.

Friday, August 12th, 8:25 p.m.

ANNIE WAS WATCHING Jake and Matty wrestle on the floor of the living room when the office phone rang. She got to it after the second ring. It was Hank.

"I thought I might drop by for a minute if you're not busy," he said.

"Sure. Jake and I are both here."

"I'm just coming up the street now. See you in a minute."

She hung up the phone. Jake looked up, a question mark on his face as she came into the room and sat in an overstuffed armchair.

"It's Hank," she said. "He's on his way over."

While Jake was distracted, Matty took the opportunity to slip free and pin his father flat on his back.

"Okay, I give up. You win," Jake announced.

Matty grinned and climbed off.

"I'll get you next time," Jake warned as he stood and dropped onto the couch.

"Yeah, I doubt that," Matty said. "Any time you want, big guy."

The doorbell rang and Matty charged to the door. He whipped it open. "Hey, Uncle Hank."

Hank ruffled Matty's hair and grinned. "Hey, Matty."

"We're in here," Jake called.

Matty followed Hank as he went into the living room, set his briefcase on the floor, and dropped onto the other end of the couch. Matty hopped up and sat between Hank and his father.

Hank said, "I got the ME's report here for Bronson, as well as the ballistics report." He reached down, clicked open his briefcase, and withdrew some papers. "I also have the report on Mrs. Bellows."

Jake took the report on Bronson from Hank, then looked at Matty. "Why don't you go do your homework, Matty? We have some boring things to discuss here."

"I did my homework," Matty announced.

"Then go read or something," Annie said. "It's almost your bedtime anyway."

"All right, I know when I'm not wanted," Matty said dryly. He jumped off the couch. "See you later, Uncle Hank."

"See you later, Bud."

Matty raced from the room and ran furiously up the stairs.

"There's not a lot of enlightenment there," Hank said, pointing to the report Jake held. "The thing of interest is, there was no exit wound on Bronson. The gun used was a twenty-two-caliber and the bullet was still inside his skull. There's not much power in those twenty-twos. Certainly enough to kill, especially at close range, but the deadly thing about them is, once the bullet gets inside the skull, it just bounces around, completely tearing apart everything inside."

Annie scrunched up her nose in distaste at the thought. "Not a nice way to go."

"No, it's not," Hank agreed.

"I don't see the difference," Jake said, chuckling. "In the head, or through the head. If I had my choice, it would be neither one."

Hank pointed at the report again. "I already assumed this, but the report states Bronson was killed elsewhere, then brought into the forest and buried."

"What about the blanket?" Annie asked.

"Nothing much to go on there. Just a regular blanket. Lots of blood on it, and a few fibers from an unknown make of car, but nothing else."

Annie frowned and looked thoughtful.

Hank continued, "I dropped by Amelia's and filled her in as well. I also asked her if she knew Mrs. Bellows. No luck there."

Annie leaned forward. "It rained a couple of days after Bronson was killed," she said. "I remember the ground was a little concave in that area. The rain probably caused that."

"Yes, for sure," Jake said. "It's almost impossible to fill in a hole and flatten the ground. There's always some air trapped inside that can go away later. Even if you stomp it down with your feet, it doesn't completely work."

Annie whacked herself on the forehead with the palm of her hand.

Jake looked at her in dismay. "What is it?" he asked.

Annie shook her head. "It completely slipped my mind. When I first saw the concave area on the spot that made me curious, I brushed away some of the leaves and twigs and saw a footprint. A child's footprint. And when I removed more leaves I saw more footprints. That's what made me suspicious. All those footprints made it look certain somebody tried to pack the ground down."

Hank whistled.

Jake was bewildered. "A child's footprint?"

"It sure looked like it," Annie replied. "At least, it was quite small. Maybe a size six or seven."

"Maybe a woman," Jake suggested.

"There aren't many woman who would use that MO. They don't bury bodies. Rarely, that is."

"Perhaps it was a young person, or someone with small feet," Annie suggested.

Hank scratched his head. Jake looked at the ceiling and frowned.

Annie got up and dashed into the kitchen. She grabbed her cell phone from a small wicker basket on the counter and raced back into the living room. "Right here," she said, tapping the cell phone screen. She turned the phone toward Hank and Jake. "I have a picture of the print."

Jake took the phone from her and stared at it. "It's a running shoe," he said. "Can't tell what size from the picture, though. There's nothing to compare it to."

Hank leaned over and looked. "You can see a few leaves there. Leaves come in different sizes of course, but I think if you compare it to the leaves, you can get an idea."

Jake agreed. "Yes, you can at least tell it's fairly small."

"You should carry a ruler with you, Annie," Hank said. "You never know when you might need it." He took the phone from Jake, looked at the photo again, and handed the phone to Annie. "Send me that picture. I'll get the lab to look at it and see if they can tell me anything about it."

Annie took the phone, and after a few more taps on the screen, the photo had been sent. "It's on its way."

Hank yawned and looked at his watch. "I'm running low on sleep," he said. "I best be getting home and catch a few." He stood, stretched, and picked up his briefcase. "Tomorrow's a new day and a fresh start."

Jake walked him to the door. "We'll keep in touch," he said as Hank left.

Saturday, August 13th, 12:01 a.m.

JAKE TAPPED ON the office door of the night shift manager of King City Foods. He looked at his watch. The midnight shift had just begun.

The door was opened by a thin-faced man, maybe in his late fifties. He was graying, with small eyes and a broad nose. He squinted at Jake through round wire-framed glasses.

"Good evening. My name is Jake Lincoln and I'm investigating the death of Chad Bronson. I wonder if I may talk to his coworkers for a moment?"

The man glared at him and said gruffly, "Can't shut down the line."

"That's okay, I just need to ask a few questions, sir."

The man hesitated before saying, "Guess it'd be okay."

Jake stepped back as the man moved from the office and closed the door behind him.

"This way," the manager said, moving down a short corridor toward a closed metal door.

He swung the door open, and they were greeted with the clatter of machinery, stamping, whirring, and humming. Jake followed him onto the factory floor.

The manager pointed toward the rear of the room. Jake could see a long conveyor belt, running along the wall, circling around, moving containers of food past various stations as they stamped, sorted, and labeled their way to the packers at the end of the line.

"Right there," the manager said, raising his voice to be heard over the factory sounds. "Doing the packing. That's where Bronson used to be. Him and Mikey over there did the packing and stacking."

Jake looked. He could see two guys picking boxes of

something off the end of the conveyor belt, packing them neatly in cartons.

"Thanks," Jake said. "I won't be long."

He strode across the factory floor, dodging workers as he made his way to where the packers were. They wore food handler gloves and hairnets to keep their hair from making contact with food.

No one looked up as he approached.

"Mikey?" Jake asked.

One of the guys glanced up briefly. "Yeah, I'm Mikey."

"I'm Jake Lincoln, and I'm investigating the death of Chad Bronson. May I ask you a few questions?"

Mikey looked stunned. He stopped working and stared at Jake. "What? Chad's dead?"

"I'm afraid so."

Mikey frowned. "No wonder he ain't been around." He picked up a container with each hand and dropped them into a carton. "What happened?"

"He was murdered. About ten days ago."

Mikey whistled. "Holy smokes. I reckon you ain't caught the killer yet or you wouldn't be here."

"Not yet," Jake said. "How long did you know Bronson?"

Mikey stood and scratched his head. "Gee," he said. "Only a few weeks, I guess. He weren't here that long."

"Did you know him well?"

"Not too well. We talked some. Not on the line too much. It's hard to talk in here, but at lunch and break. Yeah, we talked then."

"Did he ever mention anyone who may not have liked him? Anyone who may've wanted to do him harm?"

"Nope. Chad was an easygoing guy. Easy to like."

Jake crossed his arms and stroked his chin, thinking. Finally, he asked, "Did he ever talk to you about his personal life?"

Mikey turned back to the line. A few containers were starting to jam up. He swiftly packed them and answered without looking up. "Well, like I said, we didn't talk too much."

Jake waited.

Mikey straightened his back and looked thoughtfully at Jake. "There is one thing," he said, and then hesitated.

Jake raised his brows and waited.

"Well, I guess now he's dead, it don't matter. He didn't talk about it much, though." He turned and moved the full carton to another platform, where the other worker swiftly taped it shut and set an empty carton beside Mikey, ready to be filled.

Jake waited patiently.

Mikey stopped and looked up again. "He told me that, when he was younger, he'd broken into somebody's house with another guy. They got caught somehow, but because of their age, nothing really happened. So he doesn't have a record."

Jake nodded. "Yes, they seal and eventually destroy the records for young offenders. It's almost as if it didn't happen."

Mikey continued, "He never mentioned who the other guy was or anything. And he never said what house they broke into. But he said that experience really straightened him out. I believe it too. He sure seemed like a pretty good guy."

Mikey quickly packed a few more containers of food.

Jake waited. "Anything else?"

"That's about all I can tell you."

"Anybody else here who might know Chad?"

Mikey scanned the factory. "Naw, I don't think so. Like I said, he wasn't here long and he only worked this line," he said. "Geez, I sure hope you catch the guy who killed him."

"We're working on it." Jake smiled, offering his hand. "Thanks very much. You've been helpful."

Mikey slipped off one glove and shook Jake's hand. "You're welcome," he said, and turned back to work, hurrying to catch up with the never-ending stream flowing toward him.

CHAPTER 24

Saturday, August 13th, 10:00 a.m.

JEREMY WAS PLEASED there was no work that day. He never worked on Saturdays. He hated his job so much and he hated his stupid boss. Saturday was a day to do whatever he wanted, with nobody to tell him to do this, do that.

He'd had plans to work in his vegetable garden for a while. The weeds never stopped growing, and he knew if he wanted good, healthy things to grow, he would have to pull the weeds before they choked the plants and ruined all his hard work.

Today he'd slept in and was having a late breakfast. Eggs, fried potatoes, and tomato juice.

He flipped the eggs from the sizzling frying pan onto the waiting plate of potatoes, then grabbed his glass of tomato juice and a fork and carried them carefully into the living room. He set them on the coffee table and pulled the table closer.

He grabbed the remote and flicked on the television. He wanted to catch up on any news. He liked to keep up.

Channel 7 Action News was on. He listened intently as he leaned forward to enjoy his breakfast.

It was mostly boring stuff on the news. City Hall was planning a new park but the councilors couldn't agree on where. The population of cats was on the rise, and stray dogs were being rounded up and euthanized.

Jeremy liked the word "euthanized." It sounded like a happy word. It didn't sound at all like they were just killing the dogs.

Euthanized, euthanized, euthanized. It rolled off his tongue.

He laughed and continued with his meal, eating it slowly, with great satisfaction.

A story caught his attention and he looked up. Lisa Krunk was standing in front of a large building.

> *"I'm standing in front of the Richmond Hill Court building, where thirty-three-year-old Randolph Farley has just been arraigned on charges of grand larceny.*
>
> *"Police raided Farley's apartment and seized tens of thousands of dollars' worth of jewelry and electronic equipment.*
>
> *"Farley had originally been arrested when he was caught stealing jewelry from Cranston's, after video proof supplied by the retail giant had led to the raid."*

The camera panned to show a shot of two men coming down the courthouse steps. One looked greasy, slimy. Maybe a lawyer. Lisa continued.

> *"I've just been informed Farley has been released on two hundred thousand dollars' bail."*

The shot zoomed in on one of the faces, a microphone pushed at him. That must be Farley.

"Mr. Farley, do you have any comment?"

Farley scowled as his lawyer hustled him away. The cameraman followed them until they stepped into a waiting car. The vehicle drove away and the camera panned back to Lisa.

"We will bring you breaking news as it happens. In an exclusive report, I'm Lisa Krunk for Channel 7 Action News."

Jeremy had watched the newscast with great interest. He dropped his fork and sat back, frowning.

Reaching over to a small table beside him, he retrieved a pencil and scratched something down on a scrap of paper, ripped from a gardening magazine. He folded the paper carefully, thoughtfully, shoved it into his shirt pocket, and went back to his meal.

Saturday, August 13th, 10:30 a.m.

ANNIE DROPPED a bag of kitchen garbage into a bin on the back deck. She turned her head and wrinkled her nose at the smell greeting her, then quickly closed the lid.

As she stepped back through the door into the kitchen, her cell phone, resting in the wicker basket, buzzed.

It was her mother. "Hello, Mom," Annie said.

"Hello, darling. I wanted to see how things are there. Andy has gone off somewhere this morning. A special delivery he had to make or something."

"We're great here, Mom. I'm just cleaning up. Jake and Matty are in the garage doing whatever it is they do out there."

Alma Roderick cleared her throat. "You know that little

matter we talked about. I have a check here for you. I can drop it over this morning if you'd like."

"Mother, I certainly never agreed to accept any money from you. I told you, we don't need it. We're doing fine."

"Yes, but you know Matty deserves better."

"Matty is doing great where he is," Annie said with a sigh. "Please, Mom. Really, we're fine."

"I want my grandson to get the best education possible."

"He may be your grandson, but he's my son," Annie said, adding, "Jake's and mine."

"Listen to me, Annie. Your father and I have more money than we need. It's only fair we use some of it to send Matty to Richmond Academy. I insist."

"Mother, why can't you accept that we don't want, or need, your money? Jake is offended, and frankly I am too."

Alma laughed. "Don't be silly, dear. There's nothing to be offended about."

"Jake feels you look at him as not being a good provider." Annie raised her voice and added, "Let me tell you something, Mother. Jake is the best father Matty could ever hope for. And the best husband."

"Calm down, dear. I'm not threatening his manhood."

"Oh, but you are. Every time you think you know better than him, you're threatening him."

Alma laughed again, adding sharply, "I'm only trying to help. Your father agrees with me."

Annie suspected her father didn't know anything about this. Her mother was always trying to butt in to their affairs. "Mother, I have things to do. I have to go."

"Just keep it in mind, dear. Maybe talk to Jake about it."

"I don't need to talk to Jake. Goodbye, Mother."

She regretted she'd never been close to her mother. They seemed to clash over almost everything. It had been that way as long as she could remember. She loved her mother dearly, but the line between them was always there.

Her father, however, was much different. All of her happy childhood memories seemed to revolve around him. He would read her to sleep almost every night. She could vividly remember his voice as he mimicked the talking animals in her books. He could make her laugh and they giggled together and had a lot of fun.

She remembered when he would toss her high in the air, her head brushing the ceiling, and then catch her safely on the way down. She'd had no doubt he would catch her, and she always felt safe with him.

Annie stabbed a finger at the phone, hanging up. She tossed it back into the basket and shook her head in exasperation.

CHAPTER 25

Saturday, August 13th, 11:00 a.m.

LISA KRUNK unclicked her seatbelt and climbed from the passenger seat of the van. She looked at the sprawling mansion in front of her and hurried determinedly toward its double front doors.

She glanced back over her shoulder. Her cameraman, who'd been driving the vehicle, had just removed his equipment from the side door and was resting the camera on his shoulder. She frowned at him and waved for him to hurry up.

"Let's go, Don. Come on," she said impatiently.

He hurried to follow her. He knew better than to keep her waiting.

Lisa stopped for a minute and looked at the house in front of her. This was big news. An affluent family in an affluent neighborhood. Her thin lips tightened in resolve. For a moment, she dreamed about her aspirations of being a newspaper journalist and the Pulitzer she felt destined to receive some day. This job and this story was a stepping stone in the right direction. The biggest news this crappy little town had seen in a long, long time.

She raised her head. Her thin, sharp nose sniffed, and she strode on.

Don was close behind her as she reached the final step leading to the entrance of the house. She approached the door and clanked the knocker once, twice, three times, checked her microphone, and waited.

The door swung open. A young Asian girl poked her head out. "May I help you?"

"I would like to see Amelia James," Lisa demanded.

"May I ask who's calling, please?"

Lisa frowned. "It's Lisa Krunk, from Channel 7. I would like to ask her a few questions."

"Please wait here. I'll see if she's available."

Lisa waited, tapping her foot impatiently. It seemed to be taking forever. Who did these people think they were?

The door opened again. "I'm sorry, but Mrs. James says she has no comment at this time."

The door began to close.

Lisa stuck her foot in the doorway. "Just a couple of questions, please," she said. "It'll only take a minute." Her voice was a little kinder now.

"I'm sorry. She said no."

Lisa stared furiously and removed her foot, allowing the door to snap shut. She stood there a moment feeling indignant, determined.

She wheeled around and spoke to Don. "Come on. This way," she said, racing down the steps and across the lawn to the corner of the house. Don shook his head but obediently followed.

Lisa peered through a crack in a wooden gate at the edge of the house, separating the front from the back. A flagstone path led toward the backyard and the rear of the house.

She tested the gate. It was unlatched. After glancing back to make sure her cameraman was behind her, she pushed the gate open. It swung inward and tapped lightly as it came to rest against the wall.

She walked boldly toward the rear of the dwelling. Don followed.

Without breaking stride, she rounded the back corner of the house, continuing along the walkway that swung around and then widened, running across the back of the building.

Her wide mouth tightened into a triumphant smile when she saw her prey a dozen yards ahead. Mrs. James was bent over the flower bed, snipping some flowers.

Lisa strode ahead, her microphone in front, ready. Don moved slightly to the left, his camera beginning to whir.

Mrs. James looked up quickly. Her mouth flew open and she rose to her feet, her hands on her hips, a frown on her face.

Lisa was undaunted. "Mrs. James," she said as she took the last step and stopped, pushing the microphone at the woman, "I would like to ask you a couple of questions, if I may?"

"I already told you I had no comment."

"Please, Mrs. James, your daughter is missing and our viewers are greatly concerned. We want to help," Lisa lied.

Amelia hesitated. She dropped her hands and folded them in front of her, and then raised her head and took a deep breath as the frown disappeared.

"Perhaps a couple of questions would be okay," she said reluctantly.

Lisa smiled.

The camera whirred.

Amelia waited.

Lisa reached inside herself, looking for some kind words to say. It was difficult, but she knew she could fake it as well as anybody.

"Mrs. James," she said. "We all sympathize with you at this difficult time. You can be sure the thoughts and prayers of our concerned viewers are with you and Jenny right now."

"Thank you," Amelia said quietly.

"Your daughter has been missing for ten days. Do you have anything you'd like to say to her abductor if he's watching?"

Amelia looked down a moment and then lifted her head and said, "My daughter, Jenny, is the sweetest person I know. Please, allow her to go. She's never hurt anyone. I need her, and so do her friends."

Lisa loved this. Heart-wrenching stuff was always good. She kept the microphone pointed and waited for more.

Amelia continued, "If for some reason you can't let her go right now, then please, let me or the police know she's all right." She was crying lightly now. A tear reached her chin.

Lisa looked at the tear. Good stuff. Great television.

The camera whirred. Don was zooming in.

Amelia hesitated, so Lisa spoke. "As you know, the man she was last seen with has been found dead. Are you afraid the same fate has befallen Jenny?" She hoped that wasn't too cold.

It was.

Amelia dropped her head a moment, then looked up and said fiercely, "My daughter is alive." She paused and then continued in a calmer tone, "She called two days ago to say she's all right, and then she got cut off."

Lisa didn't know that tidbit of information and was caught off guard a moment. "Did she say where she was?"

"No, she didn't seem to know."

"Mrs. James, did you know Chad Bronson?"

"No, I've never met him."

"Yet your daughter seemed to know him well?"

Amelia folded her arms. "She met him through a mutual friend," she said indignantly. "She didn't know him that long, and I don't go around keeping tabs on everyone she meets."

"Of course not, Mrs. James. I only meant—"

"Please don't insinuate my daughter hides things from me," Amelia said sternly. "She certainly does not."

"I'm sure she doesn't, Mrs. James," Lisa said reluctantly. "I also understand Lincoln Investigations has been retained to aid in the search for Jenny."

Amelia hesitated. "Yes, they have."

"Do you feel the police are not doing all they can do, or should be doing?"

"The police are doing everything possible. They've been very good and very supportive."

"What, then, is the role of the Lincolns?"

Amelia seemed bewildered by the question. "Just a little extra help. That never hurts," she said. "I'm sure you're aware, Annie Lincoln is the one who found Bronson?"

"Yes, I'm aware of that, but—"

Amelia interrupted, "Please, I have things to do now. The interview is over."

"Just one more question, Mrs. James. Do the police have any suspects?"

"Not that I'm aware of. Now, I must go."

"Thank you, Mrs. James."

Amelia turned and walked toward the house.

"Mrs. James," Lisa called.

Amelia didn't respond. She walked up the steps to the back deck and went inside the house, out of sight.

Don pointed the camera at Lisa.

"We will bring you breaking news as it happens. In an exclusive report, I'm Lisa Krunk for Channel 7 Action News."

Don shut the camera off and lowered it.

Lisa sighed, "It was worth the trip, anyway."

Don nodded and followed Lisa back across the lawn, heading for the news van.

CHAPTER 26

Saturday, August 13th, 1:00 p.m.

JAKE BACKED the Firebird from the driveway. The tires left a little rubber behind as he hit first gear and touched the gas. The car jumped ahead and he sped down Carver Street. He hit his blinker and took a quick left, and then another turn onto Main Street.

There was little traffic on the road; it was never busy on Saturday. The lights seemed to be against him, turning red at the wrong time, as if some technician sat in his little cubicle, flicking switches just to annoy him.

It was blazing hot out even with the windows open, and the sun was directly overhead. It glanced off the hood of his machine, throwing a bright glare that threatened to blind him.

He squinted through dark glasses, checked his mirror, and pulled into the right lane. He had to wait behind a bus while passengers got on and off, like snails, before he could move ahead and make a sharp turn into the parking lot in front of Mortino's.

The store was busy and the parking lot was full. He zipped

up and down the aisles looking for a slot and finally opted to sit and wait until somebody moved.

He watched a young couple stroll from the store. They lazily pushed their cart ahead of them, chatting and laughing, and finally made it to their vehicle near him. Jake waited mostly patiently while the pair took their time unloading their purchases and returned the cart to the snake at the front of the store.

Finally, the spot was available and Jake eased in, careful to keep a safe distance from the other vehicles. He felt a little uneasy about leaving his car where a careless driver could open their door and mar the beautiful paint job, but there wasn't much choice.

He stepped from the vehicle, strode to the front doors of the store, and went inside. A flood of shoppers made their way haphazardly back and forth, up and down the aisles, picking out their needs and wants for the week ahead.

He dodged an old lady pushing a walker, the basket on the front stuffed with groceries, as he wormed his way toward the back of the store.

Jake knew the manager at Mortino's. He didn't like him very much, but he was the one to talk to.

The door to MacKay's office was ajar and Jake poked his head in. The room was empty.

He wandered up and down the aisles and finally happened on MacKay, reaming out a cringing stock boy. Jake waited patiently until the lecture was over and the boy slunk meekly away, then approached MacKay.

Jake offered his hand. "Good afternoon, Mr. MacKay."

"Afternoon, Mr. Lincoln." MacKay stared at him through thick glasses as he shook his hand.

"Do you have a few minutes? I'd like to talk to you about an important matter."

MacKay glanced around as if looking for another victim to reprimand, then looked at his watch and said, "I can spare a few minutes. Let's go to my office."

Jake followed him. He noticed MacKay had a strange gait. He was bow-legged, with a slight limp, favoring his right leg as he walked. He wore a butcher's hat, covering most of his prematurely bald head.

Reaching the door of the office, MacKay pushed it open and motioned for Jake to step inside. MacKay followed behind and sat at a small desk.

"Have a seat," MacKay said, waving toward a fold-up chair on the other side of the desk. "What can I do for you, Mr. Lincoln?"

Jake sat, carefully testing his weight on the tiny chair before finally trusting it would hold him. He leaned back and looked at the grocer.

"Mr. MacKay, I don't know if you're aware, but a woman was murdered in her apartment yesterday afternoon, shortly after coming from this store."

MacKay raised his eyebrows.

Jake continued, "I want to cover every possibility when it comes to who may have killed her and how it might've happened."

"Of course. Of course," MacKay agreed. "How can I help?"

"It's possible she may have been followed, and I was hoping you might have some security camera footage that could shed some light on it."

MacKay swept off his cap and tossed it on the desk. He rubbed the back of his shiny head and said, "We have a few in-store cameras. There's one covering the cash area and two at the back of the store. Nothing outside, though."

"Is everything recorded?"

"Yes, it's all on tape, and the tapes are on a one-week rotation."

"That's perfect. May I take them with me? It might take some time to go over them, and needless to say, it's important."

MacKay studied Jake a moment before sweeping up the phone. He spoke into the receiver, "Bob, I need the camera footage from yesterday." He covered the receiver and looked at Jake. "What time?"

Jake thought a moment before answering. "Everything from noon yesterday until three o'clock or so."

MacKay spoke to Bob. "Noon till three. Yesterday." Silence, and then, "Okay, great. Drop them into my office right away." He hung up and said to Jake, "It'll just take a few minutes. Bob'll bring them right over."

"Excellent. Thank you, Mr. MacKay."

The man sat back and crossed his arms. "Mr. Lincoln, how do you know the woman was here?"

"We found her shopping inside her handbag. The receipt was from Mortino's."

"I see. I see." MacKay rubbed his chin.

"The information hasn't been released to the public, so please keep it quiet for now, but inside her handbag we also found a pork chop with a Mortino's label on it. It wasn't on the receipt."

MacKay frowned. "She stole it?"

"It appears so."

MacKay shook his head and said, "We have a lot of stuff go missing. You'd be surprised what people will steal."

"I'm sure it's a headache at times," Jake said.

"Yes, it is," MacKay agreed with a sigh. "But I guess it's a fact of life."

There was a tap at the office door and it swung open. Bob

appeared with a grocery bag in his hand. "Here's the tapes, Mr. MacKay."

"Thanks, Bob." MacKay reached forward and took the bag, handing it to Jake.

Jake stood. "I'll get these back to you ASAP."

MacKay stood and waved it off. "No need to worry about returning them. We have plenty."

They shook hands and Jake thanked him again as he left.

CHAPTER 27

Saturday, August 13th, 3:40 p.m.

JEREMY'S LATE LUNCH dishes were washed, Jenny was fed, and the house was sparkling clean, just the way Mother would do it.

But right now he needed some rest to prepare himself for the task ahead. He slumped down into his favorite chair and closed his eyes.

He thought back about his first time. Joey was his first. Certainly the bully had deserved what he'd gotten. With Joey, it was intensely personal. There was no more bullying after that. The other boys had left him alone after Joey disappeared.

Disappeared. Hah. Not quite. He chuckled. He knew where Joey was. Right where he belonged.

But he was thankful. Thankful the experience with Joey in the woods that day had encouraged him. Raised him to new levels, you might say.

And then there was that Bronson character. He wondered why it had taken him so long after Joey. The rush he'd felt when he'd tasted Bronson's life on his tongue had been absolutely inspiring.

And then that old hag he'd seen at Mortino's. The filthy pig. But still, the taste of her life in his mouth had been absolutely spectacular.

He looked forward to the afternoon. It would be exactly what he needed—a refill. He shuddered once and waited until the feeling that thoroughly filled him subsided, then opened his eyes.

He climbed from the chair and walked purposefully into the kitchen. In the bottom drawer, packed safely under a stack of daisy-fresh towels, lay Father's old .22 revolver. It would hold six bullets in the cylinder. He should take it just in case. He reached into the drawer and removed it gently, then, pushing open a box of ammunition, he selected one and slipped it into the last empty slot. He spun the cylinder and tested the grip. It felt good. The revolver had a holster but Jeremy ignored it. He liked the feel of the metal next to his skin. He shoved it into his waistband, securely behind his belt, and pulled his shirt over top.

He removed his Bowie knife and leg strap from the drawer, handling it lovingly before belting the strap into place. He slipped the knife inside the sheath and covered it with his pant leg.

Everything else had been previously taken care of. He already had the guy's name, so it wasn't hard to find the address he needed. That's what phone books were for. He checked his pocket to make sure he still had the slip of paper, and then grabbed his ring of keys off the hook by the door and went outside, carefully locking up behind him.

His car came to life immediately as he turned the key. He dropped the shifter into drive and spun around on the loose gravel, heading for Richmond Hill.

Saturday, August 13th, 4:00 p.m.

RANDOLPH FARLEY sat in an aging leather chair in his apartment and looked around at the mess. The cops certainly hadn't been too careful during the search. They'd really trashed the place and hauled out almost everything that wasn't nailed down.

He cursed his luck. He knew they had him. The video was proof enough, and then the raid on his apartment had clinched it. He wished now he had gotten rid of everything.

Dumb. Dumb. Dumb.

He had hoped his lawyer could explain it away somehow but the stupid jerk hadn't even tried.

He was glad he'd had enough money stashed away in his bank accounts to cover the bail, but now his lawyer urged him to take a plea bargain in turn for a full confession. That would involve turning in the guys he sold the stuff to.

The mouthpiece said he could likely get off with a misdemeanor, or maybe even full immunity, since the fences he dealt with were big time and would lead to arresting many more fish, better than just him and his petty little crimes.

That might be the way to go, but ratting out Estefano and the other clowns might get his throat slit. Even now, he might be in danger because he knew too much.

Maybe he should call Estefano before Estefano called him.

He still had his cell phone, so he dug it from his pocket and hit speed dial eight.

"Yeah?"

Farley took a deep breath. "Is Estefano around?"

"Who's asking?"

"It's Farley. Tell him it's important."

The phone went quiet. Something banged and hummed in the background. He waited.

"Farley, you got anything for me?" It was a high-pitched voice.

"Hey, Estefano," he greeted him. "Nope, I don't have nothing for you right now. Just wanna let you know something."

Estefano waited.

"They busted me. Got caught heisting a ring. But don't worry, I didn't say nothin'."

Estefano whistled. "Busted?"

"Yup."

"Listen, Farley, you did right by not talking. It really wouldn't go so good if you said anything you shouldn't."

Farley shuddered at the thought of one of Estefano's boys coming after him. "Like I said, I didn't say nothin'. I know better."

"I'm a little concerned, Farley."

"Don't be, Estefano. No reason to be concerned."

"You remember Tommy Nascap, don't you?"

"Yes?"

"Yeah, I really liked him," Estefano squeaked. "Too bad about him."

Farley remained quiet. His hand started to tremble.

Estefano continued, "Okay, you take good care of yourself."

"I will, Estefano," Farley said, then heard a click.

He sat there for a minute. He remembered Tommy Nascap well. He would never forget him. He sure didn't want to end up like Tommy. Found under a bridge with his throat slit ear to ear. He shuddered again at the thought.

He sat back and closed his eyes, trying to relax. In few minutes, he felt a little better.

He grabbed his grimy baseball cap and slapped it on his head. At least the cops hadn't taken that. It was a wonder.

He felt hungry and decided to head on out to Phil's to grab a bite.

He climbed from his chair and headed for the door.

Saturday, August 13th, 4:35 p.m.

THE SOUTH END of Richmond Hill was considered an outer suburb of the city. Jeremy stood on the sidewalk there, on Benson Street, and looked across at a pair of structures, each with three floors. There were probably about six apartments on each floor. The building to the left was the one that drew his attention.

Pedestrians hurried up and down the sidewalk around him, not paying him any mind. He had his baseball cap pulled low over his face, just in case.

After carefully looking both ways, he crossed the street and entered the lobby of 366. He scanned the directory on the wall. Farley was listed as apartment 102. He leaned back against the wall and waited.

He didn't have to wait long. In a couple of minutes, a pair of annoying teenage girls came through the outer door, not looking at him as they yakked on about some girl who tried to mess with their BF.

Jeremy rolled his eyes and waited patiently. One girl reached into the pocket of her overly tight jeans, removed a key, and unlocked the door leading into the building. As the girls passed through the door, he stuck his foot out and stopped it from closing.

He watched until the girls disappeared into the elevator, then swung the door open and walked through.

An arrow indicated that the stairs were to the left. He had best take the stairs. He pushed open the stairwell door and went through. He stopped a moment and adjusted the weapon stuffed into the front of his pants, then climbed the steps to the first floor.

He pushed open the stairwell door and peeked into the hallway. All clear.

He walked boldly down the hall, checking the numbers on the doors, stopping at 102.

He slipped the gun from his pants, holding it firmly in his right hand, and rapped on the door with the other.

There was no answer.

He rapped again.

No answer.

Jeremy frowned. It seemed like Farley might not be home.

He looked up and down the hall, and then pulled his wallet from his back pocket and slid out his Mortino's Club Card. He stuck it in the crack of the door beside the lock and fiddled with it.

Click.

The latch moved back, and he swung the door open slowly and called, "Hello?"

No one answered.

He moved into the room and eased the door closed behind him.

His gun was ready. He called again, "Anybody home?"

Nobody was.

He poked around the apartment, checking out the kitchen and the single bedroom. A heap of clothes were piled on a chair. He smiled grimly at the sight of a t-shirt that read "Up Yours."

Farley had been here. That was the shirt he'd been wearing on the news.

He strolled back out to the living room and took a seat in the worn-out leather chair. From there, he could see the door.

He waited.

CHAPTER 28

Saturday, August 13th, 4:45 p.m.

RANDOLPH FARLEY had a full belly. Not too full, just comfortable. He pushed back his plate, sat back in the booth, and belched. A woman at a nearby table frowned at him, and he smiled back.

He ogled the pretty young waitress in the short skirt. His gaze moved up and down, taking in the sight. She sure was cute. She looked his way and he waved her over.

"Hey, baby," he said as she approached his table. "Can I get the check?"

She gave him a sexy smile and looked at him from the corner of her eye, then reached into the pocket of her skirt and removed a pad. She leafed through it, scribbled something, ripped a page free, and laid it on the table in front of him. She slipped him another teasing smile over her shoulder as she turned and walked away.

Farley watched her walk a moment and then tossed a couple of dollars on the table, grabbed the check, and headed for the cashier.

He paid for his meal and walked out to the street.

He was in a good mood now. He didn't know why, exactly. He was facing some possible jail time, but he hummed to himself as he strolled up the sidewalk.

Reaching his building, he unlocked the inner door and took the stairs to his apartment two at a time.

Slipping his key into the lock, he turned it. It clicked and snapped. He twisted the knob and pushed open the door, stepped in, and kicked it shut with his foot.

He stopped short and raised his hands halfway up, staring at the guy sitting in his chair. The guy was pointing a gun at him.

"Come in," the guy said.

"What … what do you want?" he asked, his voice wavering.

The guy pointed to the couch on the other wall. "Take a seat," he said.

Farley sat and leaned forward. "Did Estefano send you?"

"Who's Estefano?"

Farley popped his hat up and scratched his head. He straightened it again and looked at the guy with the gun. Estefano must've sent him.

Farley's hand shook, and now his voice was shaking too. "I told Estefano I wouldn't say anything. He knows I won't."

The guy stared at him a moment and then stood and came a little closer, holding the gun firmly in his hand. He was a short little guy and didn't look mean at all, but the gun pointed Farley's way frightened him.

"You're not going to shoot … shoot me, are you?" Farley asked.

Farley watched the guy move the gun to his left hand and then reach down, pull up his pant leg, and slip a knife from a sheath fastened to his ankle.

"No, I'm not going to shoot you," the little guy said.

"Then … then what do you want?" He was really trembling now.

The knife sliced through the air. Farley was thrown back as the weapon slashed his face, leaving a deep cut across his cheek and through his left ear. Blood gushed from the wound. He brought his hand up in a useless attempt to stop the bleeding.

The knife was still now, but the razor-sharp tip hung menacingly a few inches from Farley's face. He didn't move. The blood flowed.

"You think you're so smart, don't you?" the guy asked.

Farley didn't know what to say. He just shook his head.

The little guy gritted his teeth. "Things have a way of catching up with you, you know."

Farley stared. "Call Estefano," he pleaded. "Estefano will straighten this out. Please."

"I told you, I don't know any Estefano."

Farley stared, wide-eyed. He watched as the little man leveled the gun and pointed it at his nose. He watched his finger tighten on the trigger. He sat frozen as the gun exploded. He felt his head shoot forward and was vaguely aware of a spray of red in the air.

The last thing he remembered was hearing the echo of the shot and then flopping over sideways, his head finally resting gently on a fluffy white pillow perched at the end of the couch.

Saturday, August 13th, 4:46 p.m.

JEREMY CROUCHED down and cocked his head, his eyes fixed intently on the ruined face of Randolph Farley.

Blood still dripped from the gash across Farley's face, now

mingling with the flow from the neat hole just above his nose. His eyes were wide but unseeing, glazed over like breath on a mirror.

Crimson saturated the pillow beneath his head. It dripped silently onto the cushion of the couch, making its way down to the tiled floor.

Jeremy reached out and touched the gentle flow of red coming from Farley's cheek.

He drew his finger back and looked at the moist spot, not unlike the color of a deep red wine. He closed his eyes and breathed deeply, then brought his finger to his tongue, savoring the taste of Farley's life.

Jeremy held his breath and shuddered violently for a few moments, and then breathed out heavily and opened his eyes.

He stood to his feet and smiled, then suddenly turned and walked quickly to the door. As he left, he used his shirt to wipe any fingerprints from the knobs on both sides of the door.

The hallway was empty. His footsteps echoed off the wall and tiled floor as he ran. He eased open the door to the stairwell and heard footsteps. Someone was coming up the stairs.

He ducked back and ran to the elevator. It was on the first floor, and when he stabbed the button, it immediately began to rise.

The elevator door slid back and he rushed inside as the stairwell door opened. The elevator door slid shut, and his stomach dropped as it descended.

He watched the door glide open and he peeked out into the lobby. No one was around. His stubby legs carried him hurriedly to the exit door, then outside and down the walkway to the street. He mingled with the pedestrians and hurried home, a tight smile on his face.

CHAPTER 29

Saturday, August 13th, 5:05 p.m.

JAKE SEARCHED for his old VCR, packed away in a box somewhere in the storage area underneath the basement stairwell. He finally found it, lugged it upstairs, and set it on a chair next to the television.

It took him awhile to find the right cables, but he finally succeeded in getting it set up and in working order. The remote was missing, however.

He was surprised a place like Mortino's would still be using such a near defunct method of recording, and was glad he'd kept the old machine packed away.

He dug the tapes from the bag. There were three of them, marked "Rear East," "Rear West," and "Cash." The tapes could record six hours each if you ran the recorder at slow speed.

He sat on the floor by the VCR, slipped the "Rear East" tape into the machine, and gave it a push. It whirred and hummed, and then sucked the cartridge in and clunked once. He touched the play button.

The back of the store appeared on the television. He could see from one side of the store, across to the other. The view was clear near the camera but became hazy as it stretched toward the other side of the store. There was a timestamp on the bottom corner of the screen. It read "8/12 12:03." August 12th.

He wanted a view of the packaged meat counter. That seemed to be on the other side of the store, at the back. He popped the tape out and tried the "Rear West." The timestamp said "8/12 12:02."

The time of Mrs. Bellows' death was approximately 1:00 p.m.

, so that might be cutting it close. He yawned, sat back, and watched.

Shoppers were going back and forth, doing what shoppers do. A stock boy was up a ladder, piling up packages of something. Jake leaned forward a couple of times when he saw someone with a cane. False alarm.

Finally, at timestamp 12:34, his interest was drawn to an old woman walking slowly into view. The picture wasn't clear, but he could tell she carried a handbag in one hand, a cane in the other.

He leaned in. That must be Mrs. Bellows.

She stood at the fresh meat selection a moment and then walked away. A second later, she turned back and approached the meat again. He couldn't tell for sure, but it seemed likely this was the point where she must have taken the pork chop. He made a mental note of the area where she was standing—second case down, near the center. He could make a physical check of the store later, if necessary, to see whether that was the pork section.

He watched her move on and pass from the camera's view.

Jake hit the eject button and fed in the tape labeled

"Cash." He fast-forwarded it until he saw 12:30 on the screen, then let it play at regular speed. There were a dozen checkouts, but the camera was nearest the pair of "8 items or less" counters. Shoppers came in and out, cashiers were busy, and some of the counters had boys bagging purchases for the customers. He saw the short little man who had been on the ladder, wearing a Mortino's cap, whom he recognized as Jeremy Spencer. The man walked past the camera's view toward the front of the store.

At timestamp 12:36, he saw her come into view again. She went straight for the second counter, a couple of items tucked in her arms. Jake could see her face clearly now—it was definitely Mrs. Bellows.

He watched her pay, and the articles were bagged. She dropped her purchase into her handbag and left the store.

No one seemed to be following Mrs. Bellows or taking any interest in her.

He watched everything over again, looking intently for anything that appeared suspicious, and then finally sat back and shut off the machine.

All he'd proved was that Mrs. Bellows had been there, paid, and left again.

Saturday, August 13th, 5:30 p.m.

HANK WAS AT HOME catching up on some much-needed R&R when he received a call about an incident on Benson Street. He sighed and climbed from his easy chair, picked up his keys from the counter, made sure he had his badge and gun, and made his way out and down the stairs to his Chevy.

Traffic was light and he arrived at the south end of Richmond Hill in a few minutes. As he swung onto Benson Street, he saw several cruisers parked in the lot of a squat three-floor apartment building. Number 366. He pulled up beside them and climbed from his vehicle.

The building was taped off and there was a uniformed officer at the front door. He recognized Officer Spiegle.

Spiegle spoke as Hank approached. "Hey, Hank, looks like we got another one."

"Hi, Yappy. It appears so."

Spiegle opened the door and Hank entered the lobby, making his way up the stairs. The hall was taped off, entrance to and from the first floor tightly controlled. A cop leaned against the wall, inside the hallway, and he lifted the tape. Hank ducked under, went down the hall to apartment 102, and looked inside the open door.

Crime scene investigators were there, making notes, fingerprinting, packaging evidence, frowning, studying, and talking. Photos were being snapped. The medical examiner was leaning over the body, her assistant holding a clipboard and sucking on a pen.

Hank stepped carefully into the room, steering clear of evidence cones as he approached the ME.

Nancy Pietek glanced at him and smiled grimly. "I didn't expect to see you again so soon, Hank."

"Hi, Nancy," he said. "It's always nice to see you. Could be under better circumstances, though."

She stood and sighed, pulling off her surgical gloves.

Hank peered at the body and then turned to her and asked, "Any idea of the cause of death?"

She pointed. "If you look here you can see a bullet hole right above his nose. There's a huge slash on his left cheek, but at this point, it appears the cause of death is the gunshot wound. There's no exit wound, so it seems to have been a low powered weapon. Maybe a twenty-two caliber. I can't tell yet."

Hank whistled.

She continued, "Look at the soot around the entrance wound. It suggests the weapon was fired at close range.

Maybe two inches or so. The slightly downward angle of the shot suggests the shooter was standing, and the victim was sitting down when shot. There also would've been a blowback spatter of blood. The shooter, as well as the weapon, would undoubtedly have gotten sprayed."

"And the cut on his cheek?"

"It's fairly deep, but not enough to cause death. The weapon appears to have been a sharp knife with a serrated edge."

Hank stroked his chin. "Another serrated blade."

"I'll know for sure later, Hank."

"Time of death?"

"The neighbor heard a shot and called 9-1-1 at four fifty-one. Just over half an hour ago. I'm guessing that to be accurate."

Hank looked around the room. The lead crime scene investigator, Rod Jameson, was directing operations. Hank approached him.

"Rod, do you have any ID on the victim?"

Rod consulted his clipboard. "Sure do, Hank. His name is Randolph Farley, according to his driver's license. This is his place."

Hank wrote the name in his pad. "What about the neighbor who called it in?"

Rod pointed vaguely. "The guy from 104." He looked at the clipboard again. "His name is Peter Lastman."

"I'll go talk to him. Thanks, Rod."

Rod just grunted.

Hank stepped out into the hallway. Apartment 104 was next door. He tapped, and the door was answered immediately by a fortyish woman. He introduced himself and she looked at his badge as he displayed it.

"Come in," she said. "You want to see my husband. Just a minute." She turned and screeched, "Peter."

Hank followed her in, took a seat in the dining area, and set his pad on the table. In a few moments, Peter approached him. He was a middle-aged man, maybe forty-five or so, and rounded at the waist.

Hank stood and held out his hand. "I'm Detective Hank Corning."

Peter shook it. "I'm Peter Lastman," he said. "Have a seat."

They sat and faced each other across the table.

Hank said, "I understand you called 9-1-1. Can you tell me exactly what you heard, and anything else you might add?"

Peter cleared his throat. "I was sitting here having a cup of tea and reading the paper, then all of a sudden I heard a shot."

"Just one shot?"

"That's all I heard. The wife was in the bedroom and didn't hear anything."

Hank scribbled in his pad and waited.

Peter pointed to the wall separating 104 from 102. "It sounded like it came from next door, so I called 9-1-1. When I told the wife about it, she freaked out pretty good for a while. She calmed down a lot after the police came." He glanced toward the bedroom. "She seems okay now."

"Did you hear anything else? Any shouting or talking?"

"No."

"Anything from the hall?"

"No. Just the shot. That's it. But I gotta tell you, it was pretty scary. We didn't know if maybe a bullet would come right through that wall there, so we just stayed back as best we could and waited for you folks to come." He paused. "What happened over there, anyway?"

"Sorry to have to inform you, but there's been a murder."

Lastman's mouth dropped open. "A murder?"

Hank nodded. "Yes, but everything's under control now. There's no need to worry."

"You caught the guy?"

"Not yet, but we will." Hank paused. "Did you know your neighbor? Mr. Farley?"

Lastman shook his head. "Nope, never met him. Never seen him."

Hank handed Peter his card. "Give me a call if you think of anything else."

"Sure will, Detective." He stood and followed Hank to the door, letting him out.

Hank made the rounds, interviewing the rest of the residents of the first floor. There were six apartments in total, but no one in the other units had heard or noticed anything.

As he exited the front lobby of the building, he was greeted by a microphone pushed into his face. He recognized the reporter as Lisa Krunk. A cameraman stood a few feet away, aiming the camera at Hank.

"Detective," Lisa said, "what can you tell me about the incident here?"

"I have no comment at this time."

"Sources tell me a man named Randolph Farley was shot and killed this afternoon. Can you confirm that?"

Hank frowned. Lisa Krunk always seemed to have her sources. "Sorry, no comment at this time. We'll be issuing a formal statement later," he said.

She continued to follow him as he made his way to his vehicle. The camera still hummed as he pulled from the lot and drove away.

CHAPTER 30

Saturday, August 13th, 6:00 p.m.

JEREMY ENJOYED his little talks with Jenny. He'd forgiven her for what she'd done to him, but he still wasn't sure whether he could trust her.

He was busy in the kitchen. He decided to make her a nice peanut-butter-and-tomato sandwich with a dill pickle on the side. That was one of his favorites, and he wanted to share the experience with her. He put together two meals on Mother's best plates and set them on a silver serving tray along with two glasses of cold tomato juice.

He carried the tray carefully as he made his way out the door and across the yard. He balanced the tray on one hand, opened the barn door with the other, and slipped inside.

Jenny was sitting on her makeshift bed with a book in one hand. She looked up as he entered.

"I brought you something to eat," he said.

She looked at him blankly and watched as he walked over to her.

He set the tray on the blanket where she sat and smiled at

her. "I hope you like it. It's my favorite. Peanut butter and tomato."

She looked at the tray and frowned.

He handed her one of the plates. She set the book aside and took the offered meal. She continued to watch him as he took the other plate and sat across from her, balancing it in his lap.

"Enjoy," he said.

She took a tiny bite and curled up her nose. "It tastes funny."

He cocked his head and stared at her. "It'll grow on you." He took a big bite and watched her while he chewed.

"I'm not hungry," she said, setting the sandwich down. "Maybe later." She eyed the pickle. "I'll eat the pickle for now." She picked it up and took a bite.

He swallowed and put his sandwich down. "I hope you had a good day, Jenny," he said cheerfully.

She didn't speak. She took a drink of the tomato juice and looked at him over the rim of the glass.

"Today was a good day for me," he said.

She showed no sign of interest.

He continued, "Today I eliminated another scumbag."

She set the glass down. Her eyes narrowed, but she remained silent.

"Don't you want to hear about it?" he asked.

She shook her head.

"Don't worry, Jenny, he was a bad guy."

He took another bite of his sandwich and watched her. She looked away a moment, then looked down and sat silently.

"He deserved it," Jeremy said.

She remained still.

"He was a thief," he said, then raised his voice. "Why

don't you want to hear about it?"

She looked intently at him and spoke calmly. "Because I don't think you should be the one who decides."

"But they caught him, then let him go. He was going to get away with it." Angry now, Jeremy shouted, "Why can't you understand that?"

She brought her hands to her mouth and cowered silently at his outburst.

He set his plate down and rose to his feet. He paced back and forth a couple of times and then stopped and cupped his hands behind his back, staring down at her thoughtfully.

She leaned back against the barn wall and watched him.

"Jenny, if I let you go, what will you do?"

"I'll just go home. I won't tell them anything about you," she said eagerly. "I'll say I was lost in the forest."

"And what about your boyfriend?" he asked. "They found him, you know."

Jenny looked confused.

"I buried him, but they found him yesterday."

She gasped, her mouth open wide, and then she dropped her head.

"No, I can't let you go," he said, then pointed at her food. "I have to take the plate back now. Are you going to eat that sandwich?"

She shook her head without looking up.

He crouched down and gathered up the dishes, setting them on the tray. He picked up the tray, stood to his feet, and left without another word.

Saturday, August 13th, 8:30 p.m.

JAKE AND ANNIE were sitting on the deck in the backyard, enjoying the evening and a cool drink. Matty was tossing a baseball up onto the roof of the house, catching it as it rolled back down and slammed into his baseball glove.

The sky was beginning to glow red and orange on the horizon as the sun lowered. A light breeze cooled the air, and the neighborhood was quiet and peaceful.

"Hello?" a voice called.

Jake turned his head and looked over his shoulder. Hank was coming across the backyard toward them, carrying his briefcase.

Hank grinned. "I tried the doorbell. No answer, so I thought I'd find you back here."

Jake removed his feet from the lawn chair where they were resting comfortably, kicking the chair back a couple of feet. "Have a seat."

Hank sat, dropped his briefcase beside him, and leaned back. "Have you seen the news today?" he asked.

Jake shook his head.

Annie said, "Not since this morning."

"Another murder," Hank announced with a sigh.

Jake and Annie looked at each other, and then back at Hank.

"This one will interest you guys," Hank said. "Remember that jewelry thief you caught at Cranston's?"

They nodded.

Hank continued, "He's the victim."

Annie's mouth dropped open and she leaned forward.

Jake whistled.

Hank continued, "He was released on bail this morning and then shot to death in his apartment this afternoon, just before five o'clock."

Hank picked up his briefcase and set it on his lap. He snapped it open and removed some papers.

"Here's the kicker," Hank said. "I just got the ME's

report, as well as the ballistics report. It seems like we may have a connection." He leafed through the papers.

Jake spoke. "A connection to what?"

"Maybe to all three murders," Hank said. "Your jewelry thief's name was Randolph Farley. Farley was also cut across the face with a knife before he was shot. According to the medical examiner, the knife used to cut Farley was the same type used on Mrs. Bellows."

"Very interesting," Jake said.

Hank continued, "Here's where it gets even more interesting. Ballistics reports the gun used to shoot Farley was the same gun used to shoot Chad Bronson."

Jake's mouth hung open.

Annie was stunned and could only manage to say, "Wow."

Jake stood and paced the deck, deep in thought.

Finally, Annie spoke slowly. "It appears we might have a serial killer."

Hank rubbed his chin. "It sure does, but the odd thing is, serial killers don't usually mix genders. Two men and a woman. Doesn't make sense."

Jake stopped pacing and asked, "What do these three have in common? It seems unlikely they knew each other. They're all of different ages as well. One is a retired old woman, one is a professional thief, and one is just a young guy."

"That's what we need to figure out," Hank said.

Matty climbed up on the deck swinging his glove. He looked at them and sighed, "I know. Adult talk. I'll just go and watch some TV." He headed for the door.

Jake laughed and tousled Matty's hair as he went by. "We'll be in soon, big guy."

Annie watched Matty stroll inside the house, then turned back to Hank and asked, "Did the investigators find any evidence to link them?"

"Other than the weapons, no. Nothing at this point. No unknown fingerprints at any scene, either."

"And the blanket Chad was buried with?"

"Some foreign fibers found on the blanket, and on Chad's clothing, were from the trunk of a car, but they're too common to tell the make of vehicle."

"What about the footprint Annie photographed?" Jake asked.

Hank dug through his briefcase and retrieved a sheet of paper. "Forensics stated the shoe to be a size seven, but of unknown brand."

"Size seven," Annie repeated thoughtfully, frowning.

Jake sat quickly and leaned forward. He looked back and forth at Hank and Annie. "I know what they have in common," he half shouted.

Hank and Annie waited.

"I didn't tell you, Hank, but last night at midnight, I went to King City Foods and spoke to one of Bronson's coworkers. He couldn't tell me too much, but he did have one interesting tidbit of information. He told me Bronson had been involved in a B&E a couple of years ago, but because he was a young offender, his record was sealed."

"And?" Hank asked.

Annie cocked her head.

Jake continued, "This may be pushing it, but all three of our victims were thieves. Bronson's B&E, Mrs. Bellows and the pork chop, and the jewelry thief."

Hank sat back and frowned. He looked at Annie, then back at Jake. "It's possible."

"It's possible, if it's a serial killer," Annie said.

Hank agreed, "Serial killers are psychopaths. The reasons they use to justify their killing spree are usually something an ordinary person can't understand. But in their mind, it's justified."

"Assuming that's the link, then does that help us determine who the killer is?" Annie asked.

"I'm not a forensic psychologist by any means," Hank said. "But if that's the link, then what we have is a psychopath who has a need to kill thieves. A psychologist would determine that, at one point, some kind of harm was inflicted on him by a thief, and he hates them and feels a compulsion to kill them."

"Is that possible?" Jake asked.

"With a psychopath anything is possible."

Annie looked at Jake. "Did you tell Hank about the tapes?"

Jake grinned. "I've been a busy guy, Hank, and I forgot to tell you. Today I went to Mortino's and was able to get their security tapes."

Hank frowned. "I didn't get a chance to look into that yet. I had plans to go first thing in the morning." He leaned forward. "Anything interesting on the recordings?"

"I'm pretty sure I saw Mrs. Bellows take the pork chop on one tape, and another tape showed her pay and leave the store. I had to dig out the old VCR to watch them."

Hank nodded. "You know, I'm going to have to take those tapes, Jake. They're evidence, so I can't leave them here. I need to get them to the lab and let the technicians take a look as well."

"Of course. I was going to turn them over to you anyway."

"I may be able to get you a copy if you want."

"No, it's okay. I showed the video to Annie as well, and neither one of us could see anything that would shed any light on this."

"If you still have your VCR set up, I'd like to watch them before I turn them over to the lab."

"Sure, come on in. It's still set up."

They went inside to the living room. Matty was watching television and he frowned at them when they came in.

"Sorry, Matty, we have to take the TV from you," Jake said.

"Boy, oh boy."

Annie laughed and said, "Matty, it's bedtime anyway. Why don't you go on up and I'll be there in a few minutes?"

"Sheesh, Mom, there's no school tomorrow."

"I know, you don't have to go to sleep right away. Find something to do for a while." She looked at Jake and raised her brows. "Maybe Dad will read you a story later?"

"Yeah, I can do that," Jake said.

Matty got up slowly. He looked back over his shoulder as he left the room and said, "I'll just be upstairs if you need me." Then he was gone.

Jake chuckled, knelt down by the VCR, and cued up the tape to the point where Mrs. Bellows appeared. He pressed play and they viewed the tape silently.

He switched the tapes to show the "Cash" view and they watched as Mrs. Bellows appeared, paid, and then left the store.

Jake stopped the machine. "That's all," he said. He popped out the tape and put the three of them in the bag.

He handed the bag to Hank who dropped it into his briefcase.

"I assume she was either followed home," Hank said, "or the killer was waiting for her when she got home."

"No surveillance cameras on the building?" Annie asked.

"Nope."

"What about on Farley's building?"

"Nothing there either."

No one spoke for a while. Finally Hank said, "I think I'll

go home and mull this over for a while and see what I can come up with."

They said goodbye and Annie let Hank out the front door.

She closed the door and turned back to Jake. "I feel so bad for Jenny and Amelia," she said. "Another day gone and she's still missing."

Jake agreed, "Let's hope something turns up tomorrow."

CHAPTER 31

Saturday, August 13th, 10:59 p.m.

JEREMY SPENCER settled into his comfortable easy chair in front of the television. He wanted to watch the news before bedtime.

He had a bowl of popcorn tucked in his arms and a glass of tomato juice on the stand beside him.

He propped his feet up on the overstuffed footstool, picked up the remote, and flicked on the TV.

Channel 7 Action News was just coming on, and he saw the familiar face of the news anchor. He munched his popcorn and listened intently.

> *"Today's top story. Richmond Hill was shocked to see its third murder within two weeks. Here's Lisa Krunk with the story."*

The screen flickered and Lisa Krunk could be seen standing on the street, outside of a building Jeremy recognized.

He smiled grimly and listened rapturously as she spoke.

"I'm standing here outside the apartment building at 366 Benson Street, where thirty-three-year-old Randolph Farley was brutally murdered today. Police have cordoned off the area, and so Channel 7 was not able to gain access.

"Police have declined to comment at this time, stating it's an ongoing investigation. However, sources tell me Farley was first stabbed, and then shot to death inside his apartment late this afternoon.

"This makes the third such murder in the last two weeks.

"Yesterday, we were shocked to report the murder of eighty-nine-year-old Edna Bellows, also killed in her apartment after coming home from Mortino's. And as we've been reporting on, eighteen-year-old Chad Bronson was brutally murdered just eleven days ago, his body recovered three days ago.

"I spoke to police regarding the possibility of a serial murderer in the area, but again they declined to comment. They did not, however, deny my assertion.

"We will bring you breaking news as it happens. In an exclusive report, I'm Lisa Krunk for Channel 7 Action News."

Jeremy took a big drink of tomato juice and continued to enjoy his snack.

The rest of the news was boring stuff, but he watched it anyway.

He finally finished his snack, shut off the TV, cleaned up the kitchen, and went to bed.

Sunday, August 14th, 11:45 a.m.

HANK HAD CALLED Amelia and said he wanted to drop by and update her on the case. She was expecting him by noon, so she went into the sitting room to wait.

She stopped in front of the fireplace and looked at a

picture on the mantel. It was Jenny and her father. It had been three days since Jenny had called, and she hadn't heard anything since.

She gazed at the picture for some time, her mind racing back to when Jenny was young and Winston was alive. She'd had it all. A successful husband, a beautiful daughter, and her life was all she had dreamed.

She sighed. How things changed.

She'd met Winston when they were at university. She was a freshman and he was a senior. When he first talked to her, she couldn't have imagined they would end up together. He seemed a little wild and carefree, and she was much more studious and serious. Perhaps that's what had attracted her to him. He was a lot different than anyone she'd known.

They were married just after she graduated and soon Jenny came along. Precious little Jenny.

She touched the picture and sighed again.

She was startled from her thoughts by the sound of the front door knocker. Lilia was off, so she adjusted her skirt and went to answer the door.

It was Hank. He was holding a bouquet of flowers and wearing a big grin.

"Come in," she said.

As he stepped inside, he handed her the bouquet. "These are for you."

She smiled and took it from him. It was a beautiful bouquet, bursting with asters, yellow and pink carnations, and lavender daisies, arranged in a lovely crystal vase.

"They're beautiful," she said. "Thank you. Would you like a cup of coffee?"

"Sure."

"Lilia's off today," she said. "Come into the kitchen and I'll make a pot."

They went into the oversized kitchen. Hank took a seat at an elegant, oblong table of beautifully polished oak. A bouquet of fresh-cut flowers sat in the middle of the table, putting his feeble little bunch to shame.

He propped his elbows on the table and watched her as she prepared the coffee.

She produced a pair of mugs, set them on a small serving tray with cream and sugar, and brought it to the table.

While she waited for the coffee, she removed the dazzling centerpiece and replaced it with the flowers Hank had brought.

When the coffee was done, she filled the mugs and sat across from him.

Hank brought the cup to his nose. "Smells great," he said, dumping in two spoonfuls of sugar and lots of cream.

She prepared her coffee and stirred it thoughtfully. Finally, she said, "Jenny and I used to sit here a lot. Just drinking coffee, chatting, and laughing."

"And you will again soon," Hank said.

Amelia sighed wistfully, giving Hank a weak smile. "Yes," she said. "I'm sure we will."

Hank leaned forward. "Amelia, I guess you've heard about the last two murders?"

She looked up and nodded.

"I just want to assure you we're not at a dead end like the media suggests. There are a few facts we didn't release to the public."

Amelia gave him her full attention.

Hank continued, "For example, we have reason to believe all three murders are linked. And we believe we've found a common thread."

She leaned forward.

"Individually, there's not much to go on, but collectively,

there's enough evidence to give us a good idea of who we're looking for."

"And Jenny?"

"Considering the character of the killer, we believe she doesn't fit his target model," he said.

Amelia cocked her head. "His target model?"

Hank hesitated. "We believe his targets are criminals, specifically thieves."

"Like a vigilante?"

Hank nodded. "Sort of."

Amelia thought a moment. "This Chad that Jenny was seeing, was he a thief?"

"According to a coworker, a few years ago he was involved in a break and enter. Juvenile records are destroyed when the offender turns eighteen, so we aren't sure how the killer would know about his prior record. Finding out who knew that information might lead us to a suspect."

"You have no suspect yet?"

Hank hesitated. "Not yet, but I believe we're getting close. We know what weapons were used, and it's just a matter of time before we make an arrest."

Amelia smiled weakly. "I know it's in good hands. It's hard, but I'm trying to be positive and not panic."

"You're being strong, but I know what you must be going through on the inside." He paused. "Trust me, I know."

She nodded, and they sat in silence a moment. Finally, Hank said, "Don't let the news stories get you down. Everything will turn out fine."

She prayed he was right.

CHAPTER 32

Sunday, August 14th, 12:30 p.m.

JEREMY HAD BEEN busy, and his task was almost completed. In the shed near the barn, he dug around in an old wooden box underneath Father's tool bench.

"Ah, here it is."

He removed a metal ring about four inches in diameter. Like a large, sturdy eyelet that would hold a hook, it circled around and closed the gap, and then bent down at the end with a long screw. Father had used them, screwed tightly into a post, to hold a bull firmly while he put a ring in its nose.

He held it up and peered at it by the meager light shining through the dusty window.

"That should do just nicely. Yes, that will do nicely," he said with satisfaction.

He dropped it into a cardboard box on the floor.

Hanging on the wall was a chain. Not as strong as the one holding Jenny, but it would do. He tightened the chain into a sturdy vise on the bench and, using a hacksaw, he cut off a length about fifteen inches long.

"That should be about right. Fifteen inches. Yes, that's good."

He found a tape measure, measured the remainder of the chain, and dropped both pieces into the box, satisfied.

Digging in a drawer on the bench, he retrieved a pair of padlocks. The keys were in them. He tested them. They worked perfectly.

The padlocks went into the box.

He reached up onto the wall behind the workbench and brought down a crowbar. He tested the weight in his hands. He smiled as he dropped it into the box on top of his other needs.

He stood there and studied the contents of the cardboard box on the floor.

"I think that's all I need. Yes, that's all I need."

He picked up the box and tucked it under his arm. The rusty hinges creaked in protest as he swung open the aging door. He stepped outside, squinted at the sun, and then walked up the gravel drive to the house.

He stopped in the mudroom and retrieved a hammer from a hook on the wall, dropped it in the box, and then carried it into the house and up the steps, heading for Jenny's room.

He swung open the door and stepped inside.

He inspected the spot on the wall beside the door where the hole had been. He had fixed it up earlier, and it looked pretty good now, but the wall could use a little paint perhaps.

He dropped the box on the floor and picked out the hammer and eyelet. He scrutinized the floor a moment and chose a spot close to the center of the room. He bent down and pounded the screw end of the eyelet into the floor at a spot where he knew there was a floor joist. He drove it in about an inch, and then got the crowbar and put it through the eyelet, twisting it round and round until the eyelet was drawn down tight, digging into the floorboards.

He tested it with his fingers. He couldn't budge it. He sat back on his haunches and smiled with satisfaction.

"That will hold. Yes, that will surely hold."

Next, he grabbed the long piece of chain and a padlock from the box and fastened the chain securely to the eyelet. He stood, holding the end of the chain, and tugged as hard as he could.

"That's perfect."

He let the chain slide from his grasp as he stood back. He surveyed his accomplishment with great satisfaction and then packed up his tools and carried them back downstairs.

Sunday, August 14th, 1:00 p.m.

JAKE FLIPPED OPEN the trunk of Annie's Ford Escort and peered inside. The shovel and rope were still in there from her trip to the forest—from the day she'd bravely gone alone and found a buried body. He shook his head. She had spunk, that was for sure.

He took the items from the trunk and carried them to the garage. The door was already open, so he went inside and dropped them on the floor along the side wall.

He went back to the car, picked up the cooler sitting on the driveway, and set it into the trunk.

Matty came running from the house. "Don't forget these," he yelled. He ran over to the trunk and dropped a pair of baseball gloves and a baseball inside.

"Where's your mom?" Jake asked.

"She's coming. You know how women are," Matty said dryly.

Jake grinned and headed to the house just as Annie came out. She had on a straw hat and carried a blanket under one arm, a beach bag bulging with stuff in the other hand. "Get the door, will you?"

Jake took the steps two at a time, carefully retrieved the key Annie held between her teeth, and locked the door. He dropped the key into his pocket.

"I'll take that," he said, relieving her of the bag.

The bag and the blanket were packed into the trunk. Jake found a couple of lawn chairs in the garage, dropped them on top of everything else, and then climbed into the car where Annie and Matty were waiting.

He looked over his shoulder to make sure Matty had his seat belt on. The boy was struggling with it, but in a second, it snapped into place.

Jake and Annie buckled up as well, and Jake twisted the key, pulled the shifter into drive, and touched the gas.

"This is my car," said Annie. "So please, keep the rubber on the tires."

Jake laughed as he eased the car quietly, slowly out of the drive and down the street.

Their destination was a small neighborhood park a couple of blocks away. They pulled into one of several parking spots.

This popular local spot was situated on about a half acre of land, liberally covered with huge spreading maples. Picnic tables were scattered throughout the area, and Jake noticed with satisfaction there appeared to be no other picnickers around.

Jake and Matty dragged everything from the trunk over to the nearest table. Annie dug out a plastic tablecloth from the bag and tacked it to the table while Jake lounged in a lawn chair, sipping on a can of Coke, watching her.

Matty seemed to have too much energy inside him as he raced around the park, probably chasing bees and butterflies.

Sometimes they brought a portable barbecue, but today Jake had decided against it. Maybe next time.

Matty was back. He tossed a glove to his father. "Come on, Dad. Let's play catch."

Jake climbed from his comfortable chair and joined Matty, while Annie dug a John Grisham novel from her bag and settled back to read.

In a few minutes, Jake and Matty came panting back. They doused themselves inside and out with cold water and fell on the grass for a rest.

Sandwiches and salads, and of course, apple pie, were soon spread out on the table along with paper plates, plastic utensils, cups, and paper napkins. Soon the boys had recovered enough and were ready to eat.

Matty couldn't keep still, so he wandered around the park, a sandwich in either hand, looking for squirrels.

"I wish we had some solid leads to follow today," Annie said with a sigh. "But first thing tomorrow I plan on going to the high school. I want to see if they have any cameras in front of the building that might have picked something up."

"That's a great idea," Jake said.

Annie continued, "I also want to go to Mortino's and talk to Jeremy. He lives over near the area where I found Bronson. He might have seen or heard something."

"How about this?" Jake said. "You go to see Jeremy, and I'll hit the school."

Annie nodded.

Jake felt his cell phone buzzing in his pocket. It was Hank.

"Jake, I'm planning on holding a press conference this afternoon at three o'clock in front of the precinct. Do you guys want to be there?"

Jake consulted Annie.

Annie looked at her watch and then at Matty. "I think we should."

"We'll be there," Jake said into the phone.

CHAPTER 33

Sixteen Years Ago

JEREMY DIDN'T like Grandmother. Not at all. It seemed to him she was nothing but a mean old witch.

Mother had to go away. She said there was a meeting of the parole board in Kingston and she would be gone all day.

She had left early in the morning, and Grandmother came over to watch him while Mother was away.

"Now you be a good boy, Jeremy, and do what Grandmother tells you," she had warned him before she left.

"Yes, Mother," he had replied.

And now she was gone and he was stuck here with the witch.

He watched her now, sitting in Father's chair, knitting. She was a shrunken old woman. Her hair was too thin and her lips were way too tight. And the way she squinted through her glasses when she looked at him made him think about an old prune.

"Jeremy, why don't you go outside and get out of my hair?" she snarled at him.

What hair? Jeremy thought. But he decided it was better to be outside where he could forget about the old hag for a while.

On his way out he passed through the kitchen. He'd had a much-too-small breakfast that morning and his stomach was grumbling. He looked over to the counter beside the fridge and decided to have a couple of cookies.

He lifted the lid off the jar carefully, reached in, grabbed two fat chocolate chip cookies, and slipped them into his pocket.

"You little devil," Grandmother screamed.

He spun around. She was hobbling across the floor, a determined look on her face.

"You little sinner," she screamed again and raised her hand, swinging it with all her force. The blow caught him on the side of the head, knocking him on his back.

She stood over him. "You're nothing but a thief," she shrieked. "A wicked, wicked thief."

He cowered back and trembled as she leered at him. He started to cry.

"Get a tissue and clean yourself up," she screeched. She stood towering over him, her hands on her hips, a menacing look on her face.

He got slowly to his feet. She cuffed him once more on the back of the head, forcing his head to shoot forward. He stumbled, and then tripped and fell against the stove, head first, landing on his back again.

She screamed, "Get up, you horrible little creature." She pointed. "Go up to your room until I decide what to do with you."

He rose unsteadily. He felt dizzy as he staggered from the kitchen and headed up the steps to his bedroom.

A screech behind him. "I'll be up later to deal with you."

He finally made it up the stairs, stumbled, and fell through his bedroom door, then lay on his bed and cried.

A few minutes later, he trembled in fear when Grandmother's footsteps sounded on the stairs. He curled up on the bed and watched the door. Waiting.

She soon appeared, carrying one of Father's belts.

"Get your shirt off now and take your pants down," she screamed.

The tears flowed as he did as he was told.

"Now bend over the bed."

He did.

The first blow made him catch his breath. He didn't think he had ever felt that much pain in his life.

The blows continued, one after another. Finally, the punishment was over.

"Let that be a lesson to you," she screamed as she left the room.

He pulled up his pants. His back was too sore to put his shirt on, so he lay on his stomach and cried himself to sleep.

He slept and tossed most of the day. Finally, somewhere in the middle of the afternoon, he was awakened by the sound of a car crunching in the driveway. He looked out the window. It was Mother. He had never been so happy to see her.

He put his shirt on and went into the bathroom, washing his face before going downstairs.

Mother was inside and gave him a hug when he reached the bottom of the steps. He winced in pain at her touch, but smiled bravely and looked up at her.

"Welcome home, Mother."

She smiled at him. "I hope you were a good boy," she said.

He nodded up at her and stepped outside. Away from Grandmother.

Mother came out a few minutes later with the witch and they got in the car. Mother told him she was taking his grandmother home and would be back in five minutes.

And she was.

When she returned, she called Jeremy into the house. "Grandmother told me what you did," she said sternly.

He looked at her. She looked kind, but a little angry.

"I'm sorry," he said. "I was hungry."

"Next time just ask first," she said gently.

"Yes, Mother," he said meekly, looking at his feet.

"Grandmother said she had to send you to your room. She was right, and I hope you learned a lesson."

"Yes, Mother, I sure did."

CHAPTER 34

Sunday, August 14th, 3:00 p.m.

THE RECENT MURDERS in Richmond Hill were suddenly big news.

It seemed like all the national television and news media were there, nudging each other for precious space, packed like sardines, swarming about, waiting.

Behind them, news vans lined the street in both directions, some blocking passing vehicles. Officers milled about directing traffic, threatening to tow away the parking offenders. Rubberneckers further hampered the flow of cars, and many of the curious had pulled over to see what was happening.

Lisa Krunk had a prominent place in the front line. She'd been waiting all day. As soon as she heard about the scheduled news conference, she rushed over, dragging Don with her.

A small podium was set up at the bottom of the precinct steps.

Like a sudden swarm of avid wasps, the cameras zoomed

and whirled in unison as Hank stepped from the precinct doors and headed down the steps.

Amelia was at his side, holding his arm as they approached the podium.

Jake and Annie stood behind with the Chief of Police. A couple of uniforms planted themselves at either end, glaring at the crowd as if daring them to cross the invisible line of demarcation.

Lisa stepped in too close and was quickly sent back a step or two with a frown and a furious wave from one of the cops.

Hank stepped to the microphone and cleared his throat. The swarm hushed, all eyes front and center.

"Ladies and gentlemen, I want to thank you all for coming."

Hank looked down briefly, consulting his notes.

"My name is Detective Corning and I'm the lead investigator in this case. As this is an ongoing investigation, I'll need to keep this brief."

He cleared his throat again.

"As you know, this city has experienced three murders in the last two weeks. Certain items in evidence indicate all three may be the work of one perpetrator. I can't go into it specifically, but these malicious murders appear to be the acts of a serial killer."

Hank glanced at the Chief and continued, "The Chief of Police is considering the safety of the people of Richmond Hill to be of primary concern and everything will be done to ensure their continued safety."

Hank consulted his notes again.

"We're expecting an arrest at any time. This barbarous individual will be caught and face the full extent of our judicial system.

"As you probably know, sixteen-year-old Jenny James has

been missing for almost two weeks. It's known she was last seen with Chad Bronson, the first victim.

"We believe Jenny has not come to any harm at this point, and her mother would like to say a few words to her abductor."

He glanced at Amelia, who stepped forward.

The crowd seemed to slide in a few inches simultaneously. She had their attention.

"Thank you," she said quietly before taking a deep breath and continuing. "Please, if you have my daughter, or you know where she is, then I'm begging you to contact the police or let her go."

Her voice broke and she paused a moment. "Please, she's all I have left."

Amelia dropped her head to hide her tears. Hank placed his arm around her shoulder and she stepped back.

Hank leaned in to the microphone. "Thank you for coming," he said. "I have no further comments and there will be no questions." He turned away.

There was a sudden roar; the crowd was disappointed. Their questions had been cued up and waiting and they all spoke at once.

Hank disregarded them. Amelia took his arm and they headed up the steps. Jake and Annie followed them into the building.

The crowd of reporters slowly dispersed, packed up their equipment, and the once-humming street soon became just another street.

CHAPTER 35

Sunday, August 14th, 5:00 p.m.

JENNY LAY ON her back, staring at the metal roof of the barn far above her head. The door creaked open and Jeremy stepped in.

She turned her head and watched him as he drew closer. He sat on the floor a few feet away and leaned back with his arms supporting himself. He stared at her.

She turned her head back and studied the roof again.

"I just came from town," he said.

She ignored him.

He took a loud breath. "I called your mother."

She sat up suddenly and looked at him, waiting for him to continue.

"I told her you're okay."

Her eyes grew larger. She didn't know what to say.

He spoke again. "I told her not to worry about you. You're in safe hands."

"Is … is she all right?"

"I guess so. I hung up right away. I know they can trace

calls so I had to hang up. I called from a phone booth, you see. And I wore gloves, too. Have to be careful, you know."

Jenny dropped onto her back again and closed her eyes. She was hoping he would eventually let her go. Ever since the day he'd beaten her, he'd been fairly civil to her.

She turned her head and looked back at him. "If you aren't going to hurt me, then why can't you let me go?"

"You know why," he scolded.

"Please."

"Can't do it."

He was quiet for a while, and then said in a teasing voice, "I have a surprise for you."

She was silent.

"Don't you want to know what it is?"

She nodded.

"I've fixed up your room for you."

She stared at him, thinking about her bedroom at home—her nice frilly curtains, pretty wallpaper, with stuffed teddy bears everywhere. She yearned for her soft pillow, the moon through her window at night, and her warm, cuddly bed. She began to cry quietly.

He watched her for a while, then stood and pulled a ring of keys from his pocket. He selected one, approached her, and unlocked the collar from around her neck. He let it fall to the floor.

She rubbed her neck with her hand. It felt good to finally be free of the awful leather dog collar. She considered running as fast as she could. If she could make it from the room, she was sure she could outrun him. She glanced at the door, but he seemed to sense her thoughts and grabbed her arm to block her escape.

His hold was gentle but firm as he tugged at her arm. "Come on," he said.

As he kept his grip on her wrist, she followed him obediently across the rough, straw-covered floor to the doorway. He urged her gently outside.

She blinked and squinted, then covered her eyes with her free hand as the bright sunlight hit her. He paused a moment, allowing her to become accustomed to the glare.

In a moment she was fine. She dropped her hand and looked around. She hadn't been outside in a long time and she missed the fresh air. She took a deep breath.

She walked slowly as he tugged at her arm and led her down the gravel driveway from the barn, heading toward the house.

She kept one eye on the ground around her, hoping to see a weapon, any weapon she might be able to use, a rock, or a stick, anything. She saw nothing.

He led her up the steps of the house and inside. Pushing her ahead of him, he kept the hold on her arm, and they silently climbed the stairs and went into the bedroom.

It was almost a welcome sight. Certainly better than being chained up in the barn, but it also meant he seemed determined never to let her go.

The wall where she'd escaped had been repaired. The bed had been put back together, the room cleaned and organized. A bouquet of fresh flowers sat on the stand beside the bed. There was a CD player on the stand as well, with a stack of CDs beside it.

Her small measure of joy turned to despair when she saw the chain fastened to the ring on the floor.

He dropped her arm and gave her a push. "Go and sit on the bed," he ordered.

She sat obediently on the edge of the bed without saying a word.

He kept one eye on her as he picked up the short piece of

chain, a padlock hanging from it. He bent down and wrapped the chain around her ankle, and then hooked the lock through the links and snapped it shut. He tested it to make sure it couldn't slip from her foot.

Satisfied, he picked up the longer chain. It was fastened to the ring at one end, and he secured the free end to the chain on her ankle with a second lock.

He stood and dropped the keys into his pocket and stood back.

"Stand up," he said.

She stood.

"Now walk around and make sure you have enough room to move."

She walked toward the window. She couldn't reach it, but she could see outside. She moved to the other side of the room toward the door. The long chain gave her plenty of slack to move about her prison.

"I'm sorry I have to keep a chain on you," he said softly. "But I can't let you escape again."

She looked at him and nodded slightly, and then sat back on the bed and dropped her head.

"I'll be back up soon with your dinner," he said.

He left the room and closed the door behind him. The bolt rattled as he locked it securely.

She was no longer as afraid of her captor as she'd once been, but she wanted to go home, away from this awful place.

CHAPTER 36

Sunday, August 14th, 5:00 p.m.

DETECTIVE HANK CORNING slouched in the rusty chair behind his timeworn desk in the precinct. His hands were clasped as though in prayer. His fingertips touched his nose, his eyes were closed, but he wasn't praying. He was thinking, contemplating his next course of action, trying desperately to put the pieces together to form something cohesive.

He dropped his hands, opened his eyes, and reached to the clip on his belt to retrieve his ringing cell phone.

"Hank Corning here."

"Hank, it's Amelia."

He sat up straight. "Hi, Amelia."

"I just received a curious phone call." She talked fast, excited. "A man called. He has Jenny."

"Slow down, Amelia. Take a breath and tell me everything."

Amelia took a deep breath and spoke calmly. "I received a call at the house a few minutes ago. The man said he had Jenny and she was all right and in good hands."

Hank stood and paced. "Did he say where she was?"

"No, he only said she was okay and not to worry."

"Did the voice sound familiar at all?"

"Not at all, but I'm pretty sure it was a man. He tried to cover his voice by talking in a low tone."

"Is that all he said?"

"Yes, I asked him where she was, but he hung up. I dialed star 69 several times and finally got an answer. They said it was a phone booth in the plaza on Bentley Road."

"Amelia, if he touched anything in that booth, we'll get him."

"Hank, I don't know what to make of this. I'm happy, but afraid at the same time."

"It's not bad news, Amelia, that's for sure. It's actually good news."

"There's one thing that bothers me, Hank. What if it wasn't him? Maybe it was a prank caller."

Hank sighed. "There is that possibility, however, it seems slim. Keep your hopes up."

Silence a moment, then Hank said, "I need to get on top of this now. Hopefully, a fingerprinter will find something for me."

"Let me know, please. I truly appreciate your support. It's helped me a lot."

They said goodbye and he touched the "Hang Up" icon.

He arranged to get someone from CSI to go to the phone booth immediately and dust it for prints.

He prayed this was the break he was waiting for.

Monday, August 15th, 8:35 a.m.

ANNIE HAD KEPT extensive notes on whatever ideas and thoughts came to her regarding Jenny, the murders, or anything that seemed related.

She went over them again, hoping something would pop out at her from the handwritten pages.

Nothing did.

Jake walked into the office. "Anything come to you?" he asked.

She leaned back and shook her head.

He sat in the guest chair and crossed his arms. "I can't think of anything either."

"I didn't sleep well last night," Annie said. "I'm sure I woke you a few times. After Hank called and told us about Amelia's phone call, it weighed on my mind all night."

"That's what I love about you. You care so much."

She smiled.

"I keep notes too, you know." He tapped his forehead. "But mine are all up here, and even my brilliantly organized mental notes led me nowhere."

She laughed and said, "I called Hank a few minutes ago. They only found a single set of fresh prints in the phone booth. Hank was hoping to find the killer's prints, but he assumed the ones they found belonged to the person who answered the phone when Amelia called back. They'll follow up on them, just in case."

"So, another dead end."

"It seems to be."

"I'm off to school," Matty called from the office doorway.

Jake looked over his shoulder. "I'm leaving right now. I can give you a lift to school if you want."

"Dad, it's only two blocks."

"Be careful."

"Always. Bye, Mom. Bye, Dad." Matty disappeared and the front door slammed a few seconds later.

"I'm going to the high school right away," Jake said. "It

may be another long shot, but we have to try everything." He stood. "I should be back before noon."

"I should be home by the time you get back," Annie said. "I have a few things to do." She sat forward and looked at her desktop. "Some bills to pay and some invoicing."

Jake stood, leaned over the desk, and gave her a quick kiss. "See you soon," he said.

CHAPTER 37

Monday, August 15th, 9:05 a.m.

JAKE WHIPPED into the parking lot at Richmond Hill High School and pulled into a visitor's slot.

He climbed from his vehicle and looked up at the building. It was well over a hundred years old, with two stories of ancient and faded brick that had seen better days. An L wing had been tacked on to the far side since he'd last been here. That was more than twenty years ago. It looked much smaller now, even with the new section.

He made his way up the cracking concrete walkway, climbed four steps, and pulled open one of the double doors at the side entrance.

A wave of nostalgia overtook him as he stepped inside. He glanced at the familiar cream-colored paint throughout, the faded hard tiled floors, and the dark walnut trim around the doors and banisters.

He moved into the long, deserted hallway. Almost deserted. One student at the far end hustled away with a stack of books under his arm, bent forward as if leaning into the wind, probably late for class.

Jake's footsteps echoed off the floor and bare walls, and he took a left turn, strolling through the old wing of the building.

It was funny how everything was smaller now. The corridors weren't as wide as he remembered. He could almost reach up and touch the ceiling, and the once khaki-colored lockers had turned to a dismal brown.

Across the hall, three or four schoolroom doorways were spaced uniformly apart. He stepped to the nearest one and peeked in a small window. A teacher frantically waved his arms as he talked, probably trying to drum some important point into the heads of distracted students.

He stepped back quickly; he didn't want to be caught snooping.

He took another left into the next corridor and stood in front of locker number 266. That had been his, many years ago. He pensively touched the padlock, then tapped on the metal door. The sound echoed lightly down the hallway. He looked cautiously around as the echo faded, almost expecting to be caught out of class and sent to the principal's office.

He laughed out loud, then turned and continued down the hallway to the main office.

But the main office was gone.

He looked around a moment, then assumed it had been moved to the new wing.

He headed in what he thought was the right direction, and after making a couple of wrong turns, the hallway seamlessly entered the new section. The offices were dead ahead.

The principal's office was right in front of him. He glanced at the metal plate fastened to the door. Mr. Elertson. He headed toward the reception area, situated behind a large see-through wall. He eased open the glass door and stepped inside, where he was greeted by a woman who looked old enough to have been his first grade teacher.

She smiled cheerfully at him and spoke in a singsong voice. "May I help you?"

He smiled back. "My name is Jake Lincoln. I was hoping I could see Mr. Elertson for a minute?"

"Certainly, dearie. May I ask what it's regarding?"

"It's about a security matter."

The smile didn't leave her face. "Just one second," she sang, then hurried toward the principal's office.

As he waited, he looked around. Everything seemed to be running in high gear. People bustled about. Computer keys clicked, file drawers slammed, and the constant buzz of conversation and consultation filled the room.

The door to the principal's office opened and a student came out slowly, his head down, probably having been reprimanded for something or other.

The receptionist poked her head in for a few seconds, then hurried back and flashed her constant smile at Jake. "Mr. Elertson can see you now."

Jake walked cautiously into the office. Not the same room he'd visited quite a few times in his student days, but still, going to the principal's office always seemed to have a negative feeling to it.

"Hello, Mr. Elertson," he said. "I'm Jake Lincoln." He offered his hand.

Elertson stood and they shook. "Have a seat," he said, motioning to a padded chair in front of his well-used desk.

Jake sat and leaned back.

There were a few exchanges about the weather and other mandatory topics that needed to be covered when two strangers meet.

Finally, Jake got down to business. "Mr. Elertson, I'm here on behalf of Lincoln Investigations. We've been retained to look into the disappearance of Jenny James."

Mr. Elertson nodded. "That's a sad thing. Jenny was always popular around here. She would volunteer to help our office staff from time to time, and we all enjoyed seeing her."

Jake nodded. "So I understand."

"How may I help you, Mr. Lincoln?"

"The last time Jenny was seen was leaving the school. One of her friends said she was meeting Chad Bronson. He was the last person to see Jenny, and as you probably know, he was murdered that same day. He likely picked her up here after school."

Elertson nodded and leaned forward. "Did anyone see them leave?"

"Unfortunately, no. But I was hoping you had some cameras installed that might help."

Elertson shook his head and frowned. "We have some cameras in the hallways, but those are on a daily recording rotation, so anything there would be long gone."

"And outside?"

"There are only a couple of dummy cameras outside. We've been hit with budget restrictions and just can't install all the security measures we'd like to."

Jake slowly rubbed his hands in thought. It seemed like another dead end.

Elertson continued, "It's unfortunate I can't help you." He sighed. "Hopefully the board will listen to us after this and allow us a larger security budget for the future."

Jake nodded, stood, and offered his hand again. "Thank you, anyway."

Elertson stood and followed Jake from the room. "On behalf of the staff here, I certainly hope you find Jenny," he said. "And if there's anything else, please contact me any time." He took a business card from his breast pocket and handed it to Jake.

Jake took the card and thanked him again. He found his way out and back to his vehicle. He leaned against the hood for some time, waiting for a hint of inspiration that didn't come.

CHAPTER 38

Monday, August 15th, 9:10 a.m.

LISA KRUNK was always on the prowl. Today was no exception as she hung out near the police precinct waiting for a victim.

Don sat on a low concrete wall, his head down, studying the ground, the camera in his lap and a bored look on his face.

Lisa stopped her back-and-forth pacing as Officer Spiegle stepped from the precinct doors. He looked up at the sun, wiped his brow on his sleeve, and trudged down the steps. As he rounded the corner, Lisa approached him.

Don stood up, the camera ready. The red light appeared as it hummed into action.

Lisa said, "Officer Spiegle, may I ask you a few questions?"

Spiegle saw the camera and unconsciously brushed his hair back with one hand. He stood a little straighter, and his chest seemed to puff out slightly. He put on his best smile, looked at the camera, then at Lisa, and waited.

She massaged his ego. "Officer Spiegle, I understand you were one of the officers instrumental in finding the body of Chad Bronson."

He nodded. "Yes, that's correct."

"Can you tell the viewers a little bit about that?"

"Well," he said, "the body had been buried for more than a week, so when we unearthed it, it was rather a ghastly sight."

"I can only imagine," she soothed and then asked, "Do you think Mrs. Bellows and Mr. Farley were killed by the same man?"

"Yes, I believe so. We're trying to ascertain that now." He hesitated. "We think there's a serial killer on the loose and we don't know who it is."

"So then, should the citizens be worried they may be next?"

Spiegle looked confused. "Well, I sure am."

"And what gives you the indication the same individual is responsible for all three murders?"

"According to the information I … we got from forensics, he used the same gun and knife each time."

"And do you have any indication who the killer may be?"

"Not yet."

"Are you confident you'll make an arrest soon?"

"Well, I sure hope so."

"You don't sound too sure."

"Well, truthfully …" He scratched his head before continuing. "We have no idea at all who it is."

Lisa faked a smile. "Thank you, Officer Spiegle."

The camera swung toward her. She said, "In an exclusive

report, I'm Lisa Krunk for Channel 7 Action News."

She watched the cop walk away, satisfied that with a bit of editing, she would have just what she wanted.

Monday, August 15th, 9:25 a.m.

JEREMY WAS RUNNING a little late. His alarm clock seemed to be on the fritz and didn't buzz him awake.

He got out of bed late, and by the time he had packed his lunch and was ready, it was already past nine o'clock. He was expected to be at work by nine.

As he pulled into the rear lot at Mortino's, he hoped he could slip in without catching the attention of his stupid boss.

He jumped from his car and ran over to the metal door at the back of the building that led into the employee area. He eased it open and peeked inside.

All clear.

He hurried in and tucked his lunch into his locker, pulled out his cap, and he was ready.

He strode through the swinging doors, into the store like nothing had happened.

But it had.

A shipment of several skids of tissues had arrived. They'd been advertised in the flyer and were to be piled mountain high, put on special sale. That was Jeremy's job.

He was intent on straightening up some cans a careless customer moved around. A few belonged on another shelf, so he'd moved them to their correct display, and was surveying his job.

"There you are, Jeremy." The boss sounded mad.

Jeremy turned and looked at the frowning man. "Yes, Mr. MacKay."

"I've been paging you and looking around the store for several minutes. I finally assumed you weren't here. Are you late again?"

"Just a few minutes late, sir. I had a small problem."

MacKay wasn't tall, but he towered over Jeremy as he gave him his new orders.

Jeremy slunk away, cursing silently.

He set up the display of tissues as the scumbag boss directed. Satisfied with the job, he stood back and admired it.

A few minutes later, he was paged to come to MacKay's office. He walked to the back of the store and swung open the door.

"Come in Jeremy. Sit down." MacKay seemed calmer now.

Jeremy went in, sat on the edge of a chair, and looked at MacKay. "You paged me, sir?"

MacKay cleared his throat. "Jeremy, I'm sorry to say this, but I have to let you go."

"Go where, sir?"

"I'm firing you, Jeremy."

Jeremy was stunned. His mouth fell open, his eyes widened, and he stared at the boss.

"Did you hear me, Jeremy?"

"Yes … yes, sir," he said quietly. "But why?"

"Because you're always late and taking time off. I've warned you several times in the past and today was your last chance."

"It won't happen again. I promise you."

"I've heard that many times, Jeremy," MacKay said firmly. "I'm sorry, but I've already made my decision."

"But I need this job. I have bills to pay. Taxes. Food to buy—"

"I'll give you an extra week's pay, and pay you for today, but that's all I can do."

Jeremy was dazed. Now what would he do? He got up slowly and turned to leave.

"You may go home now, and pick up your pay at the end of the week as usual," MacKay said.

Jeremy left the office. He went to the break room, opened his locker, grabbed his lunch bag, threw his hat in the garbage bin, and stepped out the back, swearing to himself all the while.

CHAPTER 39

Monday, August 15th, 10:05 a.m.

BENNY FLANDERS was hungry. He hadn't had anything to eat today, and yesterday's pickings had been sparse. His stomach rumbled all night, seeking sustenance.

He sauntered lazily down Pine Street, a middle-class neighborhood in central Richmond Hill. He looked left and right.

He saw a possible opportunity—a house with no vehicle in the driveway. He crossed the road and leaned casually against an old maple tree while a car drove by. After looking up and down the street, and seeing no one, he dashed over the lawn and stopped at the side of the house.

He peeked in the window. Nobody. He crept around to the rear of the house and looked through the back door. He could see the kitchen, but no one appeared to be inside.

Moving carefully, he circled back around to the front door, climbed the steps, rang the doorbell, and waited.

He grinned. It seemed like nobody was home.

He looked around cautiously, and then jumped over a railing and hid behind a bush. A woman was pushing a baby carriage up the street. He waited until she passed, then keeping low and tight against the house, he circled back until he was at the rear door again.

He examined it. The outside screen door opened, but the inside door looked secure. He tested the knob. It was locked.

Backtracking a little, he crouched down by a rear window leading to the basement of the dwelling. He smiled grimly and removed a small knife from his side pocket. He flipped it open and worked the blade in between the window frame and the glass. He struggled with it awhile, then heard a pop. He pushed gently, and the window swung open.

He climbed through feet first, landing like a cat on the concrete floor, and then stood and looked around at the usual junk one would find in a basement. He saw old cabinets, chairs, a broken table, and a bunch of boxes full of stuff lining the side wall.

The steps to the main floor were to his right. He climbed them cautiously in case someone was about. When he reached the top, he swung open the door and stepped in. He listened intently a moment, hearing nothing. So far, so good.

Straight ahead was the kitchen, and he could see the fridge and stove from where he stood. He crept across the tiled floor and into the room. The clock on the wall ticked, the fridge hummed, and Benny breathed, but all was otherwise still and quiet.

The fridge proved to contain a harvest of food—leftover chicken, half a meatloaf, a variety of stuff to drink, veggies, and more. It was a real feast. Benny's mouth watered. He made several trips back and forth from the fridge to the table as he chose the items he planned to devour.

A cupboard by the sink contained plates. He slid one off the stack, then selected a knife and fork from the drawer beneath.

He pulled out a hard wooden chair from the table, sat, slipped a paper napkin from its holder, and tucked it under his chin.

A can of Coke fizzed as he popped the tab. He took a long swallow, then breathed out contentedly.

His plate was piled high with food, and he eagerly set about devouring it. It didn't take long, and soon he sat back, rubbed his belly, belched a couple of times, and sighed with satisfaction.

He sat a minute and formulated further plans. He assumed anything valuable would be upstairs. Maybe he could find some jewelry or something else to make it worth his while. Perhaps even some money stashed somewhere. He would try that first. Any money would be in an office, if there was one.

He got up, went to the living room, and spied a door leading off from there. He pushed it open; it was an office. He went behind the faux oak desk and plunked into the swivel chair. A computer monitor sat on the desktop along with a stuffed penholder and a small lamp. It seemed rather organized. He tried the center drawer first. It held more pens, pencils, writing paper, paper clips. The side drawers contained file folders, a stapler, a checkbook, and lots of empty space.

But no money.

He looked around for a safe. He stood and examined behind pictures, in a cabinet, and anywhere he could think of, but still no safe could be found. He folded his arms and stood still for a minute, then decided there was nothing worthwhile in the room.

He would try upstairs.

He left the office and wandered around the rest of the main floor. He spied the stairs, leading to the second floor, near the front of the house.

He hummed to himself as he climbed the steps. Reaching the top, he saw two bedrooms and a bathroom. He poked his head through the door of the first room. It looked like it belonged to a teenager; there wouldn't be anything there. He tried the closed door of the other room and it swung open silently. It appeared to be the master bedroom, and he stepped inside and looked around.

A queen-sized bed stood against the far wall, piled high with fluffy pillows, covered with a pure-white comforter. To his right was a walk-in closet. He poked his head in. Just clothes. To his left was a door leading into the bathroom, a dresser along the side wall, a vanity on the other.

He went to the vanity. It had a big mirror in front. He looked in the mirror, made a face, and the mirror made a face back. He laughed and continued looking. There was a bank of small drawers in the front, and he popped them open and closed. He saw nothing of interest inside.

On the top of the vanity were rows of little containers and holders, containing makeup, lipstick, hairbrushes, tweezers, and all kinds of other junk he had no interest in.

Then he spied a small jewelry box over to one side. He slid it forward and lifted the lid. It held a couple of rings, a necklace or two, and some earrings. It didn't look like a major score, but he dumped the contents of the box into the side pocket of his overcoat, patted his pocket shut, and tossed the box back.

He took another quick look around, decided there was nothing else worth scrounging, and headed for the door.

His work here was done.

He stepped into the hallway and stopped short when he heard someone moving around downstairs—a tap, tap of shoes across the tiled floor that led from the front entrance to the kitchen.

He held his breath. Should he dare to creep down the stairs and make a dash for the door?

He heard a gasp. It sounded like a woman, and it was coming from the kitchen. He heard her running around, and then the unmistakable tone of a cell phone dialing. Three numbers. He swore to himself. She was calling 9-1-1.

She must've seen the food and plates he'd left on the table. He cursed to himself again and wondered what to do.

He made a decision. He crept down the stairs, but the steps that had been so quiet when he went up now decided to squeak.

He was sure she would've heard it.

He took the rest of the steps three at a time, reached the front doors, then saw a blur behind him. He twisted the knob. She must've locked it as she came in. Too late. He felt a glancing blow on the back of his head. It stunned him briefly, and he ducked down and half crawled, half ran, into the living room.

She chased him, swinging a pot—one he'd left on the table.

She didn't seem to be afraid as she pursued him. He jumped behind a couch in the center of the room, making a barrier between them, and then spun around and faced her.

She was probably in her midthirties, and he couldn't help

but notice she was pretty good-looking. But she also looked to be in good shape physically and could likely beat him into meat patties if she caught him.

She hesitated, probably not sure whether to chase him around the couch, or to wait.

"You're trapped," she said.

"I didn't mean no harm," he whined.

"I don't mean any harm either. Just step over here and I'll show you that, you coward." She raised the pot menacingly.

"Just … just let me go. I didn't take anything."

She advanced a step or two. He crouched, ready to run.

"I called the police," she said.

He was trembling now, his hands shaking. His voice shook as well as he said, "Please lady, I was just hungry. That's all I did was eat a little food."

"We don't keep food upstairs."

He didn't say anything.

"I can wait here all day," she said. "Until the police come."

He looked back and forth, and then at her. He couldn't find any way out except past her and the pot she gripped.

She reached into a pocket in her skirt, pulled out her cell phone, and dialed 9-1-1 again.

"I called a few minutes ago," she said, giving her name and address. "I have him trapped in the house."

She listened a moment, then grinned. "He doesn't appear to have any weapon, but I do. I'm holding him off with a pot."

She lowered the phone and looked at Benny. "The police are on their way."

Benny looked around again. He had to make a move.

She left the phone on, and as she slipped it into her

pocket, he made a mad dash for the door. She swung the pot and he thought maybe she'd broken his backbone. He stumbled to the floor, rolled a couple of times, slammed against the wall, and jumped to his feet.

She hit him again. The pot sang as she caught him on top of the head. He fell again, and then he was up, stumbling into the kitchen toward the back door. He twisted the lock and then the knob, yanked the door open, and dove through head first, landing on his back with a thump.

The pot connected with his shoulder as he rolled to his feet. He lost his balance, staggered a moment, and then dashed across the deck. He jumped the three steps to the lawn and vaulted the hedge.

"Police. Stop."

He looked over his shoulder as he ran toward the neighbor's property. A cop was leveling a gun at him. He didn't stop. He felt sore all over, a little dazed by the blow to the head, but he continued to run.

He glanced over his shoulder again. There were two cops now, and they were gaining on him.

He rounded the neighbor's house and headed for the street. The cops followed, ordering him to stop.

The police car was parked at the curb in front of the house. He dashed toward it and whipped open the door. The keys were in it. He jumped in, started it up, and sped away, the driver-side door swinging on its hinges as he careened down the street.

In the rearview mirror he saw the cops chasing him on foot. He chuckled. He took a left at the intersection without looking, bumped over a curb, and spun back onto the asphalt.

Main Street was straight ahead, so he gunned it. He

touched the brake to avoid a pickup truck as he spun through a red light, making a left onto Main. The truck whipped around, tires squealing, and came to an abrupt stop, its wheels plowing sideways into the curb.

Benny stomped on the gas pedal again.

Dead ahead, out of nowhere, a cruiser sat at right angles on the street, blocking his path. He slammed on the brakes. The car spun sideways, did a hop, and then plowed broadside into the tail end of the cruiser.

He saw two armed cops in front of the other cruiser as he kicked the door open and tumbled to the street. They yelled at him to stop, but he staggered and made tracks the other way.

He was tired and sore, and though he did his best to make his getaway, it was not to be.

He was brought crashing to the asphalt, overtaken and tackled from behind. One cop sat on his back; the other one had his gun pointed toward his head. His hands were expertly cuffed behind him, and he was dragged roughly to his feet.

They threw him over the hood of the smashed cruiser and searched him. They relieved him of the knife found in his pants pocket, and then dug into the pockets of his overcoat.

"Well, well, looky here," one of the cops said. "He has a jewelry store in his pocket."

The other cop laughed.

Benny just scowled.

He was sore all over, and bending over the hood, hands secured behind his back, just made it worse. Right now, he wanted to be tossed into a holding cell where he could get some rest.

In a couple of minutes, another cruiser pulled up. A cop

jumped out and opened the back door.

"Watch your head."

Benny didn't think another knock on the head would make much of a difference, but he watched his head as he was helped into the cruiser. The door slammed shut behind him.

He laid his head back and closed his eyes. Now he felt better.

CHAPTER 40

Monday, August 15th, 10:15 a.m.

JEREMY WAS NOT a happy camper as he jumped into his vehicle and headed home.

He always carried his trusty knife with him, strapped to his leg, and now he wished he'd sliced old MacKay's throat with it. That would teach him a lesson. Or maybe he should just drive home, grab his gun, and shoot the top off his bald head. He deserved it.

He continued muttering and cursing as he drove down Main Street. Traffic was slow. He saw some red lights blinking up ahead. As he drew closer, he saw three cop cars parked in the middle of the road. It appeared two had been in an accident.

Stupid cops. Didn't they know how to drive?

He inched forward. One cop directed traffic, but it was still slow going.

He wanted to shoot them, too. He was mad at the world and hated everybody who got in his way.

As he was directed past the scene of the accident, he could

see some old man in the back of a cruiser. He looked like he was sleeping.

Finally, he made it through the mass of cars and sped up again. He ran through a late orange at the next intersection and pulled a quick left. Five minutes later, he was speeding along County Road 12, bumping over potholes and bulging pavement as he made his way home.

He peeked up at Jenny's window as he crunched over the gravel of his driveway. He saw her appear at the window. She had probably heard him coming. He parked in his usual spot by the front door and climbed from the vehicle.

He wasn't sure what to do. He had no job and a whole day ahead of him. He didn't think much of his prospects of finding a job any time soon. Tomorrow he would have to look, though. Maybe his idiot former boss would give him a recommendation if he asked nicely. Or if he stuck his revolver down his throat.

He unlocked the front door of the house and went straight through into the mudroom at the back. He grabbed a basket of gardening hand tools off the bench and went out the back door.

Maybe he would work in his garden for a while. That always calmed him down.

Monday, August 15th, 10:20 a.m.

ANNIE PASTED a stamp on the last envelope, ready to mail. She had filled out a few invoices for clients and paid a stack of bills. She stuffed them into her handbag and stood from her desk.

She clicked off the computer monitor, dug her key ring from her handbag, and made her way out the front door, locking up behind.

Her Escort chugged as she touched the gas. She sighed. It was time for a tune-up. She stopped at the corner, dumped the mail into a big red mailbox, and sped away.

Traffic on Main Street was a little slow. A couple of tow trucks were busy towing away a police car, and one lane was blocked in either direction.

Her cell rang as she was stopped in traffic. It was Jake. "Hi, honey," she said.

"I just left the high school. No luck there, but I wanted to let you know, I'm going to drop by and see Hank at the precinct for a few minutes. I should be home by noon."

"Okay," she said.

"Where are you now?" he asked.

"Just on my way to Mortino's to talk to Jeremy. I'm stuck in traffic right now, though."

"Traffic?"

"Yeah, a police car got in an accident. I don't know what happened. They're towing it away."

"Okay, see you soon."

They said goodbye and she hung up.

Traffic started to move again and she finally got past the obstruction. In a few minutes, she pulled into the parking lot at Mortino's.

Once inside the store, she checked up and down the aisles, looking for Jeremy. She didn't see him. Perhaps he was out on a delivery. She made her way to the back of the store and approached the manager's office.

She tapped on MacKay's door. There was no answer. She wandered around the store until she found him, straightening up some boxes of cereal on an overloaded shelf.

"Good morning, Mr. MacKay," she said cheerily.

MacKay stopped his task and glanced over his shoulder, smiling when he saw Annie. "Good morning," he said, turning around to face her.

"I'm Annie Lincoln—"

"Yes, I remember you and Jake. He was in here on Saturday to pick up some surveillance tapes. Were they helpful at all?"

"They did shed a little light on things. It may be too early to tell yet."

"It's a real shame about what's going on in this town right now. My wife's a little nervous about the whole thing. I told her not to worry. Just be careful, and she'll be all right, I told her."

Annie agreed, "The police are on top of this. I'm sure they'll catch him soon, and we're doing what we can as well, on behalf of a client."

MacKay nodded and smiled. "So, what can I do for you today?"

"As you know, the first victim's body was found along County Road 12. One of your workers, Jeremy Spencer, lives out near there. I was hoping to talk to him and see if he heard or saw anything. I didn't see him around here, though."

MacKay frowned. "Unfortunately, I had to let him go this morning."

Annie raised her brows. "Oh, that's too bad."

"Yes, it is. I felt a little bad about it." He paused and shrugged his shoulders. "But you know how it is."

Annie nodded. "Perhaps I can catch him at home. Thanks, Mr. MacKay."

"You're welcome," he said, and turned back to the shelf.

Annie looked at her watch. She had a few things she needed to buy, so she would grab what she needed now. There was nothing perishable, so she wouldn't have to drop them home first. She could head straight out to Jeremy's place and get back by noon.

CHAPTER 41

Monday, August 15th, 10:25 a.m.

HANK GLANCED UP from his desk as an officer rushed toward him. It was Officer Spiegle.

"He's here," Spiegle said in an excited tone.

Hank leaned back in his chair, looked sideways at the cop, and frowned. "Who's here, Yappy?"

"The guy I saw."

"What guy?"

"The guy in the car."

Hank swung his chair around. "Yappy," he said calmly. "What car?"

"The stolen car," Yappy said impatiently.

Hank shook his head in frustration. "We get stolen cars in here all the time. What's so special about this one?"

"The guy who ran the car into the bush. You know, he stole that dead guy's car."

Hank sat forward. "Are you telling me the man who had Bronson's car is here?"

Spiegle waved his hands as he talked. "Yes, yes, he's here."

Hank stood. "And you're sure it's him?"

"Yes, yes, I'm sure."

"Where is he?"

"In the holding cell."

Hank turned to Jake, who was sitting on the other side of the desk. "I'll be right back." He brushed past Yappy and strode across the precinct.

Yappy followed Hank downstairs to the holding cells, where an officer opened a secure door and let them into the hallway.

There were six holding cells, three on each side of the passageway. Prisoners were held here awaiting arraignment or temporarily before transport to prison, and sometimes the cells served as an overnight "drunk tank."

Hank followed Yappy to the second cell on the left. The officer pointed through the bars.

Benny was flat on his back on an uncomfortable-looking woven, metal bed. He was sound asleep, his shoe tucked under his head, serving as a pillow, his arms folded in front of him. Snoring filled the room.

"That's him," Yappy said.

"You're sure?"

"Yup."

Hank turned without a word and went to the central control room. It was staffed by deputies in the holding cell area.

He spoke to one of the deputies. "The prisoner in cell two. What do you have on him?"

The deputy picked up a stack of papers, leafed through them, and selected one. "Benjamin Flanders. Fifty-eight years old. Not arraigned yet. Arrested and charged for break and enter, car theft, and other charges pending." He handed the paper to Hank.

Hank looked it over briefly and handed it back. "Get me a copy of this, and get the prisoner up to interview room one, will you?"

The deputy nodded. "Right away." He turned around. The photocopier hummed for a minute, and then the deputy handed Hank a sheet of paper.

Hank took the paper and went back up the steps to his desk. He looked around. Jake was talking to a couple of cops near the watercooler.

Jake glanced over as Hank approached.

"They're bringing him up to the interview room," Hank said. "You can watch through the glass if you want."

Jake nodded. "That would be great."

It took a few minutes to rouse Benny and get him upstairs. They waited until the deputy signaled the prisoner was ready.

Jake followed Hank down a short hall and through a door. They entered a small room containing only a desk and three or four chairs. The far wall was largely a two-way mirror, an adjoining room visible through the glass. Jake took a seat as Hank went through a door beside the glass and into the connected room.

The interview room was a small, soundproofed area, with three chairs, two on the near side of a metal desk, one on the far side, facing the mirror. The room was brightly lit, with barren, blank walls, a small camera in one corner.

Benny was on the far side of the table, facing the mirror, his hands cuffed to a ring. He sat up straight in the uncomfortable chair, a sullen look on his face. He looked up as Hank entered.

Hank pointed to the empty chair. "Mind if I sit?" he asked.

Benny just stared.

"May I call you Benny?"

Benny nodded slightly.

Hank pulled the chair back and sat. He consulted the paper, then leaned in. "You're in a bit of trouble," he said.

The prisoner remained quiet.

"I'd like to help you if I can."

No response.

Hank looked back at the paper. "They have you here for break and enter, grand theft, car theft, failure to obey a lawful order, assault on a police officer, and a whole host of traffic violations." Hank looked up and whistled. "Looks like you're going away for a long, long time."

Benny frowned. "I didn't do none of that."

"Benny, Benny. This is all solid. We have witnesses for everything here." Hank consulted the paper again. "Who's the judge going to believe? The cops, or a man who has a pretty long record already?"

Benny shrugged and looked at the table.

"I can make some of this go away," Hank said.

Benny looked back at Hank. His face showed a flicker of interest.

"Are you interested?"

"Maybe."

"But you have to help me."

"Help you how?" Benny mumbled.

Hank sat back. "Last Wednesday you were driving a white 2000 Toyota Tercel. An officer saw you, chased you, and witnessed you crash the vehicle and run away."

"Weren't me."

"Come on, Benny. We know it was you. We have you cold here. The witness was a cop."

Benny was silent a moment, then asked, "What about it?"

"All I want to know is where you found the vehicle. You tell me that, and we'll forget you stole it, or you ever saw it."

Benny considered that. "What about them other charges? The break and enter and stuff?"

"I can't do anything about the B&E, but the theft of the officer's vehicle, I can get that reduced to public mischief and make all the traffic violations go away."

"What about the assault?"

"What assault?"

Benny looked around the room, at the ceiling, at Hank, at the floor. He seemed to be thinking, but said nothing.

"It's a good deal, Benny," Hank urged.

Benny looked at Hank and nodded slightly. "Okay, then. If you do what you just said, I'll tell you." He paused. "I'll tell you 'bout the car, but I ain't gonna admit none o' that other stuff till I see a lawyer."

A lawyer couldn't get him off the B&E charges, so Hank was satisfied with that. He nodded and leaned in. "That's fine. Go ahead, Benny."

"What do you wanna know?"

"Tell me exactly how and where you found the car."

"Well, I was just out for a walk, see. And I seen this car parked, and the keys were in it, so I just decided to take it for a little ride. Didn't really steal it."

"I know, Benny. You just took it for a joyride. But where did you find it?" Hank urged.

"It were in the parking lot over at Walmart."

Hank leaned back. "Excellent, Benny. Now can you tell me what part of the lot you found it in?"

"Right near the back row. Over by where people shove the grocery carts in when they're done with 'em."

"And the car wasn't locked?"

"Nope."

"And the keys were in it?"

"Yup."

"Anything else you can tell me?"

Benny thought a minute. "Well, I had to move the seat way back just to get in."

"Did you take anything from the vehicle when you left it?"

"Nope. Weren't nothin' worth taking."

Hank leaned back and folded his arms. "I think that's all, Benny. You've been a big help."

"So you'll do what you said? Make them charges go away?"

"Don't worry, Benny, I'll do exactly what I said." Hank stood, went through the door to the viewing room, and sat beside Jake.

"Very interesting," Jake said.

"Yes, it is. It appears the killer tried to hide Bronson's vehicle in plain sight."

Jake nodded. "Now we have to figure out what this all means."

An officer poked his head into the room and looked at Hank. "Captain Diego wants to see you right away."

"What about?" Hank asked.

"An armed robbery just went down at the Commerce Bank. Apparently, the security guard shot the robber, but he escaped. Diego needs you down there right away. Says it can't wait."

Hank frowned. "Can't he get anyone else?"

The officer shrugged. "You'll have to talk to Diego about that. I'm just the messenger, but since it's your department, he needs you."

Hank turned to Jake. "It looks like I'm going to have to put this on hold awhile. I'll talk to you later." He stepped from the room, shaking his head as he went toward Diego's office.

The city was growing, crime was growing, and the

department needed more cops. But until then, as head of RHPD robbery/homicide, and the only detective that could handle the situation, he knew the captain had no other option but to call on him.

He wanted to follow up on the lead Benny had given him, but that would have to wait, and he would be forced to put the search for Jenny on hold for a few hours.

CHAPTER 42

Monday, August 15th, 10:30 a.m.

ONE CAN ONLY work in a garden for so long. There are a limited number of weeds to pull and one can soon run out of rows to hoe.

Gardening had kept Jeremy busy for some time, but he still felt rejected and dejected. He was still mad at the world.

Whenever he'd felt this way in the past he would talk to Mother. She would always have a sympathetic word or two, maybe a hug, and it always made him feel better.

But she was long gone. She had left him to fend for himself. He adored Father, but he was gone as well. All he could hope to do was carry on Father's work—doing his part to rid the world of scum. That was important, yes, but he needed a job as well.

He swore and threw the hoe across the garden, mashing one of his prize tomato plants. He didn't care. He lay down on the grass and looked up at the sky. The clouds moved gently across the endless expanse, drifting from one horizon to the other without a care in the world.

He wished he were a cloud. No, he wished he were a rain cloud. Full of thunder. And lightning. Maybe a tornado. He'd rain havoc down and wouldn't care.

He jumped up and strode to the house, slamming the door behind him as he went into the mudroom. He went through the room and into the kitchen, where he took the .22 revolver from the drawer.

He cocked it and held it to his temple. His hand trembled. Sweat appeared on his brow. He held his breath and closed his eyes, clenching his teeth. His finger tightened on the trigger. He held motionless a moment, and then his grip loosened, and the gun slipped from his hand and clattered to the ceramic floor. His breath came out in a rush, and he stood still, breathing slowly. He finally opened his eyes and looked at the floor by his feet.

He stared at the gun a moment and then picked it up and put it back into the drawer, covering it carefully with the towels before gently shutting the drawer.

He dropped his hands into his pockets and trudged up the stairs to the second floor. He slid back the dead bolt on the door of Jenny's room and opened it.

Jenny was sitting on the bed, propped up by pillows, reading a book. Classical music came from the set of speakers under the window. She looked up.

Without saying a word, he went over, moved the chain to the side, and sat on the edge of the bed at the opposite end.

He stared at her.

She stared at the dejected look on his face, then reached over to the CD player, turned down the music, and waited for him to speak.

"I got fired today," he said calmly.

She cocked her head. "What happened?"

"The boss said I was late too often."

She was silent.

"So, he fired me."

"Now what'll you do?"

"I don't know."

She waited.

"Perhaps I'll sell the house," he said. "If I can't find another job."

"And … what about me?"

"Yeah, that's a problem."

She waited.

"I really like you, Jenny. You're the only one who listens to me."

"I … I like you too, Jeremy," she lied.

His brows shot up. "Really?"

"Yes."

He frowned slightly and studied her face. Did she really like him, or was she just saying that?

"You've been treating me well, and have been kind to me," she said.

His eyes narrowed as he studied her. Finally he said, "I might take the chains off if you promise not to try to get away again."

She smiled. "I won't."

"Promise?"

"Promise."

He watched her for a couple of minutes. She seemed honest and sincere. Maybe she had changed. Maybe she now understood he really was a good man, trying his best to take care of her.

He stood suddenly, reached into his pocket, and pulled out the ring of padlock keys. He bent over and grabbed her foot, dragging her leg toward him. He put a key in the lock and twisted. The long chain fell loose. He unlocked the one holding the small chain around her ankle, and then the chain from the ring in the floor. He picked them all up and tossed them into a corner along with the padlocks.

She drew her leg in and rubbed her ankle. "Thank you," she said.

"Do you want a shower?" he asked.

"Yes, please."

He went to the door, opened it, and stepped outside the room. She picked out one of his mother's old dresses from the closet and followed him. He stood at the top of the steps to block her way to the stairs, motioning down the hall. She slipped down the passageway and into the bathroom.

He sat on the floor and waited, listening to the shower running. In a few minutes the toilet flushed and the door opened again.

He stood and motioned toward the bedroom. She went in and sat on the bed, watching him.

He followed her in.

"Thank you," she said. "I feel better."

He smiled and said as he left, "I'll be back soon with your lunch."

CHAPTER 43

Monday, August 15th, 10:55 a.m.

ANNIE SHUDDERED as she drove past the forested area where she had found Chad Bronson's body just two or three days before. She took a quick look down the lane, then forced her eyes back on the road and hummed to herself, trying to remove the scene from her mind.

She continued along for perhaps a mile and turned into the Spencer driveway. The gravel under the tires snapped as she drove toward the house, coming to stop behind a blue Hyundai she assumed was Jeremy's.

She climbed from her car and looked around. She'd never actually been on this property before, although she'd driven past it many times. To her right, a couple of hundred feet away, further down the driveway, she saw the old barn. She thought again of the day she heard about Jeremy's mother hanging herself from the beam overhead.

To her left was a field, now unused and overgrown with

weeds. A little further past, a forest extended for a couple miles or more, with the swamp dominating a large part at the center of the vast area of land.

The old farmhouse sat straight ahead. She climbed the aging wooden steps to the large front porch and knocked on the door. She waited and knocked again.

The door opened a few inches and Jeremy poked his head out, looking at her quizzically. "Yes, Mrs. Lincoln?"

She smiled at him. "Hi, Jeremy. May I talk to you for a few minutes?"

"What about?" He seemed guarded, a little uneasy.

She tried a new approach. "I went to Mortino's to talk to you. Mr. MacKay said he let you go. I'm sorry to hear that."

"Yeah." He sighed. He seemed a little more at ease.

"It must be hard on you," she said in a concerned voice.

He opened the door further and shrugged. "Can't do much about it, I guess."

"I don't want to bother you if you're busy. I have a couple of questions for you, if that's okay?"

He stepped onto the porch, took a couple steps forward, and leaned with his back against the railing. Annie turned to face him. She smiled down at him again to assure him she was harmless.

"What questions do you have?" he asked.

"As I'm sure you're aware, a man was killed on August second, two weeks ago, and his body was found over there in that forest." She pointed to the tree line. "I'm wondering if you saw or heard anything at all that day that was unusual or out of the ordinary?"

Jeremy glanced toward the trees, then back at Annie, squinted, and shook his head. "Nope. Didn't see anything."

"Or hear anything?"

"Nope." He paused and eyed her carefully. "You're the

one who found him, aren't you? I saw it on the news."

She nodded slowly. "Yes, I found the body. A couple of days ago."

"What was that like?"

She laughed lightly. "It was kind of spooky."

"Yeah, I guess it would be."

Nobody spoke for a moment.

She was about to thank him and leave when he asked, "Do you want to see my garden?"

She looked at her watch. "Sure."

She followed him down the steps and around to the back of the house to a large, well-tended garden.

He pointed. "I've got carrots there, and lettuce just starting to come up here."

He walked between some rows of onions and pointed again. "And there're some beets, and there're my tomatoes." He stopped in front of a tomato plant with a broken stem. "That one got broken. Must've been an animal here. Maybe a raccoon. Stupid animals."

She looked down at the plant. The break looked fresh.

And that's when she saw it.

She took a quick breath and stepped back.

It hit her like a tidal wave. Mortino's. Mrs. Bellows had been at Mortino's. Jeremy worked at Mortino's. He was on the video heading for the front of the store as she'd left. The place where Chad was buried was near Jeremy's house. But the thing that brought it all together was right there on the ground at her feet.

The footprint.

Jeremy's footprint in the garden was the same one she'd seen at Bronson's grave. She was sure of it.

"Are you all right, Mrs. Lincoln?"

"Yes … yes. I'm all right."

He looked at her and cocked his head. "Are you sure?"

"I have to go now," she said. She turned quickly and strode back around the house to her car. She opened the door, climbed inside, and dug in her handbag for her cell phone. There was no signal, but she dialed 9-1-1, praying it would go through.

The phone was struck from her hands. It flew up and hit the floor on the passenger side.

"Who are you calling?" Jeremy snarled.

She reached for the keys in the ignition but found herself being choked from behind, his arm around her neck as he dragged her from the vehicle. She felt the cold steel of a knife on the back of her neck.

"You know, don't you?" he asked.

"Jeremy," she managed to say. "What are you doing?"

"How did you know?"

"Know what?"

He kept his arm around her throat and dragged her around the car. He opened the other door, picked up the phone with his free hand, and dropped it to the ground. He stomped on it, once, twice, three times. The case shattered, then the knife was at her throat.

She heard a tapping, a banging, like knuckles on glass, and she looked up. A girl peered from a window on the second story. A blond girl.

It was Jenny.

Jeremy followed her eyes to the window. "I'm sorry, but now that you know, I can't let you go."

He moved the knife from her throat, grabbed her by the wrist, and twisted her arm behind her back. He put the knife between his teeth and grabbed her other arm, twisting it back as well. He held her wrists together with one hand and retrieved the knife. She struggled, but he was stronger than he appeared, and she couldn't break free.

"Jeremy, you have to let me go. The police know I'm here and so does my husband."

"You're not a good liar, Mrs. Lincoln." He tightened his hold and pushed her across the driveway, holding the point of the knife to the back of her neck. "Now walk straight ahead. To the barn."

The sharp point dug into her skin and she obeyed, walking slowly forward, prodded by the knifepoint. It could cut into her neck if she didn't take careful, easy steps.

Finally they reached the barn.

"Open the door," he commanded.

She pulled on the handle and it swung open. He marched her over to the far wall where a blanket lay on the floor, a chain fastened to a massive post.

He removed the knife and tripped her from behind. She fell onto the blanket face down, and he jumped onto her back, pinning her down. She heard a rattle of chains, then something cold and stiff was wrapped around her neck. She heard a click, and the weight on her back was gone.

Chains rattled as she jumped to her feet. She brought her hands to her throat. It felt like a leather collar around her neck, padlocked to the chain.

He stood back out of reach and watched her.

Annie was terrified. She knew what he'd done to Bronson, to Mrs. Bellows, and to Farley. She cowered in fear, her back against the wall of the barn, watching him carefully.

"Why'd you have to come poking around here?" he asked angrily.

"I … I didn't know."

"Didn't know what?"

"I … I just wanted to talk to you. I didn't know it was you who … killed those people."

"Now that you know, I can't let you go," he said flatly.

"My husband will find me, and find you," she said. "You can't get away with this."

"I have no choice."

"I saw Jenny in the window. You can't keep us both here for long."

Jeremy seemed to consider that and started pacing. Finally, he stopped and shouted at her, "It's your own fault and hers too. Both of you should never have been here. She should never have been here. She wasn't supposed to be in the car with him. And you shouldn't be here. You should have minded your own business. And if your husband comes here I'll have no choice. I'll have to shoot him. He's too big for me. Yes, I'll have to shoot him."

"And the police?"

He was ranting and pacing. "The police won't come. The police here are not very smart. No, they're stupid, and if they come, I'll shoot them too." His voice got higher, more frantic. "Yes, I'll shoot the police. I'll shoot everyone. I don't care. Father would shoot them all if he was here. Father would kill them all."

He stopped ranting and breathed heavily, his eyes wild, frenzied.

The knife whistled as he swung it back and forth in the air. Then he lowered it and walked quickly to the barn door, then back again, and again, and again.

"I won't let them catch me," he screamed. "Never. Never. Never."

He moved toward her, still frantic. He held the point of the knife close to her face. "Sit down and shut up," he snarled. "Or I'll have to cut you right now."

She slunk to the floor and sat quietly on the blanket, afraid to move.

He stared down ferociously at her a moment, then turned quickly and strode from the barn, screaming obscenities as he went.

The barn door slammed and he was gone.

CHAPTER 44

Monday, August 15th, 12:30 p.m.

JAKE WAS GETTING worried and he looked at his watch again. Annie should've been back awhile ago. He had tried her number many times, and each time he was informed her phone was off.

He paced the living room floor a while and then called Hank. The detective was still at the scene of the bank robbery and hadn't heard from Annie. He said not to worry, she'd show up soon and they'd laugh it off. He reminded Jake of the time she'd had a flat tire and a dead phone and came home late.

But something didn't seem right.

Jake tried to remember what Annie had told him. He was pretty sure when he'd called her earlier, she'd said she was on her way to Mortino's and then would be right home.

She might have had to stop somewhere, but she surely would've let him know.

He tried her number again. Same result.

He called Chrissy. She answered on the first ring.

"Chrissy, it's Jake. Have you heard from Annie today?"

"No. Not at all, and that's unusual for her. She must be rather busy."

"That's the problem. I haven't heard from her either, and I can't get her on her cell."

"Sorry, can't help you, Jake, but I'm sure she's all right. Maybe her battery is dead or her phone is out of range."

"You're probably right," Jake said and hung up.

He wasn't convinced and didn't feel as optimistic as Chrissy. Something was wrong. It just wasn't like Annie.

He paced the floor awhile longer and then stopped. He hurried into the office, spun the Rolodex, found the number for Annie's mother, and dialed it.

"Hello."

"It's Jake. Is Annie there?"

"No, she's not here. I haven't seen her today."

He didn't say anything.

"Is everything all right?" she asked, sounding annoyed.

"I … I can't find Annie."

She gave a loud, impatient sigh and spoke sharply. "I hope you didn't get her into any trouble. Getting her involved in missing people and murder. I told her it's not safe."

"I didn't get her into anything. She has her own mind. Please, if you see her, tell her to call me."

He hung up abruptly. He could picture Annie's mother staring at the phone, probably yelling, maybe cursing. He smiled grimly at the thought. That was a woman he just didn't like, and he couldn't figure out how Annie had turned out so good.

He called Annie's number again. There was still no answer.

He stood still a minute, thinking, and then shoved the phone back into his pocket, grabbed a piece of paper from the printer, and scribbled a note. He left it on the desk where Annie wouldn't miss it, grabbed his keys from a hook near the front door, and stepped outside, locking the door behind him.

He hurried to his car.

Monday, August 15th, 12:45 p.m.

JEREMY NEEDED a listening ear again. Just someone to talk to and perhaps a kind word or two. He was frustrated things weren't going well. His plans were all messed up and he didn't know what to do any more.

It seemed like Jenny was the only one he could talk to. She was the only one who would listen to him and could understand his mission.

He stopped pacing the kitchen floor and climbed the steps to her room. He slid back the deadbolt, gently turned the knob, and opened the door.

Jenny was in her usual place, propped up on the bed reading. The CD player was playing quietly. She looked up as he peeked in.

"I hope I'm not disturbing you," he said.

"I'm just reading." She closed the book and laid it on the bed beside her.

He stepped inside and sat on the bed opposite her. It seemed to him she was content to be there now. He looked at her, a weary expression on his face.

She cocked her head. "Who was that woman?" she asked.

"She was just snooping around."

"I saw you take her to the barn."

He shrugged. "I had no choice."

"What did she want?"

"I told you, she was snooping around."

She looked at him a moment and then asked, "Does she know what you did?"

He sighed heavily. "Yes, she knows."

Jenny frowned deeply. "So you locked her in the barn?"

"Yes, I had to. I hid her car in the garage."

"So now what will you do?"

"I don't know." He hung his head and sighed again.

"You aren't going to … hurt her, are you?" she asked cautiously.

He looked up. "I might have to."

"Why?"

"Because I can't let her go and I can't keep her here. I can't afford it. I have no job, you know."

She nodded.

He studied her. Jenny really did seem to understand him. "She's a private detective," he said.

Jenny looked surprised.

He continued, "I don't know what to do. She told me her husband knows where she is and he'll come looking for her. She also said the cops know where she is and they'll come too." He dropped his head.

A sudden glimmer in her eyes indicated she seemed pleased, maybe a little excited to hear that. She smiled slightly, but the smile disappeared as he raised his head and said, "I think maybe I'll have to kill him. If he comes, that is. Maybe she's just lying."

"What if he kills you?" she asked carefully.

His eyes blazed and he spoke sharply. "He can't. It's impossible."

"Impossible? Why?"

"Because the good guys always win. You know that." He motioned toward the bookcase. "It's in all those books you read and always on TV and in the movies. The good guys always win. So, in the end … I will win."

"Because you're the good guy?"

"Of course." He sounded annoyed. "You know that."

"Yes, I know that," she lied.

Monday, August 15th, 12:48 p.m.

ANNIE WAS AFRAID. Afraid the crazy, insane little man would come back and kill her.

She knew Jake would be frantic, but she was optimistic he would find her. She'd been able to piece it all together and was confident Jake, or the police, could do the same.

But would it be in time?

She sat on the blanket, leaned against the wall of the barn, and looked about her gloomy surroundings. High above she saw a beam, a piece of rope still attached. She shuddered when she realized what it was—the place where Annette Spencer had hanged herself. She forced her eyes to look away from the dreadful sight.

She had struggled with the leather strap around her neck but was unable to work it loose. The chain holding her was fastened securely to the post. She had studied it for some time, but could see no way to remove it. She had tugged and twisted, but it remained solid.

She thought about Jenny, looking from the upstairs window. She was thankful Jenny was still alive and appeared to be safe, but Jeremy was insane, and she couldn't predict what he might be capable of.

She stood and moved across the barn floor, testing the length of the chain. It was about ten feet long. She searched every square inch of the floor as far as she could reach, brushing back the straw, looking for something that might help her cut through the collar around her neck.

Her search turned up nothing.

She tugged at the floorboards, looking for a loose board, anything she could use as a weapon if he came back. She pulled and strained for a long time.

Her fingers felt sore and her arms ached, and she dropped back onto the blanket in frustration.

Suddenly, she stood to her feet and picked up the chain. She held it at either end, swinging it, testing it, looping it around, practicing. Perhaps if she used it as a sort of lasso, she could catch him with it, maybe wrap it around his neck if he came close enough.

She kept at it, over and over.

She was determined to protect herself when he came back.

CHAPTER 45

Monday, August 15th, 12:55 p.m.

THE WALMART in Midtown Plaza was busy as always. Parking spots were scarce and Jake didn't have time to wait. He pulled up in front of the store, parked under a no parking sign, and swung from his vehicle.

He didn't know where on earth he would find the manager's office in such a massive store, so he approached the greeter and asked her.

She pointed vaguely toward one side of the store. "Over there."

Jake strode to where he'd been directed, dodging serious shoppers and casual browsers.

He found the manager's office close to a set of huge double doors leading to the warehouse behind. He stepped aside to avoid a motorized dolly speeding carelessly through the doors.

He tapped on the manager's door and it swung open. He peered inside. A middle-aged woman with a well-curved business suit looked his way.

"Yes?" she asked.

Jake stepped in. "May I sit down?"

She motioned toward a chair that looked more expensive than it probably was. He sat.

She raised her brows and looked at him.

He leaned forward and offered his hand. "Jake Lincoln," he said. "From Lincoln Investigations."

She shook his hand and sat back. "What may I do for you, Mr. Lincoln?"

He cleared his throat. "I'm investigating the murder of Chad Bronson. His car was found parked in this lot last Tuesday, August ninth."

"Yes?"

"I was hoping you might have some security camera footage from that time and going back to August second. It may show us how the car got here and when it was picked up."

She frowned. "We can't give our security video to just anyone."

Jake pulled a business card from his pocket and handed it to her. "It's very important. It may be related to the disappearance of a young girl, and we'd very much like to find her."

The manager studied the card, then looked at Jake thoughtfully. "I think I've heard of your organization, but it doesn't seem likely we would have footage that old," she said, picking up the phone. She touched a number and waited. "Give me security."

Jake's foot tapped the floor as he eagerly waited.

"It's Ms. Stanley. Do we have security footage from August second on?" Silence. "From outside—in the parking lot." More silence, then, "Okay, hold on."

Jake waited.

She looked up. "I'm sorry, Mr. Lincoln, but any recordings beyond seven days are long gone. However, there are cameras in front of the store covering much of the lot, and we have digital recordings for August tenth, if that would help."

August 10th might show Benny taking the car, but Jake was interested in finding out who dropped it there on the 2nd.

He said, "That would be a help."

Ms. Stanley spoke into the phone. "Bring me what you have from August tenth, Brian. As soon as possible." She hung up.

"Mr. Lincoln," she said, "you might want to check with the plaza management office. They have cameras in the lot as well and may be able to help."

Jake brightened. "That would be great. I'll check there immediately."

She motioned toward her left. "Just go down here past two or three stores and you'll see the door. Management is on the second floor. I'll call up there and let them know you're coming."

In a few minutes, Brian appeared. He held up a flash drive, handing it to Jake as the manager motioned toward him.

Jake stood. "Thank you, Ms. Stanley. You've been a big help."

She smiled at him. Jake nodded at Brian as he left.

He jogged through the store and out to the sidewalk. He turned left and soon he saw the doorway. He went inside, took the stairs two at a time, and knocked on the door below a sign that said, "Midtown Plaza Management Office."

He turned the knob and went in without waiting. A pleasant-looking girl sitting behind a desk looked up and smiled at him.

Jake stepped forward. "I'm looking for the security office."

She pointed behind her. "Just tap on that door and Eugene will help you." She smiled again.

"Thank you," he said, hurrying past.

He tapped on the door and it was opened by a stout man, maybe in his thirties.

"Yes?" The man sounded way too cheerful.

Jake explained who he was and what he needed.

Eugene looked at him and frowned. "Do you have a warrant?"

Jake was stunned. "Uh—"

Eugene almost fell over laughing. "Just kidding," he said. "Come on in and sit down." He hooked a chair with his foot and swung it over toward Jake. "Ms. Stanley called me and vouched for you."

Jake forced a laugh and sat.

"You're in luck," Eugene said. "We used to erase everything after a week and reuse it, but last winter some guy said he slipped on the ice and hit his head. He decided to sue us. We didn't have the footage and it was a big headache. We finally won, though. But memory is so cheap these days, we put in a bunch of new servers and now we keep everything for a month. Just in case, you know." Eugene laughed again.

Jake didn't know what Eugene was laughing at, but he smiled and said, "If I can get the footage from August second, as well as August tenth, that would be perfect."

"No problem."

Eugene whipped open a drawer and pulled out a flash drive. "This baby can hold a lot," he said. He pushed the drive into a port on his desktop computer and hit a few keys. In about two minutes, he pulled the drive out, snapped the top on, and handed it to Jake. "Voila. Finito."

Jake took the drive, thanked him, and left.

He hurried down the steps, hopped in his car, and flew from the lot.

He didn't want to waste the time going home, setting up their equipment, and trying to fudge his way through the video by himself, so as he turned onto the street, he pulled out his cell phone. He punched a few keys and heard the phone dialing. He pinched it between his chin and shoulder, and waited.

"Jeremiah Everest."

"Geekly, it's Jake."

"Jake, what's up?"

"I need your help."

"Sure. What can I do for you, my good man?"

Jake knew Geekly was always home. He ran a web design and computer consulting business from his house. It seemed like he never left his chair.

"I'm on my way over now. Do you have time to check out some video for me?"

"Sure do. Come on over."

Jake hung up and tapped the brakes, swerving down a side street. He slapped the shifter into high gear and touched the gas again. A couple of lefts, and then a right, and he screeched to a stop in front of a row of townhouses.

He swung from the vehicle and ran up the steps of number 633. The door opened as he approached it.

"Come on in, Jake."

Jeremiah Everest was appropriately nicknamed Geekly for obvious reasons. He looked the part. Hair down over his ears, a fruitless attempt at a goatee, true geek glasses, and a face that would've been enough on its own to spell "geek" even without his other enhancements. He actually took great pride in his appearance and loved his nickname.

Jake slapped him on the back and followed him in.

The whole house seemed to be an office. A desk was in the living room. There was no normal furniture around except an easy chair in the corner facing a television perched on a coffee table. The walls were lined with makeshift shelving containing computers, printers, and a variety of electronic stuff Jake didn't recognize. His desk contained only a pair of monitors and a mouse.

Jake suspected even his bedroom had computer parts and other stuff lying around.

There was, however, besides Geekly's well-worn chair, one other that spun over toward Jake as Geekly gave it a shove.

"Have a seat, Jake. Let's see what we have here."

"Do you have a paper and pencil?" Jake asked.

"Paper? Who needs paper when I have a computer?" He chuckled and opened a drawer at the side of the desk. "Are these the obsolete items you were looking for?" he asked, handing Jake a pad and pencil.

Jake laughed and scribbled down the dates and times he was interested in viewing. He handed Geekly the paper.

Geekly fitted the flash drive from Walmart into a slot on the tower. In a moment, an icon appeared on his desktop. He glanced at the paper and then double-clicked the video icon that appeared inside the drive. A window opened containing a video. A timestamp read midnight on the 10th of August. He made the video a little larger, and then dragged a small bar at the bottom of the window. The timestamp blurred. Spiegle had called in to dispatch at 5:02, so Geekly expertly maneuvered the bar until the timestamp read 4:30 and let it play.

The camera was some distance from the spot where Benny had said he found the car, and the image was small and unclear. Jake saw the spot where the shopping carts were parked. He pointed to the screen. "The car would've been right about there." He leaned forward and squinted. He could vaguely make out a white Tercel in among other parked vehicles.

He looked at the timestamp. "Can you speed it up little?"

Geekly touched the keyboard and the video sped up to three or four times normal speed.

In a couple of minutes, Jake shouted, "Stop."

Geekly stopped it, backed it up, and played it forward in slow motion. A man could be seen bending down and looking in the window. In a few seconds, he climbed in the vehicle and pulled from the spot. Jake saw the side view, certain that was the car. He looked at the timestamp. 4:52.

"Try the other drive. There should be two videos on it. Let's see August second," Jake said.

Geekly tucked the other flash drive into another slot and repeated the process. The camera was still not close enough to make out details, but it showed a much better shot of the area in question. By comparing the two videos, Jake narrowed down the exact slot where the Tercel would be. The video started at midnight, August 2nd, and the slot was empty.

"We have no idea of the exact time, so can you play it at super fast speed?" Jake asked as he touched the screen. "Watch that spot. When a car appears there, that should be it."

They watched.

The video was playing so fast the car seemed to appear in the slot like magic. Geekly stopped the video, moved the bar back until the car disappeared, then played it at normal speed.

Jake leaned in a little more.

Soon. "There it is."

The Toyota came into camera range, turned into the slot, and stopped. Jake held his breath as someone climbed from the car, his face turned toward the camera.

"Stop."

The video stopped.

"That's him," Jake said. "Can you enhance that?"

Geekly shook his head. "Nope. You can't enhance a video in real life, only in the movies. You can't see any information that doesn't actually exist."

Jake frowned.

Geekly said, "Have you ever looked at a TV screen from a few inches away? Everything is just a blurry mess, but if you sit back a few feet, it becomes clear."

Jake cocked his head. "So?"

"So," Geekly said. "If I blow the image up large on the screen, and then you stand over there by the wall, it'll appear much clearer."

Jake stood back a few feet. Geekly blew up the video until the face filled the monitor.

"I don't believe it," Jake shouted.

"You know who it is?"

"I sure do. Thanks, Geekly. I owe you one," he called, running toward the front door.

Two or three pedestrians spun around to stare as a bright red Firebird squealed from the curb, roaring away from their startled eyes.

CHAPTER 46

Monday, August 15th, 1:30 p.m.

IF THEY CAME looking for him, he had to be ready.

Jeremy pulled out the drawer by the sink and retrieved the knife sharpener. It made a gritty squawk as he drew it through each serration on the blade of his hunting knife, first one side, then the other. Again and again. He tested the blade with his finger. Perfect. He smiled grimly, tucked it back into its sheath, and dropped his pant leg.

He leaned down and slid open the drawer where he kept Father's trusty .22. He lifted the towels and picked up the gun, caressing it lovingly, and thought of Father. He spun the cylinder, then tucked it behind his belt buckle next to his skin.

He hadn't used Father's old hunting rifle for some time. Not the same one Father had used to eliminate the dirtbag thief who'd destroyed their lives many years ago—the police had kept that one—but his other one would do just fine.

He flicked on the basement light and went down the aging wooden steps. The stone-walled basement smelled musty, and the air was thin and damp.

He walked over to a gun rack hanging on the far wall, lifted the semiautomatic off the rack, and wiped the dust off with a cloth he found on a shelf. He grabbed a handful of ammunition from a box by the stand and dropped them into his pocket. The rifle had a five-shot magazine, and he loaded it up from the box and carried it upstairs.

He went to the living room and stopped in front of a window facing the driveway. He opened it a crack and poked the barrel of the rifle through, testing the range, swinging the gun back and forth. From there he would be able to see the whole front of the property. He wished the rifle had a scope, but he didn't think there had ever been one. He would have to make do without it.

He couldn't carry the rifle around with him everywhere he went, so he decided to leave it in the mudroom. He tucked it back out of sight on a low shelf of the workbench where he could find it quickly if necessary.

Digging on another shelf, he found a spike about four inches long. He picked a hammer off a hook on the wall above the bench and went to the front door. He selected a spot and pounded the nail in, fastening the door securely to the frame. He stood back and smiled grimly.

He had one more thing to do. He went to the phone in the kitchen, grabbed the receiver and unplugged the cable, tucking it under some towels in a cupboard drawer.

He was anxious to get back to work. There were a lot more scumbags out there whom he needed to kill and he didn't want this distraction right now. He hoped this would all blow over soon and he could continue his task.

He didn't know for sure if anyone would come. He knew Mrs. Lincoln was a filthy liar, but … just in case.

He went into the living room, dropped into his chair, and thought for a while. There didn't seem to be anything else he could do. He was as ready as he could be.

Suddenly he jumped up, went to the mudroom, retrieved the rifle from the workbench, and brought it back to the living room. He dragged his chair closer to the front window and sat. He adjusted the location of the chair a few times, finally satisfied he had a clear view of the front of the property and the driveway.

He sat back down and put the barrel of the rifle on the window ledge, the butt resting in his lap.

He watched and waited.

CHAPTER 47

Monday, August 15th, 2:22 p.m.

WHEN JAKE LEFT Geekly's, he had a nagging suspicion. He grabbed his cell phone and dialed directory assistance. He wanted the number for Mortino's.

"May I speak to Jeremy, please?"

"I'm sorry, Jeremy no longer works here."

He was correct. His face was grim as he poked at the phone, hanging it up.

He spun across oncoming traffic, made a left turn, then dialed another number.

"Hi, it's Hank. Leave a message."

"Hank, it's Jake. I'm on my way to the Spencer house out on County Road 12. Pretty sure Jeremy Spencer is the killer, and Annie is out there. Give me a call."

He was traveling well over the speed limit now. He whipped past a couple of cars, spun around a few more turns, and then he was on County Road 12. He slowed the vehicle.

The road was too rough to do top speed, and he bumped and rattled around as he flew.

Soon he approached the Spencer house. He pulled over a hundred feet short of the driveway, shut off the car, and jumped out.

He climbed through the ditch, leaped over the fence on the other side, and approached a copse of trees that hid the farmhouse from view.

He crept cautiously into the trees, advancing slowly until he saw the house. He crouched down and studied it a moment. There was no movement.

Keeping as low as possible, he edged forward, stopping often to listen and watch. A few birds chirped, hidden somewhere in the trees above. A squirrel skittered up a tree and rustled in the branches above his head. All was otherwise still and quiet.

He edged forward a little more.

A rifle shot broke the silence and echoed as he heard the smack of a bullet slam into the tree beside his head.

He heard another shot, and he dropped flat and lay still, out of sight of the shooter.

Crawling on his stomach, he backtracked until he was out of sight of the house, almost at the road again, and then crouching and keeping low, he skirted around the edge of the copse until he was parallel with the side of the house.

He carefully watched a pair of windows in the side of the building for a few moments. He saw no movement. Satisfied, he dashed toward the house, expecting at any moment to hear a shot and feel a bullet rip into him. None did.

He reached the wall safely and leaned back against it, catching his breath, then dug out his cell and hit speed dial.

"No Signal."

He shook his head and shoved the phone back into his pocket.

He needed to formulate a plan. Annie had said she was going to talk to Jeremy. He was sure now she had come here. He had to find her or her body. He winced at the thought and it made him more determined.

He had to find Jeremy. He wondered if he should go toward the front of the house where the shooter was and surprise him, or go around the back way and work his way through the house. The problem was, he wasn't sure whether the shooter was on the lower level or upstairs.

He decided to go around to the back of the house, trying desperately to calm his anxiety and control his anger.

Keeping against the wall, he moved slowly along. He glanced around the back corner. It was all clear.

He rounded the corner, crept along several feet, then crouched down under a window. He slowly raised his head and peeked inside. It was a small room, maybe a den or an office. He could see across the room and through a doorway, into the kitchen, but nobody appeared to be around.

The back door was just a few feet ahead. He took a couple of slow steps and stood in front of it. There was no window in the door. He tested the knob and it turned in his hand. It was unlocked.

He eased open the door a few inches and listened. He heard nothing, so he pushed it further, stepping to the side. The door creaked open.

He waited until he was sure it was safe before stepping inside. He was in a mudroom, another door ahead of him, probably leading to the kitchen.

He cautiously opened the door to the kitchen a crack and listened. He swung the door fully open and stepped aside. No sound. He crouched down and moved into the kitchen. The room was clear.

To his right was the den he'd looked into through the

window outside. Nobody was in there, but he went in and looked around, just in case. Still nobody.

Back in the kitchen, he saw a doorway leading down a short hallway. There was a bathroom on the right, the living room further down and to the left, and then a set of steps to the right, leading up.

Keeping his back to the left wall, he slid down until he could see into the bathroom. All clear. A few more inches and he could see up the steps. All clear. Another cautious step and he was near the archway on his left, leading to the living room. He ducked down and took a quick look into the room.

There was a chair pushed up near a window, facing out to the front of the house. The window was open. He saw a couch and a television, some bookcases and other knickknacks spread about, but the shooter was not there.

Jake guessed he had been shot at through the open window, but the chair was now empty.

He assumed Jeremy was upstairs.

He moved to the bottom of the steps and looked up. He knew if the killer was up there waiting and he was caught halfway up, he would be trapped and could easily be shot at before he could get back down to safety.

Thoughts of Annie forced him to take a chance. He moved up the first step and listened.

Silence.

He moved up to the second step. It squeaked. He listened.

Nothing.

He took one step at a time, stopping to listen after each one.

When he was halfway up, his head was at floor level, and he peered through the bannister, down a passageway to the bathroom. There was a bedroom halfway down the hallway with an open door. At the top of the steps, straight ahead, was another door. It was closed, and there appeared to be a sliding bolt lock on it.

He reached the top of the steps and hugged the wall as he moved to the bedroom with the open door. Looking in quickly, and seeing no one, he stepped in and looked around. The room was tidy and clean, but obviously a man's bedroom. It was probably Jeremy's.

He opened the closet door, checking under the bed and any other possible hiding places. No one was there.

He moved back into the hallway and went to the bathroom. He stepped aside as he pulled back the shower curtain. Nothing.

He frowned. There was only one place left. The other bedroom.

Approaching the door, he saw the bolt lock was closed, the door locked from the outside. Jeremy couldn't be in there.

Just in case, he slid back the bolt quietly and pushed the door open a crack.

All was quiet.

He peered through the crack. His mouth fell open when he saw a girl lying on a bed by the far wall. She faced the door, but her eyes were closed.

He swung the door open. It banged slightly as it hit the wall.

She opened her eyes and gasped.

He hurried toward her. "Jenny?" he asked.

"Yes. Yes. I'm Jenny," she said excitedly. She sat up and asked with a frown, a little more cautiously, "Who are you?"

He smiled. "Your mother sent me. My name is Jake."

She let out her breath and sat still a moment. Then a few tears leaked from her eyes and she sobbed, slowly at first, then uncontrollably.

Jake sat on the bed beside her, his big arms around her as she clung tightly to him.

"It's all right. You're safe now," he soothed.

Finally, she looked up at him. "Where … where's Jeremy?" she asked weakly.

"I'm not sure. He was here but now he's gone, and you're safe."

Her sobbing had lessened and she wiped at her tears.

"My wife and I are private investigators," he said. "Your mother hired us to find you."

She looked up and drew in her breath sharply. "Oh, no. He's got her."

"My wife?" Jake asked.

"Yes. It must be her. He said she was a private detective." She motioned toward the window. "I watched him take her to the barn."

Jake stood and walked to the barred window. He looked to the left and saw the old barn, maybe two or three hundred feet away, further down the gravel driveway.

He turned back to Jenny. "I have to go and find Annie," he said.

She grabbed his arm, holding on tight, and pleaded, "I'll come with you. I don't want to stay here anymore."

He nodded. She reluctantly let go of him, following him as he moved toward the door.

"Stay behind me," he said.

She followed him out the door to the top of the steps leading down.

"Stay up here," he ordered. "Until I make sure it's safe."

He went slowly down the steps and into the hallway. It was all clear. He motioned for Jenny and she came down.

He poked his head into the living room to be sure Jeremy

hadn't returned and then led her through the kitchen to the mudroom.

He opened the outside door and peered out. It was all clear. He motioned for Jenny to stay back and he stepped outside.

CHAPTER 48

Monday, August 15th, 2:45 p.m.

JEREMY PULLED the barrel of the rifle from the window ledge and dropped the weapon into his lap.

"Got him," he screeched.

He had seen someone moving through the trees at the front of the house. When he'd fired the first shot, he was sure he'd hit him, and when he'd fired the second one, the guy had dropped.

He watched the spot for a while and saw no movement.

He grinned. His grin turned into a chuckle, and then a laugh.

"That'll teach him," he shouted. "Yes, that'll teach him."

He slid the window open and climbed out. He pulled the rifle out after him, and holding it in a ready position, he moved forward slowly.

He didn't know whether the guy was dead or just injured, and he might have a gun, so he would need to be careful.

He crossed the small front lawn, and then the driveway, heading for the copse of trees.

He kept his eyes on the spot where he was headed, his rifle cocked and aimed in case the invader was still alive and had a weapon.

He breathed heavily, excited and a bit nervous as he walked.

He reached the spot and frowned. There was no body. There was no blood.

He spun around looking, looking for a sign, any indication of where the trespasser was. He saw nothing.

He looked through the trees in front of him, then back toward the house.

That's when he saw him.

The intruder was at the side of the house, just going around the back corner.

Jeremy swore and hurried toward the building, around to the side, and then back.

He peered around the corner. The invader was standing at the doorway to the mudroom. Jeremy raised his rifle and stepped out, his finger tightening on the trigger.

He lowered the rifle and swore silently as the trespasser stepped inside the house, out of sight.

He was disappointed, but then realized the burglar was trapped. He had nailed the front door shut, and the back door was the only way out.

He swore as he realized he had left the front window open and hoped the intruder wouldn't see it. If not, the back door was the only way out and he could nail him then.

He stepped back around the house, hurrying for the forest that began at the side edge of the property.

Once he was safely in the darkness of the woods, he circled around through the trees extending across the back of the property, starting maybe fifty yards or so from the house.

He crept forward slowly until he reached the tree line. He

lay down on his stomach, shielded by a bush, his elbows bent, the gun ready and trained on the mudroom door at the back of the house.

He waited, muttering to himself.

He wanted to nail the trespasser, the intruder, the thief who had broken into his house and now deserved to die. There was no doubt about that.

He gritted his teeth and watched, waiting.

Minutes went by. He didn't move. More minutes. He remained still, anticipating the kill. It would be for sure this time. Any minute. Just wait. Wait.

Now.

The scumbag stepped from the mudroom door.

Jeremy squeezed the trigger.

He missed.

He squeezed it again.

Missed again.

The trespasser was moving fast along the back of the house. The gun swung and exploded again.

The dirtbag had disappeared around the corner of the house. He watched for a while but saw no movement, and he knew for sure he'd missed him this time.

He stood and aimed carefully toward the corner of the house. Then he saw a face, just the top of a head, and a pair of eyes looking at him. He pulled the trigger.

The gun was empty.

He hastily pulled out the magazine and fumbled in his pocket for more ammunition.

Suddenly the intruder was coming his way, running through the garden. He would be here before Jeremy could get the gun reloaded.

He swore as he turned around and ran.

He had lived here all of his life and knew the property

well, every tree, every bush. He ran straight, crashing through the trees, his breath coming in gasps.

Suddenly he stopped short. He could hear his pursuer behind him and he would need to be quieter. He couldn't hope to outrun him, so he had to outsmart him.

He saw a fallen tree to his left, big enough to hide behind. He vaulted the tree, lay down and loaded the magazine, ramming it in, and aimed the rifle toward the sound of the approaching pursuer. He waited.

CHAPTER 49

Monday, August 15th, 3:13 p.m.

JENNY HEARD the sound of the shot and dropped down. She saw Jake jump sideways, and then she heard another shot, and then another. Then silence.

She crawled forward carefully until she could see through the mudroom door and across the backyard. She saw the forest beyond and Jeremy holding a rifle. She watched as he turned and ran, Jake racing into the forest behind him. The sounds of the chase grew quieter.

She waited a few minutes and then cautiously left the house. Keeping low, she ran around the corner to her right, hurried forward, and down the gravel driveway toward the barn.

She knew Jeremy had taken Annie there, and she wanted to see if the woman was safe. Jenny also knew she would have a better chance by hiding in the barn until Jake came back, rather than staying in the house. It would probably be safer than running to the road or trying to get away in any other direction.

The barn door was hooked on the outside, so she lifted the hook, unlatched the door, and swung it open.

The woman she had seen being pushed toward the barn now sat on the blanket, leaning against the far wall. Jenny was relieved she appeared to be safe, but the woman was chained up the same way she had been.

That must be Annie. Jake had said her name was Annie. She hurried over.

Annie jumped to her feet when she saw Jenny.

"Annie?" Jenny asked.

Annie's mouth was open and she stared a moment. Finally, she said, "Yes, I'm Annie. Jenny, it's you."

Jenny ran to Annie and hugged her. The chain rattled as they cried, laughed, and held on to each other.

Annie stepped back, still holding Jenny by both hands. "What happened?" she asked. "I heard gunshots. How did you get free?"

"Jake," Jenny replied. "Your husband. Jake came and found me. He let me out."

Annie looked worried. "Where's Jake now?"

"He's chasing Jeremy," Jenny replied, pointing behind her. "Back there in the forest."

"And the gunshots?"

"Jeremy has a gun," Jenny said. "But don't worry. He missed every time."

Annie frowned, a worried look on her face. "Jake's smart and knows when to be careful," she said, then paused, her eyes on the barn door. "But still, he's rather impulsive at times, and Jeremy has a gun." She turned back to Jenny and asked, "Are you all right? Did he hurt you in any way?"

"I'm fine. Really. I don't know how I'm going to feel a little later, but right now, I'm all right."

"Did he molest you?"

Jenny shook her head. "What about you? How are you?"

"I'm all right, too. Pretty frightened, though."

"Me too," Jenny said. "I was chained up here for a while."

Annie raised her brows. "Oh?"

"At first I was in the bedroom upstairs. I crashed through the wall, but he caught me and chained me up here." She shuddered. "Finally he took me back up there again."

"I suppose you didn't find any way to get out of this collar?"

"I tried. It's hopeless."

Annie forced a smile. "It's not hopeless now. Jake'll call the police and they'll catch Jeremy."

"Yes, they will," Jenny said. "I'll stay here with you until they come. It's safer here for me, and I can hide if necessary."

They sat on the blanket together. Annie held Jenny's hand, her other arm around her shoulders, their heads touching, as they watched the barn door and waited.

CHAPTER 50

Monday, August 15th, 3:12 p.m.

AS JAKE STEPPED from the mudroom door he heard a shot. A bullet whizzed by his ear and he dropped down.

His first instinct was to dive back into the house, but he didn't want to endanger Jenny. The shooter was straight ahead of him so, thinking fast, he dove to his right and ran for the corner of the house.

He was chased by two more bullets before making it around the corner and safely out of sight.

He dug out his cell phone. Still no signal.

He waited a moment and didn't hear any sound, so he chanced a quick look around the corner. Jeremy was aiming the rifle straight at him.

Jake dropped to the ground and looked again. The rifle was down and Jeremy was fiddling with it. It was hard to be sure from that distance, but he appeared to be reloading.

Now was his chance.

Jake sprang to his feet and sprinted toward the fugitive. Jeremy's head shot up, then he turned and dashed the other way.

Jake was thinking as he ran. Should he turn back and find Annie? No, she was probably tied up, and if Jeremy came back, they would be helpless. Should he run to the road and hope for a passing vehicle? There wasn't enough traffic on this road, and even if he chanced to find a passing car, it would be too late before any help could arrive.

He had no choice. He followed his instincts and kept running.

Jeremy crashed through the forest ahead of him. Jake saw him disappear as trees blocked his view, and then he appeared again.

Then there was silence. Jake couldn't see or hear the fugitive.

He crouched and went ahead slowly, dodging from tree to tree. He had to be careful—he was certainly no match for a man with a rifle.

Suddenly he heard an explosion and he dropped to the ground. It came from behind a fallen tree to his left. He heard another explosion and felt a searing pain in his leg.

He was hit.

The killer fired again as Jake rolled a couple of times and came to rest against the trunk of a large maple. He was sheltered from the view of the gunman, but now what?

His leg was burning and he bit his lip. Blood seeped from the wound, soaking his pant leg.

He heard a snap and the sound of feet, fading away. He poked his head around the trunk. The killer was running the other way.

Jake stood and tested his leg. He could stand, but it was painful; the bleeding was the problem.

He dropped to the ground and took off his t-shirt. He struggled and finally managed to rip a strip from the bottom, then rolled up his pant leg, wrapped the strip around the wound a couple of times, gritting his teeth as he tightened it snugly.

The blood stopped oozing from the wound and he stood, testing his leg. He would be okay for now.

He lifted his head and looked through the forest. Jeremy appeared to have run directly ahead in a straight line.

He wondered what the killer's plans were. Jeremy had tried to shoot him several times. Would he come back to finish him off? Or would he head back to the barn, or the house, or just run away as far as possible?

If Jeremy ran, he wouldn't get far, and Jake realized the fugitive's only chance of escape would be to eliminate any witnesses. That meant Jenny, Annie, and himself were targets.

Ahead of him, but over to the right, he heard a flock of birds taking to the air. Jake watched them. Undoubtedly, Jeremy had disturbed them.

He was circling back.

He was heading for Annie.

Jake spun to his right and ran. With his sore leg he couldn't possibly make it to the barn before Jeremy. He decided to try to cut the fugitive off, somewhere between where Jeremy was now and the barn.

Here in the forest he wasn't sure how far that would be, so he stopped often to listen.

Finally, he realized he must be getting close, so he ducked behind a tree and waited.

Soon he heard the unmistakable sound of someone coming, perhaps a hundred feet away, but getting closer.

Jake listened carefully, calculating the distance. His estimate was off. He needed to be another twenty feet ahead if he was going to have any chance of intercepting the killer.

He gritted his teeth and disregarded the pain. Careful not to give himself away as he sprinted, he watched the ground carefully, keeping low, struggling to avoid any twigs or debris that could betray him.

His calculations were correct. He stopped behind a tree and waited as the steps came closer. He heard loud breathing, panting. The killer was out of breath, making much slower progress.

Jake crouched, ready to spring.

Jeremy came into view a few feet away.

Jake dove from his hiding place, remembered his football days, and made a perfect tackle.

They hit the ground. The rifle was knocked from Jeremy's hands and landed ten feet away. Jake winced as a sharp pain ran up his leg. He was stunned a moment, and his prey broke loose as Jake stumbled and fell.

Then he rolled to a crouch, ready to pounce again.

He raised his head and looked straight into the barrel of a .22 revolver.

The gun exploded and a bullet whipped past his ear as he rolled behind a tree.

Another bullet skinned the bark beside him. He had to get away.

He jumped to his feet and ran in a zigzag pattern for a few seconds, then chancing a look over his shoulder, he saw the killer running the other way.

Toward the barn.

The rifle was still on the ground where it had fallen. Jake ran back and scooped it up.

The magazine was missing.

In frustration he threw it aside. His leg was paining him, but he had to get to the barn before Jeremy.

Before long he realized he wouldn't make it in time. He stopped briefly and checked his leg. It was bleeding again, so he tightened the makeshift bandage and gritted his teeth.

Thoughts of Annie forced him to his feet and pushed him forward. He bit his lip, endeavoring to take no notice of the throbbing pain he felt with each step.

He needed to be cautious in case he had misread the killer's intentions. Jeremy may be waiting ahead for him.

He limped forward, glancing back and forth in all directions as he cautiously made his way through the forest. He finally reached the tree line and could see the barn, not far in the distance. No one was in sight. He stopped, listened, and looked around for a few moments.

There were no sounds or movement warning him of any imminent danger, so he continued on, keeping low, stopping often to listen.

The barn was close. Annie was close. He prayed she was all right.

He stumbled the last few feet and looked for a crack in the barn door—some way he could see inside. The only way he was going to be able to see inside was to open the door.

It was unlatched so he drew it back an inch. He couldn't see clearly. Another inch.

Then he saw them.

He eased the door closed and thought a moment on what he had seen.

Annie was on her knees near the far wall, her eyes closed. Jeremy was crouched behind her, holding the revolver to the side of her head.

He didn't see Jenny. She was probably still in the house waiting for him to come back.

He fought back a sudden panic, but it was quickly replaced by anger. If Jeremy hurt Annie, he would tear the filthy coward apart, limb by limb.

He had no choice now. He had to go in. Jeremy could have killed Annie at any time, but he didn't. Now Jake knew why.

The killer was waiting for him. He was the real target now.

He opened the door and stepped boldly inside.

Jeremy faced the door. He grinned evilly, laughing as he tightened his grip and swung the gun toward Jake.

Annie's eyes popped open. Jake saw terror on her face mixed with relief at seeing him.

He moved forward and stopped twenty feet away. "Here I am," he said.

Jeremy scowled. "Come closer." His voice was low, guttural, hostile.

Jake shook his head and said nothing.

Jeremy moved the weapon back to Annie's head. "I'll kill her," he gritted through clenched teeth.

"No you won't," Jake said. "It's me you want."

The killer glared.

"Put the gun down," Jake demanded.

"Never," Jeremy screamed.

"The police are on the way," Jake said calmly.

"I don't care. If they come, I'll shoot her right through the head and I won't care."

Jake put his arms halfway up. "You can have me, but leave her alone."

"Come closer." Jeremy was shouting.

"Come and get me," Jake said, struggling to keep his voice as calm as possible. "I won't move."

Jeremy glared, breathing heavily. He looked frantically from Jake, to Annie, and back up again. He seemed to come to a decision.

Jake waited.

Jeremy stood and moved the gun to the top of Annie's head, glaring down at her. "Get up," he shrieked.

His hand tightened on the back of the collar as Annie rose slowly to her feet. The gun moved down again, the steel pushing into her neck, just below her ear.

He prodded her forward a step by the firm grip on her collar, keeping his eyes on Jake.

The chain rattled as they moved another step.

Then one more step. The chain rattled. Then one more. Now they were ten feet away.

Jake abruptly took three strides to the right, then two steps forward.

"Stay still," Jeremy screamed, spinning toward Jake. "What are you doing?"

"Sorry," Jake said mildly. "It won't happen again."

Jeremy stood as if paralyzed, glowering for almost a full minute, his eyes fixed on Jake, unmoving, unblinking.

Then he shook his head, blinked, and prodded Annie forward one more step.

Jake put his hands all the way up and stood still.

Jeremy drew the revolver away from Annie's neck and pointed it at Jake's head. He was just a few feet away, and he couldn't possibly miss.

Jeremy's hand began to squeeze the trigger just as Jenny stepped out from behind a large wooden pillar and slammed a two-by-four into the back of his head.

He went down. The gun flew from his grasp.

He lay unconscious on the straw covered floor of the barn, directly below the massive beam where his mother had hanged herself all those years ago.

EPILOGUE 1

JENNY WAS CURLED up in a comfortable chair, reading. She dropped the book into her lap, looked up, and smiled. "I think I'll go to bed and leave you two lovebirds alone."

Hank laughed. "Goodnight, Jenny."

"Goodnight, my dear," her mother said.

Jenny climbed from the chair and dropped her book on the side table. She gave a teasing smile over her shoulder as she left the room.

Amelia looked deep into Hank's eyes. She gave him a long kiss and sighed, snuggling up close. "My hero," she said.

Hank held her tighter. He knew he wasn't the hero. Annie and Jake had been mostly responsible. He was pretty sure Amelia knew that as well, but even two months later, she still called him a hero, and he was happy to hear her say it nonetheless.

"It's great to see Jenny has finally gotten over her ordeal," Hank said.

Amelia nodded. "She's a strong girl."

Hank reluctantly removed his arms from around Amelia and stood. He yawned. "I need to be going home now. It's getting late and tomorrow I have a bank robber to catch."

Amelia stood and followed him to the door. They kissed long and passionately before she finally let him go.

"Goodnight, my darling," she said as Hank opened the door.

Hank grinned. "See you tomorrow."

He was still grinning as he shut the door behind him and left.

EPILOGUE 2

ANNIE STUCK a stamp onto the final envelope and tossed it into the "Out" bin. She picked up a newspaper from the desk and looked at it again.

Since Jenny had been found, the news coverage had been tremendous. The story received national attention, and there were more phone calls than they could handle. Not just from news people, but from prospective clients. It seemed as though they were going to be rather busy.

Jake limped into the office and plopped down into the guest chair. He gave a groan and rubbed his leg.

Annie sat back in her chair and smiled at him. He had been so supportive, helping her through the first rough days after the ordeal in the barn. She just couldn't bear to tell him she knew his leg was better. So she pampered him anyway. He deserved it.

She had chided him gently for endangering his own life, perhaps being careless in trying to rescue her. He had taken it good-naturedly and promised to be more careful in the future. But she loved him all the more because of it, and knew she would likely do the same for him if necessary.

"So, what's our next job?" he asked.

"I have an important mission for you," she said.

He cocked his head. "Oh?"

"It involves a beautiful woman."

"And?"

"And a room upstairs." She looked at his leg and said, "Oh, but I don't know if you're up to it."

He grinned. "I'm up to it."

EPILOGUE 3

THE CHAINS around his ankles rattled and clanked as he was led down the passageway. The heavily barred door behind him slammed shut. Another one ahead squealed open.

He was prodded through.

The cuffs bit into his wrists. The smell of sweat was in the air and he could taste it. The constant echo of metal on metal assaulted his ears.

Other inmates yelled and whistled, slamming and shaking the bars that contained them. They hooted and howled at him as he was pushed forward.

He faced one last door. It swung open, and a hand on his back thrust him into the small room. The leg constraints were removed, and then the cuffs binding his wrists fell loose.

Finally, the crash of a massive latch ground into place and he was left alone.

He looked around, then stood gripping the barred door for a while, contemplating his situation.

It might not be so bad, he thought. There could be opportunities here.

Jeremy chuckled as he turned and sat on the lower bunk. He didn't have his knife or his gun with him, of course, but he was resourceful. He could make do.

He was in the perfect place to find all the bad guys he could handle.

He laughed out loud. His voice echoed in the small room, finally blending in with the continual low roar of Cell Block A.

###

32475452R10192

Made in the USA
Middletown, DE
06 June 2016